Noble Lies

Books by Charles Benoit

Relative Danger
Out of Order

Noble Lies

Charles Benoit

Poisoned Pen Press

Copyright © 2007 by Charles Benoit

First Edition 2007

10 9 8 7 6 5 4 3 2 1

Library of Congress Catalog Card Number: 2007924784

ISBN: 1-59058-450-7 Hardcover

Poisoned Pen Press
6962 E. First Ave., Ste. 103
Scottsdale, AZ 85251
www.poisonedpenpress.com
info@poisonedpenpress.com

Printed in the United States of America

To Rose
My Super Queen

Acknowledgments

Some good people did their best to make this a better book. In Thailand they include the dozens of people who shared their tsunami stories with me, a great kindness that I will never forget. Thanks also to the many prostitution, corruption, piracy and smuggling experts—both official and otherwise—who provided details so fantastic I couldn't have made them up. As promised, you remain anonymous. Thanks, too, to Bill Smith for the beachfront hospitality and inspiration. Special thanks goes to Vitida Vasant, co-author of *Thailand Fever: A Road Map for Thai-Western Relationships*, for her help in comprehending the incomparable, Zoë Sharp for her weapons expertise, and to Joanne LaFave and Deana Costanza for all the red ink. Where things are right, they get the credit; where they aren't, you can blame me.

Chapter One

What he needed was a knife.

He had sold his good knife in Cairo, a court official demanding a much larger bribe than usual, and last month, somewhere north of Delhi, he had left his backup knife in the thigh of a French bootlegger. He was sure the man was eager to return it, but he saw it more as a gift than a loan.

An ice pick would work, and he used to own one, kept it right under the front seat of his car, but that was several lifetimes ago, and besides, he was in Thailand now. Not a lot of call for ice picks this close to the equator.

He tried using the stub of his thumbnail, but it just clicked against the plastic. He stopped, paused, took a deep breath and tried again, his eyes throbbing in and out of focus, his nail pushing against the edge, the foil backing bowing up then clinging down, fusing with the clear plastic.

They were right there. Two Extra-Strength, non-drowsy Sinutabs. Childproofed for his protection.

In his experience with hangovers—and in his thirty-three years he had a lot of experience with hangovers—he knew there was no instant cure, but there was relief. And it came in the form of two—or four, depending on whether it was beer or whiskey—acetaminophen-heavy sinus pills downed with a can—or two—of a warm cola; any brand as long as it wasn't caffeine-free.

Getting the moisture-seal foil off the back of the little plastic dome, well now, that was the challenge, wasn't it? It separated the stumbling drunk from the merely hung over; the drug company's final protection against lawsuits. *Your honor, if he was sober enough to remove the safety backing, surely he knew not to exceed the recommended dosage.*

Then the knocking at the door started up again, a long I-know-you're-in-there string of knuckle raps. Whoever it was must have heard the lone kitchenette drawer slam shut. Five white plastic sporks, an ashtray and handfuls of wooden chopsticks, but not one goddamn knife.

More knocks. He sighed a cotton-mouthed sigh and shuffled toward the door, favoring his left leg more out of habit than need. Only two people knew he was there and one of them had a key. The other was probably still in the hospital. He checked the fly on his shorts, ran a hand through his hair, and unlocked the door. Whoever it was, he hoped they came with a knife.

It was a girl. The hallway was filled with bright mid-morning light and he had to squint, bringing a hand up to cover his eyes, but he was sure it was a girl. That wasn't unusual—it was that kind of hotel after all, the kind where you brought your own sheets and signed someone else's name. What was unusual was that she was blonde. In a land of coffee-colored skin and jet-black hair, a pasty-white blonde with ice-blue eyes was noticeable, no matter how hung over you were. She wore a well-filled peach tank top and a pair of tan baggy shorts, with a new backpack slung over her shoulder, the airline tags still tied to the straps.

"Are you Mark Rohr?" There was something about how she said it, the way her nose curled and how she leaned back as she spoke, that told him she'd be disappointed with the answer.

"The one and only." He was hung over and nauseous and his eyeballs felt ready to pop, but he smiled his best smile, instinct taking over.

She smiled back. "They told me I could find you here. The woman in the bar downstairs."

"Did she?" Mark let the smile fade.

"Yes," she said, shifting her feet, holding her smile.

"Now why would she do that?"

"Well, I just got here and I didn't know what else to do, so…"

"So you knocked on my door. Sorry, not interested," he said and shut the door. He took two steps before the knocking returned, sharper and more urgent now. She was still knocking when he pulled the door back open. "I told you I'm not interested."

"It's not what you think," she said, stepping forward.

"Let me guess. You were backpacking with your friends and you got lost or they left you or you got ripped off and now you're *all alone* and all you need is fifty bucks so you can call your folks back in Iowa or Texas or Mayberry, and you'll pay me back just as soon as they wire the money and, *gosh*, you'd be oh so grateful, and *whatever* could you do to say thank you?" He smiled again. "Like I said. Not interested."

"No," the girl said, stopping the door with her hand. "That's not it at all. I want to *hire* you."

Mark leaned against the doorframe and waited.

"I asked the bartender," the girl said, pointing down the hall to the stairs that led to the nameless hotel's nameless bar, "and she told me I should talk to you."

He looked at her, at her straight blond hair, her pale shoulders, her athletic build, her long smooth legs and her painted fingernails. Maybe she could get past the childproof seal. "Come on in," he said, stepping aside as he swung the door open.

It had never been a large room but someone had converted it into a studio apartment, someone who liked things cramped and musty. A fan dangled down from the ceiling, the motionless blades tied together by thick spider webs; gray-white sheets hung over a pair of open windows that let in the stuffy back-alley air and moist tropical heat. There was a sagging bed in the center of the room, a desk, a bar stool, two lamps—one missing its shade and bulb—a TV and VCR on a wheeled cart, a kitchen counter with a sink, three metal cabinets and the knifeless drawer. A shower curtain blocked the view of the squat-style toilet and the chest-high spigot that served as the shower.

"Make yourself at home," he said, smiling to himself as he watched her reaction. She stepped around the bed to get to the bar stool, careful not to brush against the piles of sheets and tee shirts that littered the floor. She sat down and set her backpack by her feet.

"Have you lived in Thailand long?" she asked.

"Is it Monday or Tuesday?"

"It's Friday."

"That makes it four days. What about you? Aren't you on the wrong side of the island? Nothing to see in Phuket City."

"I just got in this morning."

"And you came straight to see me? I'm touched."

"No, it's not that. Well, I guess sort of…" She swallowed and ran her tongue across her lips, and by the way the light filtered through the sheets on the windows he could see her eyes begin to water. "My name's Robin Antonucci and I need your help."

"And you're going to pay me?"

She nodded.

"For what?"

Robin reached down for her backpack. He watched as she undid the plastic clips and zippered open the main compartment, pulling out a videotape. "Does that thing work?" she said, pointing at the TV and VCR with the tape.

"No idea. Never turned it on." He sat at the edge of the bed and swung the rolling cart around. The wheels squeaked and the whole thing wobbled but it moved. He hit the power buttons and a dubbed episode of *Friends* filled the screen.

"It should be ready to go." She moved the stool closer as Mark worked the remote. He put the tape in and squeezed the green button until the word play appeared in the upper corner. The VCR whirred and clicked and after a fluttering, slanting start, the program began.

With the CNN logo floating over his right shoulder in a cloudless blue sky, a handsome, olive-skinned man in a red polo shirt walked along a beach, pointing out to the sea and up to the beach as he spoke, the sound too low to hear what he was saying. Along the bottom of the screen the sports ticker ran updated scores—Patriots at the Jets, Lakers at the Bullets, Suns at the Timberwolves. "This is from a few weeks ago," Mark said, feeling the buttons on the remote with his thumb. "I lost twenty bucks on the Pats. Didn't cover the spread."

"December twenty-sixth," she said, looking deep into the screen as a row of bright orange volume level squares paraded by.

The postcard shot of the beach was replaced by a shaky amateur video, out of focus and badly lit. It took a moment for Mark to comprehend what he was watching. A torrent of water raced down a city street, pouring through shattered windows, washing furniture and people out of busted doors and through collapsing walls. In the middle of the churning brown water, sprawled atop the roof of a submerged car, a woman held onto a screaming baby, her makeshift raft lurching, rolling slowly sideways, upending as it passed from view. A quick cut to a knot of people holding on to a telephone pole, their heads above the water and just below a jumble of sparking wires, then a hurried pan up the street as a pair of lifeless bodies floated by. Another shot, a high balcony view, the camera trained down the length of the beach, capturing the moment when a towering, white-topped wave plowed over the roof of a three-story seaside hotel to crash down on an outdoor market two hundred yards from the shore, an inch above the final from the Monday night game. In a booming James Earl Jones voice, the announcer read the text that appeared on the screen. *CNN Special Report—Tsunami—A Year of Recovery.*

Robin took the remote from Mark's hand as the man in the red polo shirt spoke of psychological shock and long-term trauma.

"My brother moved to Thailand three years ago. He was working at a beachfront hotel here on Phuket—a small place, local owner, right up on the water. He gave scuba lessons, took tourists out on dives. He used to email all the time. Sent these great pictures of the sunsets. He loved it."

On the screen, footage of tropical resorts and bustling town markets were interspaced with images of debris-filled streets and collapsed buildings, a then-and-now montage that faded to black and then cut back to the man in the polo shirt and the golden-sand beach. Robin pointed the remote at the VCR and raised the volume.

"But for some the scars run much deeper. Shock, denial, confusion, anxiety, forgetfulness, recurrent headaches and menstrual problems, sudden outbursts and anger issues, a growing dependency on drugs and alcohol…" the man in the polo shirt gave the sentence a three-beat dramatic pause before continuing. "All classic symptoms of Post Traumatic Stress Disorder, or PTSD, a serious mental health threat made more complex by the region's societal norms and cultural traditions."

Robin pressed the fast forward button, the images of health workers, victims, experts, blue skies, and palm fronds blurring past. She watched the screen, thumb above the play button, as she spoke. "We talked to my brother Christmas Eve. It was already Christmas Day here I guess. Usually we just emailed, phone calls are kind of expensive, but it was Christmas, so we called. He made me promise I'd come and see him at Easter." Mark watched as she chewed on her lower lip, her eyes fixed on the screen.

"Over two hundred and sixty people died on Phuket, half of them tourists. Many of the bodies were never found. Pulled out to sea probably. We called everybody we could think of calling, but nobody could tell us a thing. We kept on waiting for an email or the phone to ring. It would have been just like him to walk in and ask what's for dinner."

She hit the play button, the tape slowing down to normal speed, the VCR's whirring replaced by a Ford commercial and the flashing graphics of the CNN Special Report. The red-shirted man was back on the beach, a different one this time, the dense vegetation and tall beachside palms hinting at a remote location. Below, the sports ticker continued its endless loop.

"This part's in either Southern Thailand or Northern Malaysia," Robin said, and Mark tried to place the region on a fuzzy mental map.

The camera panned the shoreline, zooming in tight on a small group of dark-skinned, hard-bodied fishermen that stood around the tail end of a long, low boat that was pulled high on the beach.

"There," she said, mashing down the pause button, the fishermen jittering from side to side as the VCR held its place. She leaned forward and put a finger to the screen, holding it there as she turned to look at Mark, her clear blue eyes wide and bright.

"That's him. That's my brother. He's alive. We've got to find him."

Chapter Two

The bartender pulled the tall tap back and let the beer slide down the side of the pint glass. She angled the glass, letting a thin head build on the top of the Singha lager, leveling it as the last drops disappeared into the foam. Behind her, hidden among quarter bottles of Mekong and Sang Thip whiskies, a Fosters bar clock read two minutes after five, its hands super-glued in place. Outside it was ten till noon, but here it was always Happy Hour.

She rubbed the bottom of the glass on a damp towel before setting it down in front of the bar's only patron and said, "You should never drink tequila. It makes you stupid."

Mark Rohr picked up the glass and took a long sip. He ran his tongue along his top lip, feeling for the foam trapped in the mustache he had shaved off weeks ago. He wanted to say something clever—not smart-assed, just clever—but the moment passed and he knew it, so he said nothing.

She picked up the five pound note next to the glass and punched open the cash register, looking up as she did the math, tossing a short stack of Thai bhat back on the bar. She hadn't changed much since he had seen her last, divvying up the take after an all-night rave, miles out in the Jordanian desert. She was younger than him but not by as much as she claimed; still petite though, her burgundy-red hair a wild mess of frizzy natural curls that bounced just off her shoulders. Her hazel eyes sparkled in the neon light and when she smiled—which she did often—it was beautiful. He didn't ask Frankie Corynn how she came to own a run down bar that fronted a whorehouse on the roughest street in Phuket City, and she didn't say. He had known her too long for those kinds of questions.

"You went too far, Mark," Frankie said.

"You hired me to be a bouncer. So I bounced."

"*Sawatdee krup*," a raspy voice said behind him, and in the mirror over the bar Mark watched as a greasy-haired Thai with a pencil-thin mustache strolled into the bar and over to the pool table.

"*Sawatdee kaa*, Ronnie," Frankie said without turning around.

The man pinched a cigarette tight to his lips and sucked as if he was trying to finish it off in one drag. He moved around from pocket to pocket, rolling the balls to one end of the table, then stood there counting and recounting, going back to double check the pockets, the cigarette held in place.

"See, Mark? I told you not to use a pool ball, but did you listen?" Frankie said, her back still to Mark as she organized the cash register, separating out dollars, pounds, bhats, dinars, and rupees.

"I was busy at the time," Mark said, curious now, wondering if the man had noticed that the rack was missing too. "I figured it was better to use a pool ball than to put him through the window."

"Neither was an option you know."

Mark shrugged. "Maybe."

Using his fingers, which seemed freakishly long for his stubby hands, the man grouped the remaining pool balls into a rough triangle, the cue ball sitting in for the missing striped fifteen. He held them in place then tapped the cue ball free, chalking up a cue he slipped from the rack. He bent down and lined up the shot, drew the stick back but then closed his eyes and turned his head away, pausing for a moment before finishing the stroke, breaking the balls in every direction. He kept his eyes closed long enough for the balls to stop moving, then turned to survey the damage.

"Why does he do that?" Mark said to Frankie's back.

"Close his eyes? He says it makes it more interesting, creating all that mess and then trying to figure a way out of it."

"The same thing would happen with his eyes open."

"Probably," Frankie said, slamming the drawer shut, turning to rest her thin forearms on the bar. "But then where's the surprise? And speaking of surprises, you do realize you're fired, don't you."

Mark nodded.

"Suppose that one guy's knife didn't get stuck on the chair? Oh yeah, you smile now, but you wouldn't look so cute with one ear."

"And what was I supposed to do, let them go on like that?"

"Okay, they were getting a little out of hand, but once you had them down you didn't have to keep hitting them. And now I'm out a pool ball."

"It seemed like the best thing to do at the time." He took a long drink of his beer. "Still seems like a good idea."

"It's funny."

"See? It *was* a good idea."

"Not that," she said shaking her head. "When Mahmoud told me you were coming to Thailand part of me wanted to hide. You know I love you, Mark, but you can be a real pain in the ass."

"That's not what you said in Nairobi."

She rolled her eyes. "Okay, but that was different. They were armed."

"And Jaipur?"

"That was totally *your* fault. I had everything under control so don't even think of blaming me for that one. Besides, I can always bring up that little incident in Alexandria…"

He winced. "I wish you wouldn't."

She picked up a wet rag and ran it across the bar. "Did I tell you I Googled your ass a few months back?"

Mark looked up but didn't smile. "Now why would you do a thing like that?"

"I wanted to see if you were still alive. Interesting stuff." She tilted her head and gave him a knowing look. "How long have I known you?"

Too long, he thought but said nothing.

"You were a Marine."

"Don't hold that against me."

"You were in the first Gulf War."

Mark focused on finishing his beer.

"There was a nice story online from your hometown paper. Canajerry?"

"Canajoharie. It's in New York."

"Never heard of it."

"Nobody has."

"Anyway, the paper there had a nice little write up about you, about a big firefight in Kuwait, how you got a Bronze Star—"

"Less talk, more pouring," Mark said, waggling his empty glass.

Frankie picked up the glass held it under the Singha tap. "Some other things came up on that search too, something about a warrant for you in Ankara?" She filled the glass and handed it to him, slipping a hundred-bhat note from the stack. "Then there was a blog entry from this woman in Macedonia…"

"Is all this going somewhere?"

She punched open the register and slipped in the hundred, pulling out three tens which she dropped in the tip jar. "I figured that with all your experiences you could handle a simple job like bouncer."

"I handled it. It's over."

"Yeah, well if the cops come in here looking for a fat bribe to keep it all quiet I'll tell them the Marine said it's over."

"Speaking of jobs," Mark said, trying to change the subject, "why'd you send that girl up to my room this morning?"

Frankie leaned on one elbow, propping her head up with her hand, her fingers lost in the red curls. "She came in as soon as I opened. Some cab driver dropped her off right out in front. Totally ripped her off. The kid was a wreck—jet lagged, crying, obviously lost. She said she's never been overseas, never been out of frickin' Ohio if you can believe that. She tell you about her brother?"

He nodded. "Is that why you sent her up to me, to help her find her brother?"

Frankie smiled at him. "I knew you were out of a job and didn't have a place to stay—"

"What about the room upstairs?"

Still smiling, she shook her head. "It goes with the job."

"Damn. And I was gonna make curtains."

"I think the hotel her brother worked at is over in Patong, but I don't go over there much anymore. I know a guy there, owns a hotel. It's cheap but it's close to the beach. You can start with him, he might know some people to talk to, then you can—"

"I told her no."

Frankie dropped her hand to the bar. "You said *no?*"

He could feel her staring at him as he drank, waiting while he set his beer back down and ran the back of his hand across his mouth. "It's not the kind of work I usually do. You know that."

"Who cares?" she said, her voice rising an octave. "It's five thousand dollars. And in case you haven't noticed, that's a lot of money around here."

"That's if we find him."

"*Plus* she's willing to pay all expenses. Food, shelter…*beer*. That alone ought to be enough. Take the job."

Marked looked across the bar and into her eyes. "There is no job. A guy missing that long is either dead, or he doesn't want to be found. Trust me on that."

"She says she's got proof that he's alive."

"She hasn't got proof. What she's got is some guy in a video that she's convinced is her brother. A lot of guys have tattoos, a lot of guys have a certain way of walking. It's all coincidence."

"Then help her," Frankie said, leaning in as she spoke. "Take her around, let her look. It might do her a lot of good, help her bring some sort of closure."

"I told her she was wasting her time and that she should go back to the States and get on with her life. Coming all the way over here just because she thinks she's going to find her brother, it's stupid."

Frankie stood up and pulled a clean glass from the dish rack below the bar. She shook out the excess water and poured herself a Coke. She watched the foam settle and said, "That's a real bastard thing to say."

"Well that's me. A real bastard."

Frankie looked up. Her face was soft but she wasn't smiling. "This girl, Robin, she's got reason to believe her brother is alive. Okay, it's not much, but she's got something. She's got hope. If I thought my brother was alive somewhere, if I had *half* the proof she's got, I'd be there in a second. I wouldn't care what it cost or what it took to find him or what people thought about me. If I had that hope, that's all I'd need. But I don't get that hope. I watched my brother die. I went to the hospital every day and watched him get worse. At the end he weighed less than me." She took a small sip of her Coke. "But as you say, I got on with my life."

A pool ball clattered into a corner pocket. Cue stick in hand, the man moved around the table, rolling the balls all to one end, arranging them into shape. He stepped back and balanced the stick against a chair and from his shirt pocket he drew a loose cigarette. He flicked open a Zippo and lit the cigarette, pinching it to his lips as he considered the possibilities of the lopsided formation.

"You don't do these kinds of jobs, you apparently don't need the money and you don't owe me shit," Frankie said, and she waited until Mark met her gaze before she continued. "Help this girl."

Behind them, eyes closed, the man snapped the pool cue forward, the balls scattering across the table.

Chapter Three

The old woman with the chicken got off at the fifth stop.

She waited until the subcompact pickup came to a complete stop, listening for the ratcheting of the emergency brake before setting the chicken on Mark's lap, smiling up at him until he wrapped his hands around the bird's scrawny body. She stooped as she stood but was still far below the curved roof that covered the bed of the pickup. She inched her way down between the facing wooden benches, pausing to catch her breath halfway along. One hand on the railing, she eased herself down the two steps that hung below the bumper and onto the packed dirt along the pavement, pausing again to check her balance. She reached up, and Mark handed her the chicken, smiling first at Mark and then to the driver who hung out the window of his door.

The driver tooted the horn and drove off and got the pickup up to five miles an hour before slowing to a stop twenty yards away where five grade school students waited at the end of a narrow trail. Giggling, they climbed aboard, the boys in their white shirts and blue shorts sitting on one side, the girls in their matching shirts and blue jumpers on the other, all of them heading back for afternoon classes. They passed small coins up through the open window and pointed to a pair of their classmates a hundred yards back up the trail. The driver turned off the engine, ratcheted down the break and watched the boys approach, hanging an arm out the window to flick the ashes from his cigarette.

"This is going to take forever," Robin said, turning to check on the tardy boys who had stopped to throw rocks at a tree stump.

Mark stretched his long legs out the open back of the truck. "What's your rush?"

"No rush, it's just that on the map it looked like it was only about ten miles to Patong Beach. At this rate it'll take an hour."

"They always do," Mark said.

"I thought you said you've never been to Thailand?"

"I haven't. But these kinds of cabs, they're all the same. Matatus in Mombassa, jeepneys in Tuguegarao, tuk-tuks in Lahore, auto-rickshaws in Hyderabad. They're a great way to test your patience."

Robin sighed. "I seem to be getting a lot of that." Done with their rock throwing, the boys were wandering toward the pickup, kicking an empty beer can ahead of them. Robin set her backpack on her knees. She looked up at him, smiled. "Thanks again for agreeing to help me."

Mark smiled back. "I never agreed to help you."

It took a second to sink in, then her shoulders sagged and her mouth dropped open. "But...but you said...at the hotel..."

"I said you could hire me."

"What's the difference?" She shook her head, her hair shimmering in the light.

"The difference is five hundred dollars US a week, plus expenses and a five grand bonus if I find your brother. Dead or alive."

"And if you *were* helping me?"

Still smiling he said, "I'd just expect the bonus."

With a final kick of the can, the boys jogged the rest of the way to the truck. "Hello sir, hello ma'am," they both said, smiling blinding white smiles as they squirmed past Mark and Robin to squeeze in beside them on the wooden benches. The driver held a hand through the open window and the boys passed up their coins. The driver glanced at the coins before tossing them in a wooden box on the dashboard. He started the truck and continued down the road at a walking pace. The boy next to Mark settled in, pulling a wrinkled and incomplete homework sheet and a chewed stub of a pencil from his book bag. He jumped right in on question two while down the bench the schoolgirls looked at the paper with unveiled disgust.

Robin zippered open a large pocket on her backpack. She reached inside and took out a manila envelope, yanked the pocket closed and dropped the backpack to the floor. She slid a small stack of photos from the envelope. "This is my brother." She handed Mark several of the pictures. "They're from a vacation a couple summers back."

The photos could have passed for candids from a Calvin Klein shoot—the dark-haired man, muscled body glistening with sun block and sweat, grinning at the camera. She picked up the third shot, a close up, looking at it for a long moment before handing it to Mark.

"You sure this is the guy in the video?"

"I'm sure. On this one you can see his tattoos. He's got one like this Celtic chain on his upper arm. And you can see part of the one on his shoulder, the dragon." She reached up and patted her own back to show the area. "He was a little thinner in the video and his hair was longer, but yeah, it was Shawn."

"That's your brother's name? Shawn?"

"Yup, Shawn Keller."

Mark tapped the edge of the photo. "I thought your name was Antonucci?"

She seemed surprised by the question. "It is," she said. "I got married."

"When?"

"A few years ago. Didn't last a year."

Mark looked at the picture. "How much older is he?"

"Five years. He just turned thirty last month."

"Why's he in Thailand?"

Robin opened her mouth to speak, and the way she held her chin high and stared up at nothing, Mark could tell she was debating what she would say, how she would spin it. When she closed her eyes and gave her head a slight shake, a deep breath starting as a sigh and ending in an ironic laugh, Mark decided she would tell him something close to the truth.

"Shawn was the classic stoner. He smoked a *lot* of dope. Hash, too. Thai stick, sinsemilla, Santa Maria, Afghan Gold. Never got into the hard stuff but with as much as he was smoking it probably didn't make much of a difference. Before school, between classes, after school. He was all into that *High Times* lifestyle, saw himself as a real connoisseur, even got snobby about it. You know the type?"

Mark knew the type. There were a lot in high school, not as many in the Marines, but more than their squeaky clean image implied. He didn't know as many now. The stuff was still around but the people he encountered were more interested in moving it than using it. "Thailand's a long way to go just to catch a buzz."

"He went for the drugs, but not how you think. Shawn's been clean and sober for over five years but he likes to test himself, prove how committed he is. He hangs around stoners and party people, waiting for someone to pass him a joint or a pipe just so he can smirk and pass it on. He's like a recovering alcoholic who still keeps a stool at the bar."

"Dangerous, isn't it? Easy does it, one day at a time, one hit away from addiction, that sort of crap?" Mark said, trying to remember how that bumper sticker put it.

Robin shrugged. "That's why he does it. It's dangerous. He swapped one high for another."

"And the biggest highs are in Thailand?"

"That's just the latest stop. He's been to Colombia, Mexico, all these little Central American countries. Haiti. Some place called Marrakech," she waved her hand, the gesture suggesting dozens of forgotten drug filled locales. "He liked it in Thailand. Had a job with a hotel, they gave him a little place to stay. He took groups out for dives, scuba lessons, snorkeling."

"You didn't approve?"

"All I know is that if he didn't have that stupid job he wouldn't have been there when the wave hit." There was an edge to her voice that he didn't expect, and he could see her clenching her teeth as the pickup slowed to a crawl.

A lanky teen stood at the side of the road, his arms somehow crossed behind his back. It looked painful and the pose accentuated every peak of his angular frame. He smiled a gapped-toothed smile when the driver waved him over to the passenger seat, young enough to enjoy the thrill of riding shotgun, old enough to twist around to check out Robin's legs. Mark followed the boy's gaze. The kid was young but he had a good eye.

"I know it's stupid to blame the hotel," Robin said, "but I can't help if that's how I feel. That tsunami really screwed things up for me."

"How inconsiderate," Mark said, knowing how it sounded and saying it anyway.

"The good thing is that he's still alive," she said, missing or ignoring his tone. "All we've got to do is find him."

"I told you, he may not want to be found."

"I heard you."

"Besides, living through something like that, watching all those people die, everything just ripped away, it affects people, screws with their heads. Why did they survive, why didn't they do more, what are they going to do next..."

Her eyes narrowed. "What are you trying to say."

"There's a lot of drugs out there." He was going to say more, tell her about the Golden Triangle and the opium trade, about uncut heroin cheaper than Jack Daniels, and amphetamine-laced caffeine pills, tell her about the bands of strung-out Westerners, the hepatitis, and AIDS, but by the way she looked at him he could tell she knew.

"First we find him," she said.

Chapter Four

The man behind the counter smiled at them and said, "Fuck it."

Mark Rohr set his bag down on top of the registration desk. "Excuse me?"

"Fuck it," the man said again, his big, toothy grin framed by the patchy strands of his blond beard. "That's what everybody says when they come in here. Fuck it."

Mark hadn't planned on saying anything, deciding that since she was footing the bill Robin should handle the hotel registration, but when they had entered the lobby she had dropped back a step, allowing him to take the lead, shrugging now when he looked over his shoulder.

"Usually it comes out like, Fuck it?" the man said, changing his voice to indicate a hesitant question. "But it's not. It's the p h that messes people up."

"The p h?"

"They see the p h and think phone," the man said, punching numbers on an invisible mobile. "Or maybe photograph or physics, I don't know; I should ask. Anyway, they say fuck it."

Mark was reaching down for his bag, ready to agree, when it clicked. "Phuket."

"Yeah, that's it," the man said, the loose curls of his dreadlocks bouncing as he nodded his head. "*Poo*-ket."

"As in Phuket Inn by the Sea?" Mark pointed at the sign above the man's head.

"*Exactly.*"

"Except that it's not exactly by the sea…"

"True," the man said, curls bobbing, "but we're not much of an inn either. Inns are homey places, with room service and afternoon teas and maybe a communal living room; you know what I mean? Us? Got a busted Coke machine in the stairwell and as far as communal space, you're in it, man." He waved his hands around the cramped room, taking in the potted plant in the corner, the end table covered in dive shop brochures, and the condom machine next to the tourist map tacked up on the wall by the door.

"I'm sure it's wonderful," Robin said, setting her bag down on the counter and pulling out her passport and wallet.

"No, it's a dump," the man said, laughing as he said it.

Mark looked around the room. "Okay. But I wouldn't let the owner hear you say that."

The man laughed as he reached his arm across the counter and held it there till Mark shook his hand. "John DiMarco. Or Jason DiMarco. Whatever. Just call me JJ. And I'm not about to fire my best employee."

"And you're telling us that your hotel is a dump?"

"It's true," JJ said. "I'm not going to lie to you. Half the plumbing don't work, when it rains the stairs are like little waterfalls, the mattresses are paper thin, and the rats, well they're not as bad as they used to be before we got the dogs but now you got to put up with the howling."

"You're a hell of salesman, JJ."

JJ waved off the compliment then pushed the rolled-up sleeves of his white cotton shirt higher on his arms. "You're not stupid. You can see what kind of place this is. We don't ask many questions and whatever you do up in your room is cool as long as nobody gets hurt and you don't get the police at my door. It's live free or die, am I right? Now I suppose you want a room…"

"Two rooms," Robin said, pulling a pen from her backpack to fill out the form JJ slid across the counter.

JJ raised his eyebrows but didn't comment. "You want them adjoining, you know, with a door?"

Robin shook her head. "No thank you."

"Right," he said, turning to scan the row of keys that hung on nails on the back wall, a long, thin finger flicking each key in the line. "Third floor rooms are two-thousand bhat a night—fifty US—ground floor rooms are four hundred bhat. About ten bucks."

"Is there a better view from the third floor?"

"Nope," JJ said, still flicking the keys. "All the rooms look out to the side of the Patong Princess Resortel."

"Why so much more for the third floor?"

"Because when the tsunami hit they were the only rooms above the water."

Robin looked up. "Were you here that day?"

JJ laughed as he turned around to rest his bony elbows on the counter, his thin leather necklace dangling an Italian horn amulet like a tiny golden pepper. "I had a girl that worked here, Noi, older bar-beer girl looking to settle down a bit. She had hooked up with some Brit just before Christmas, wanted to spend as much time with him as possible, maybe get him to fall in love or something, I don't know. Anyway, it was the day after Christmas, what the Brits call Boxing Day, and Noi wants the day off in case this guy's feeling generous. Fine. So it's like the first thing in the morning, I haven't even had coffee yet." He stood up and pulled his dreads behind his head, holding them in place a moment before letting them drop; Mark watching his eyes as memory came into focus.

"I'm just hanging out, you know? And I hear this boom, Boom, BOOM." JJ's eyes widened, his shoulders jerking with the sound, each one louder than the last. "I'm thinking, ah shit, terrorists. I mean it's Christmas and this place is packed. Well not *this* place but the real resorts, you know? We had a lot of guests, maybe half full, Noi had a room on the first floor, some Aussie tour group took most of the top floor…"

"The boom," Robin said, leaning forward. "What was it?"

"It was the *wave*, man," JJ said, his voice dropping to a whisper. "Smacking into the beachfront hotels. You could feel the walls shake. Then the screaming starts. The only thing I could make out is run, so like an idiot I run out into the street, I gotta see, right? Well I saw, all right."

Mark rocked back on his heels and looked out the picture window. "Ocean that way?" he said, pointing down the side street, past the row of dumpsters behind the Patong Princess.

JJ nodded. "That's Sawatdirak Road at the corner. I see these people—not many, you know, it's Sunday morning—and they're running that way," he said, his thumb jerking over his shoulder and up the surrounding hills, "everybody looking back. And then like that," he said, snapping his fingers, "the wave came, a big brown roller, fifteen feet tall easy, just pushing everything out of the way. Cars, trees, people—it's ripping down poles and wires, whole storefronts, just snapping off, tumbling." JJ's hands moved as he spoke, the gestures growing in size and speed.

"And there was this…this *roar*. But you felt it as much as you heard it. They didn't get it in the news and you don't hear it in those videos people made, but ask anyone who was here, they remember."

"So, did the water come down the street?" Robin said.

"Oh, it came," JJ laughed a nervous laugh. "Like I said, I'm looking up at Sawatdirak Road and the wave, it's pushing all that shit in front of it, and there's these people climbing on top of car roofs and trying to hold on to street signs, and they're getting pulled under. I see this guy, Laang, did some painting work for me, he's floating on this freakin' deck chair from some resort, and I'm looking at him just as he falls off to the side into the water. Gone. Then I notice that the water is coming down the street at me. Not as much, sort of like a side wave, but it's knocking through storefronts and swallowing up cars, and I still got no idea what's going on. I mean, did you even *know* the word tsunami before then? So I hear the screams right behind me, and that roar. I look back, see the same thing happening on Bang-la Road. It was funny, it was like a wall of scooters—I mean everyone here's got one, right?—well the wave's just pushing all these scooters right at me, and I'm thinking, wow, that's a lot of scooters; and the next thing I'm hip deep in water and I can't stand up and it's half dragging me, half pushing me and I'm stepping on those scooters and all this wood ramming into me and it's like I'm getting gang tackled and I'm thinking, I'm dead."

JJ stopped and, tight-lipped, drew a deep, whistling breath through his nose. Mark glanced at Robin, her eyes locked on JJ's tanned face, the pen shaking in her hand.

"But, as you can see," JJ said, hands out to his side as he did a wobbly pirouette, "I lived to die another day. See that utility pole, the one that sunburnt guy's walking by? I grabbed a hold of that and started climbing, got up to that roof there. Me and about twenty others up on that little space—you can't see from here but it slopes a lot in the back. That's where I sat it out. Two hours later I'm ID-ing Noi's body over at the morgue they set up at the school. Sucked her right out of the hotel room. No idea what happened to her Brit."

JJ stood looking out the window at the rooftop across the street and the memory that was as clear and as vivid as the afternoon sky. Mark recognized the silence that filled the room. It was the same silence that had hung in the air after he had told his friends back home what it was like to come up against a squad of Iraqi troops, the troops that were supposed to be poorly trained and too scared to fight.

"Anyway," JJ said, clapping his hands together like he was closing a book, "let's get you a couple rooms. Third floor, right?"

Chapter Five

Straight rows of over-size umbrellas and rented lounge chairs lined the beach, filled with jet-setting university students on an early Spring Break; while beer-gutted retirees in Speedos and topless grandmothers strolled the shore looking for sea glass and shells. Standing off from the crowd, Mark stared over the low waves of the outgoing tide to a point just above the horizon, a million miles away.

Mark remembered the shaky videos of the hundred-foot wave hitting Patong Beach, the same beach where tanning tourists now dozed in the late-afternoon sun. It was all over in one day—the first wave, the unexpected waves that followed, the retreating water—a handful of hours the survivors would replay for the rest of their lives. A year later it was almost as if the wave never happened. Almost.

Above the wide open doors of the beachfront shops—shops that had been drowned under tons of debris-filled dark waves—deep gouges in the concrete showed where boats had been hurled inland, fifty feet off the ground. The marks had been painted over and some had been patched, but that only made them more obvious. Along the edge of the beach, guy-ropes held dozens of newly planted palm trees in place, filling in the gaps between fat-trunk giants, rare survivors with scars high among the palm fronds. The evidence was there, if you went looking for it; something neither the tourists nor the locals seemed eager to do.

Robin stepped down off the low wall that separated the narrow grass park from the beach and kicked off her sandals, slapping them together as she walked, knocking free the sand and letting him know he had company. She had changed into a light color tank top and khaki shorts, the bottoms rolled up to expose the top of her thighs to the sun. "You were right about the cold shower," she said and flicked her still-wet hair behind her head. "That took care of the jet lag."

"It'll take a few days. Tomorrow will be the toughest." He looked at her bare shoulders as she sat down in the sand. "You got sun block on?"

"It's okay, I don't burn. I tan." She smiled as she said it, closing her eyes as if willing herself bronze.

Mark pulled a plastic bottle out of one of his deep pockets, dropping it in her lap. "We're in Thailand, not Tampa. Put it on."

Rolling her eyes, Robin flicked open the lid and squeezed a white dollop onto each knee. Mark watched as she rubbed the lotion into her legs. She had dancer's legs, muscular but with the right shape. She finished with her legs, wiping the excess off on her forearms. "Put some on my back." She held up the plastic bottle and he squatted down behind her and squeezed some lotion between his sandy hands.

"So what's the plan?" she said, bunching her wet hair into a ponytail that she held out of the way.

"We start with the dive shops, see if any of them know anything. After that we work our way down the beach, hit the bigger hotels, then the shops, then the bars."

"You think we'll find him here?"

"No."

She turned her head to look at him, letting her hair fall to one side. "That's not very positive thinking."

"It's realistic thinking," he said. He wiped the last of the lotion on the base of her neck then stood up. "This place is connected. Phone, Internet…it's all here."

"So why can't he be here too?" She reached out a hand and he helped her to her feet.

"He could be. It's just that if he is, we won't find him."

"And that's realistic because...?"

"Because if he were here it would have been easy for him to contact you. But he didn't. So he's either someplace not as connected, or he doesn't want to be found. Or both. But if he is here, he'll know quick that we're looking for him and he'll make sure we don't find him."

She looked at him as she brushed the sand off her shorts, her head nodding slightly as if noticing something she'd overlooked before. "Okay," she said, the word coming out slow. "If he's not here then where do you think he is?"

"Anywhere. But just for fun, let's assume he's still in Thailand. He could have gone north, up to the mountains. Might not be as easy to get in touch from up there. He's a scuba diver, maybe he took a job on one of those live-aboard dive boats. Hell, he could have joined some Buddhist monastery."

Robin laughed. "Shawn as a monk? I don't think so."

"Fine. Then maybe he found himself a little bungalow somewhere, kicking back, spending his days on the beach, a sweet little Thai girl to keep him company, maybe one of those Norse goddess bathing beauties; there's certainly a lot of them around. Maybe he's been too busy to call, that kind of lifestyle can be exhausting for a guy."

"Shawn's not like that," she said, the anger rising in her voice.

"What? Human? I'm just trying to be realistic here. Now put some of this on your face," he said, handing her back the sun block. "You're getting a bit red."

She glared at him, and for a moment he thought he had pushed too hard, that she would storm off and he'd be fired twice in the same day. Not that he'd mind. But then she sighed and flicked open the cap. "You don't get it," she said, squeezing the lotion onto her fingertips. "And the reason you don't get it is that you don't know Shawn."

"Come on," Mark said and started across the beach to the row of small hotels that lined the road, "I've got five thousand very good reasons to meet him."

Chapter Six

With a pearly-white smile and a deferential bow, the waitress set the plate on the table, backing away as she wished him a goodly breaking fast time. Mark poked at the pile of noodles, moving the tiny legs on the freakishly large prawns with the tips of his fork. Spicy pad thai shrimp at seven a.m., the chef's special, highlighted on the breakfast menu.

"Your friend not a morning person?" JJ said as he sipped his tea. Other than a Swedish couple, a round German retiree plowing through a second bowl of white rice, and a Thai security guard—his forehead resting on the napkin dispenser as he got an early jump on his first nap—Mark and JJ were the only people at the restaurant, the empty beach visible over JJ's shoulder, just beyond Thawlwong Road.

Mark considered the little he knew about Robin before shrugging his shoulders.

"I always liked mornings," JJ said. "Everything seems possible in the morning. But then the next thing you know it's noon and you start to wonder if you'll get anything done, and before you know it it's like five-o'clock and you're like, fuck it, I'll worry about it tomorrow." He poured himself a second cup from the teapot the waitress left at the table. "Wasn't always like that. I used to own my own business. A construction company. Not some nickel and dime thing either, a real construction company with bids and contracts and out-of-state jobs, all that shit. It's true," he said, reading Mark's mind. "It was great for a while, maybe ten years. Then one night I'm watching the Travel Channel, an eight-minute piece on Phuket comes on. A month later I'm signing the whole thing away, a dime on the dollar. A month after that I'm buying a hotel." He shrugged his shoulders, a gesture that could mean a thousand things. "That's Phuket for you."

Mark wasn't sure what he had expected to find in Phuket. What he didn't expect was for it to look as developed as most second-tier beach towns he'd seen in the states, with souvenir shops shoulder to shoulder down the main strip, interspaced with McDonalds, KFCs, and 7-Elevens. The beach road hotels peaked at four-stories, but away from the sand twenty-story chain hotels rose up, oddly angled on oversized lots to assure every balcony a sunset vista.

And he didn't expect so many tourists: college kids from Europe, lugging backpacks heavier than anything he had to carry in the corps, their matted hair twisted into dirty-blond dreads; retirees from Australia with sagging folds of skin as rich-hued as the leather purses that hung on racks outside the designer knock-off shops; and bands of Japanese tourists, sticking close behind the tour director's yellow umbrella.

There were Thais, of course, but none looked as if they were on vacation. Their English was good—their survival depending on it—and by the time he and Robin had walked a mile they had heard ten variations of the what-is-your-name-where-are-you-from-please-come-to-my-shop monologue from the gentlemen, and the piercing, drawn-out offers of something called a Thai massage from girls not old enough to order a beer.

But more numerous than the backpackers and the retirees and honeymooners and the souvenir shop touts and the scantily clad masseuses were the legions of single white men, nursing hangovers as they slept in deck chairs that lined the beach or, sunburnt and peeling, lounging in hotel bars, waiting for the tropical sun to set. There were some in their twenties and some pushing eighty, but most were what would generously be called middle-aged, with middle-aged paunches and middle-aged hairlines and middle-aged fashions, and girls young enough to be their daughters on their arms. And at night they crowded three deep into the open-front bars of Bang-la Road, packed tight with giggling Thai girls whom they ogled, and pounding techno that they pretended to like.

He had planned on starting with the hotel Robin's brother had worked at, checking with the dive shop to see if anyone had seen Shawn Keller since the tsunami; but although it was still marked on the tourist maps, there was only a vacant lot where the beach-front hotel had stood, a rare empty space as conspicuous as a missing tooth. He showed Shawn's picture around the shops along the main drag, the employees glancing at the photo for a full second before launching into their sales pitches. By seven p.m. they had run out of shops and hotels and headed to Bang-la Road.

"So if you came in on the beach end you probably started with the Free Bird," JJ said, eyes closed, mentally building a map of the street. "The Pussy Cat bar-beer used to be there on the right hand side, but the tsunami took that out. Was the bartender's name Nitaya? A short Thai girl with long black hair, parted in the middle, small tits but really pretty?"

Mark raised an eyebrow. "That sort of describes every Thai woman I've seen since I got here."

"You'd remember Nitaya. Sweet kid. Great smile. A real high-pitched laugh though, like somebody cleaning glass."

"Like I said…"

JJ swirled the tea in the cup, bits of tea leaves rising to the surface to cling to the white ceramic rim. "Nitaya might know where to look for your brother."

"It's Robin's brother. And I asked at the bar, passed the picture around, told the bartender I was looking for this guy. She told us I should check over by the Royal Paradise Hotel."

"I'm sure she did," JJ said with a laugh. "The Thais call 'em *katoey*—sort of means lady-boy. Transvestites."

"Some of them, yeah," Mark said, recalling the short skirts, broad shoulders, and the bouncing Adam's apples, "but not all of them."

JJ shook his head and smiled.

"I'm telling you, JJ, there were some really hot looking women there. Models, most likely."

"*Katoey.* Trust me. Just be glad you didn't learn the hard way. Okay, so I assume you went back to the bar-beers on Bang-la."

Mark skewered a tamarind-coated prawn and pulled off its crispy tail. "Are you sure?" he said, his fork bobbing in time with the words. "I mean, a couple of those women…"

"Positive. So, you're back on Bang-la."

"Right. Back on Bang-la," Mark said, shaking his head. "There was this huge place, open air, big fiberglass crocodile with a guitar out front."

"Ah yes. Know it well."

"We go inside, Robin's like the only blonde in the place. Well, natural blonde," Mark said, wondering now if she really was. "It was crowded but we found a seat. Next thing you know there's like a dozen women hanging all around our table, rubbing my shoulders and giving Robin these dirty looks."

"Unfair competition," JJ said. "They think all Western women give it away. Obviously they didn't know my wife."

"Anyway, I buy them a round of drinks and I show them the picture of Robin's brother. One of the girls spoke English pretty good so I told her why we were here, how her brother was supposed to have been killed in the tsunami but how he may be alive." Mark paused, letting the moment build, a confident smile growing. "The girl explains to her friends what I was saying and the next thing you know, they're all talking at once, pointing at the picture and nodding. Every one of them said they've seen this guy since the tsunami. Apparently he comes in that bar all the time," Mark said, biting off half of the giant prawn.

"Sure they have. And I bet they all said that it would be easy to find him, and that he's healthy and safe and doing really well…"

Mark looked across the table as he chewed on the prawn, JJ waiting as he washed it down with a short glass of pineapple juice. "So they all lied?"

"See, now that's a typical Western reaction," JJ said. "A Thai told me something that's not true, therefore she lied to me. Maybe, but it's not that simple."

"Seems pretty simple to me."

"That's because you're not Thai. If you were, you'd understand. Thais call it *ruksaa naa*," JJ said and even Mark knew that he had butchered the pronunciation. "The Noble Lie. It's better to have a wrong answer than no answer at all."

"Better for who?"

"For everybody. You get an answer—which, if you know Thais, you realize may or may not be true—and they save face by not looking stupid."

"They save face with a wrong answer? Doesn't *that* make them look stupid?"

"You asked a question, they had an answer. Believing everything you hear, now *that's* stupid."

Mark stabbed his fork into a second prawn, the tiny legs splaying out flat on the plate. The waitress shuffled over to their table, her flip-flops sliding across the sand-covered concrete floor. JJ said something to her in Thai that made her laugh, Mark guessing it was more the way he said it than what he said. They both watched as she shuffled back to the open-air kitchen, her long black ponytail swaying in time with her hips. Mark waited until she stepped behind the counter before breaking the reverent silence. "If everyone's worried about saving face, how will I know if someone is telling me the truth?"

"Simple. You move here, immerse yourself in the culture, master the language—a tonal language by the way—unravel the social norms, become one with the ways of the Buddha, learn to read the gestures and body language, gain the trust and respect of the locals and, if you are so inclined, marry a wonderful Thai girl and willingly take on the burden of supporting her and her entire extended family for the rest of your life."

Mark nodded. "I'm a bit pressed for time."

JJ sighed and shook his head, his dreadlocks swinging back and forth. "See? That's what I had to get away from. You're a slave to time, man. You get one life; live it. Just let go and let God." Mark waited, winding the thin rice noodles around his fork like it was spaghetti.

JJ sighed again, a louder, disappointed sigh. "I've got some friends, Sailor Bill and Chao. They know everything that's going on in Phuket. I'll give 'em a call, tell 'em about your brother. Right, Robin's brother. I'll see if I can get some answers for you."

"Answers I got," Mark said, helping himself to some of JJ's tea, the hot liquid steaming up the sides of his juice glass. "What I need is the truth."

JJ closed his eyes and tilted his head back, his bronzed face welcoming the morning sun. "You want everything, don't you?"

Chapter Seven

"I can't believe we're back here two nights in a row."

Mark stepped off the sidewalk and through the wall-sized opening that served as the doorway of the Super Queen. Even with Robin at his side, he noticed a quartet of bar-beer girls peel off from the mob of British divorcees cheering on some rebroadcast of a Premier League match-up. They clomped across the hardwood floor, the unsteady gait of teenaged legs on eight-inch spiked heels, high-pitched voices giggling a welcome at once both grating and erotic.

"We were in a different bar," he said. "We've never been here before."

"Seen one testosterone-soaked, techno-blasting beer garden loaded with fat old men and petite size-two Thai hookers," Robin said, glancing from side to side, "seen 'em all."

Jet lag had caught up with her shortly before noon, heading up to her room "just for a few minutes," coming back down after the sun had set, asking JJ if there was a place nearby that was still serving breakfast. As she rubbed the sleep from her eyes and ate a bowl of noodles and shrimp at a beachside restaurant, she kept checking the clock by the cash register, debating which clock to trust.

"I talked to Sailor Bill," JJ had said when they returned to the hotel, shaking his head as he spoke. "The stories that guy's got. Anyhow, he tells me you gotta see Won at the Super Queen."

"Which one?"

"Won," JJ said. "Not one. She's a bar-beer girl from way, way back. Hangs out at the Queen. Part housemother, part madam. Bill says that she's the person to ask."

"So Won's the one," Mark had said as he and Robin turned to leave.

"Yeah," JJ had yelled to them as they stepped outside, "but who's on first?"

Even with a hundred people in the bar—one-part tourists, three-parts hostesses—the Super Queen was too cavernous to seem crowded. The white-skirted bar-beer girls wore yellow and black rugby tops, knotted high to the side to reveal flat stomachs, silver bellybutton rings, and the occasional Disney character tattoo.

"Hello sir, hello m'am," the quartet said. "You party with us?"

"Sorry ladies, we're on our honeymoon." Mark swung his arm around Robin's shoulder and he could feel her step away from his embrace.

"Not true," one of the girls said, poking him playfully on the arm. She smiled up at him with her tiny white teeth and he could feel himself smiling back. "Not married. No ring."

"Rings are old fashioned," he said, waggling his fingers. "We're a modern couple."

"Ooohhh," the girl said, translating for the rest of the quartet, each nodding, repeating the rapid-fire Thai words, shouting back a high-pitched response.

"You modern. That's okay for us. We give you discount."

Mark rubbed his chin with his free hand. "It's tempting," he managed to say before Robin ducked out from under his arm.

"We're looking for Won," Robin said to the girl.

The girl's eyes widened. "Just one? Okay for me."

Mark tried not to laugh as he listened to Robin draw in a deep breath.

"There's a woman who works here, her name is Won. Do you know her?"

The girl smiled a real smile, brighter and more attractive than the first. "Sure. Everyone know Won. She the best." She reached out and took Robin's hand, her fingers lost in Robin's small palm. "Come."

The girl led them past the football fans and around the chain of island bars that dotted the dance floor to a large booth in the back, too brightly lit to interest the bar's customers. Crowded on one side of the booth, three uniformed bar-beer girls held plastic bowls up to their chins, shoveling in wads of noodles with blurred chopsticks while crushed in next to them two more girls tapped out text messages on their mobile phones with electric-blue nails; a final girl, balancing a butt-cheek on the rattan bench, bobbed her head to the synthetic beat.

Alone on her side of the booth, an old woman took a long drag on an American cigarette.

She was thin and small, smaller than the tiniest girl in the bar, with skin as lined and wrinkled as a balledup roadmap. She wore her hair—or her wig—short and fire-red. She blew the smoke straight up out of the corner of her mouth, her cracked lips pressed tight together; and Mark noticed Robin staring at the woman's long earlobes, dangling down like flattened fingers, heavy gold hoops hardly noticeable.

"Excuse me," Robin said, stepping into the light that pointed down from the ceiling to the center of the table. "We're looking for Won. I mean we're looking for a person named Won, not…"

"Stop," the old woman said, holding up her hand, her cigarette pointing back at her nicotine-weathered face. "I hear every Won joke in the world, the last time I hear original it by Marine heading to Vietnam, so do not try."

"Sailor Bill sends his regards," Mark said.

The old woman looked at him as she inhaled, the end of her cigarette glowing hot, then blew the smoke out toward the dangling light. She knocked a knuckle on the tabletop and shouted something at the row of girls as if they were a block away. They slid out of the booth and wandered toward the bar, noodle bowls and phones still in place. Won gave her wrist a flick, inviting them to sit, Robin sliding in, Mark taking the end.

"Sailor Bill, huh?" Won gave a smoky snort. "When he first got here he was Ski Bum Bill, then he was California Bill. One girl called him Big Dick Bill but she was new and she want him to buy her things. The best when we call him Dollar Bill. He spend the whole night talking some poor girl down ten bhat." She laughed, somehow puffing on her cigarette at the same time. "He was fun. Then he got married." She paused and took another puff. "Bastard."

Mark smiled. "My name's Mark. This is Robin." He reached across the table and shook her hand, her skin like warm leather. She smiled up at him as she ignored Robin's outstretched arm. "Your English is better than mine," he said. "Accent's a bit heavy…"

"I gotta brush up on my English. Gotta brush up on my German, too," she said, pausing a beat before adding, "just as soon as he gets here." She laughed again, and her face disappeared behind a cloud of blue-gray smoke. "This how you tell how long a girl's been here. The better her English the longer she's been bar-beer girl. I tell girls, don't let on how much you know. Guys come in looking for sweet, farm-fresh virgin. They don't want some worn out whore."

"Interesting. I was wondering if you can help me. I'm looking for my brother." Robin pulled a photograph from her purse. "This is his picture."

Won looked across at Mark and raised an eyebrow. "She your wife, Mark?" Won gave her head a slight nod in Robin's direction.

"No."

"Smart man." Won pulled a fresh cigarette from behind her ear, offering it first to Mark before lighting it off the stub of the old one. "So what your friend's problem?"

Mark chose the simple answer. "Her brother went missing during the tsunami."

"Lot of people went missing that day," Won said.

"She's got reason to think he's still alive."

"What you think, Mark?" Won flicked the dead butt out to the dark dance floor. "You think he alive?"

"Yeah, maybe."

Won kept her eyes on Mark as she drew on her cigarette, blowing the smoke out through her nose this time. "No you don't. Besides, been over a year. If he alive you would know by now."

"Possibly. But Robin here thinks he could still be in shock."

"I don't suppose you've ever heard of Post Traumatic Stress," Robin said, trying to hide her impatience as Won watched a smoke ring float up past the hanging lamp to the dark rafters twenty feet overhead. "He might still be in shock and not thinking clearly. His brain may not be working right. I'm *sure* you understand that."

"Shock, huh?" Won wrinkled her lips, exaggerating her smirk. "Sound like bullshit to me. If he alive you know it. Unless he don't want to be found."

Mark could sense Robin tense up and he reached over to pick up the photograph before she could say something stupid. "Ever see this guy before?"

Mark held the photograph out, Won making him wait as she took another long drag, holding it in as she propped her cigarette in an ashtray, exhaling slowly as she reached for the picture. She glanced at the photo then handed it back to Mark. "I not seen him."

"That's it?" Robin said, her voice rising. "You didn't even *look* at it."

Won looked at Mark and gave a slow-motion shrug. "He not been in."

"This was a waste of time," Robin said, turning, pushing on Mark's arm to move him out of the booth. Mark reached over and put a hand on Robin's leg, shoving her back down.

"He hasn't been in," Mark said, and he mirrored Won's smirk. "But you know who he is."

Robin stopped squirming. She looked first at Mark, then across the table at Won, easing back down as the old woman's smirk slid into a grin. Won forced another drag out of her cigarette, keeping her eyes on Mark. "I think I let Pim explain to you."

"Who's Pim?" Mark said.

Won paused, an eyebrow arching up. "Let's say she a bar-beer girl."

"One of the girls here?"

"No. Over at Horny Monkey. Not on Bang-la, but not far."

"A real girl, right? Not some lady-boy."

She clicked her tongue as she shook her head, her earlobes flapping like JJ's dreads. "Pim all girl. Just like me."

Mark smiled and leaned forward. "A sweet thing like you, you wouldn't tell me a story just to save face now, would you Won?"

"Sweetie, after fifty years in this business, I not have any face left to save," she said, and gave him a wrinkled wink.

"Excuse me," Robin cut in, the irritation clear in her voice. "This Pim person, what can she tell me about my brother?"

Won's smile dropped as she turned to face Robin. "More than you want to know."

Chapter Eight

Not counting the two diners that sold beer and the one restaurant that had a three-bottle wine list, there were fourteen bars in Canajoharie, New York.

They all fit a pattern—dimly lit, a pair of TVs mounted on either end of the bar, a jukebox that hadn't changed since the seventies, template sports posters from Budweiser and Miller, a vinyl banner announcing that TK 99 was The Home of Classic Rock!, and an interchangeable clientele that knew theirs was the best bar in town. The music was better at the strip club but the beers were more expensive, the same girls everyone had seen naked since high school, the stretch marks hardly visible in the half-light. He hadn't been back since the late nineties but he knew that it was still the same. And they wondered why he left in the first place.

Despite what the locals like to think after a night of pounding back dollar drafts, there were no tough bars in Canajoharie. There were bar fights and once or twice a month the cops would be called when some drunk pulled a knife or fired off a few rounds in the parking lot, but in every bar on any night you'd find retirees, sipping away their pensions, the other patrons stepping out of the way as they shuffled past with their walkers.

Mark knew more than a few tough bars. Back road juke joints a day's ride from Camp Lejeune, after-hours hip-hop clubs in Dar-es-Salaam, back alley opium dens in Pakistan, a Kingston rum shop far off the tourist track. There was something about them, something primal, something that told you that this was no place to fuck around. They never had bar fights—at least not in the Hollywood sense—and the cops would never be called, never show up if they were, the crowds staying in the shadows, nobody watching the drug deals go down, nobody jumping up to stop the three-on-one beating, nobody saying nothing when a backhand flattened a mouthy hooker.

The Horny Monkey was one of those bars.

Unlike the wide-open bar-beers on Bang-la Road, Vegas-bright and Carnival Cruise-naughty, the windowless walls and steel door of the Horny Monkey kept the casual tourists away, drawing only those who knew what they would find. A tight spring yanked the door shut behind them and Mark felt the muscles in his arms twitch.

Inside, a couple dozen people leaned on the bar, slouched in a dark booth or clumped around the pool table, the hanging low-watt lights giving form to the blue-white bank of cigarette smoke. The men in the bar—Thais, Chinese, a few Europeans—either ignored them or stared straight at them, looking for a reason to start something; and Mark knew he was standing taller, sending a clear message.

There were fewer women than the other Phuket bars but more than he would have found in any bar in Canajoharie, and there was no uniform at the Horny Monkey, the women dressing to please themselves, not some Western tourist's fantasy, all jeans and black tee shirts, baggy and unrevealing. And where the bar-beer girls were sweet and bubbly, the women of the Horny Monkey didn't play that game—no flirtatious bullshit, just business. They were older, harder and, pound for petite-little-spiked-heel pound, the most dangerous people in the place.

"Two-drink minimum, each," the barmaid shouted over the music, a high-pitched Thai pop singer and a drum machine squealing through a cover of last year's number one. She held her arm out straight, two fingers pointing level at them like a forked stick. "You pay now."

Mark peeled off a five-hundred bhat note and set it on the bar. "Four Leos," he said, pointing at the beer light on the back wall.

"You think this a cheap dump?" the woman shouted, her voice cutting through the din. "Twelve-hundred bhat. You pay now." She popped the tops off the four beers to seal the sale.

Mark added more multi-colored bills to the pile, and when the woman reached over to grab them he covered the bills with his hand and said, "I'm looking for a girl named Pim."

If he hadn't been watching for it he wouldn't have noticed her hand stutter when he said the name. Chin down, the woman raised her hooded eyes, trying to read something in Mark's expressionless face. He moved his hand an inch to the right, revealing a pair of thousand bhat notes. The woman glanced down at the bills, her tongue darting out to wet her lips, glancing from side to side to see who was watching. With one hand, Mark passed two warm beers back to Robin, leaning in as the woman's sweaty palm slid across his hand, dragging the bills down under the bar. He waited, wondering if it was him that made her so nervous. The woman turned to look up at the TV, a cricket match live from Lahore, and rubbed her nose with her knuckles, the gesture obscuring her lips. "Back of the room, by dance floor. White dress. That Pim."

Mark took a long pull on his beer before turning around, Robin handing him an empty bottle to set on the bar. Despite the surroundings, her hips moved with the music, a sway that was subtle and instinctual.

"Well?"

Mark took a minute, draining his first beer as he let his eyes adjust to the light. "She's here," he said, Robin looking at him as he spoke. "But something's not right."

"Not right? How do you know?"

He could tell her about the darting look in the bartender's eyes or about those two guys at the end of the bar, the bad actors who were pretending to be watching the cricket match but were watching them, or how everyone near the pool table all held a cue even though no one was playing. Instead he said, "I've spent a lot of time in bars." He set the empty on the bar, taking a swig of his second beer. It reminded him of an Odenbach lager but too warm to enjoy. "Things might get difficult. If you're not comfortable with that..."

"I can deal with it," she said, her thumb peeling through the green and white beer label as she spoke.

"You don't even know what 'it' is," he said and, ignoring the strange looks, he led Robin to the dark end of the room.

A row of high-backed narrow booths hugged the wall and above each, a dim-bulbed lamp hung down from the ceiling, spilling a feeble pool of yellow light on the table. Cigarettes glowed red in the darkness and a low-hanging bank of wispy gray smoke rolled overhead with each exhale. Some of the booths were empty, a few others appearing empty, their occupants pushed far back into the shadows. He was sweating in a featherweight sport shirt but there were plenty of jean jackets and leathers in the room. In the corner, the lamp over the table a bit brighter, a girl in a white dress worked through a word-search puzzle. She didn't look up as they approached; and as Mark and Robin stood at the end of her booth and sipped their beers, the girl ran her pen diagonally across the page, putting a tight loop around Pandorasbox.

She wore her hair like every other Thai woman, long and straight, parted in the middle and pushed back behind her ears; and, like countless other Thais, she was naturally thin, with tiny features and bee-stung lips, narrow hips, and a small chest. He watched her scan the rows of letters of the Mythic World! puzzle, her painted nail gliding under each line, her measured pace never changing. Later that night, as he stared up at the slowly turning fan in his hotel room and thought about all the things that should have made her so average, he couldn't decide what it was that made her so much more beautiful than the others.

"Excuse me," Robin said, her voice apologetic and sweet this time, "we're looking for someone named Pim."

The girl clicked shut her pen, setting it in the fold to mark her place before closing the magazine and pushing it to the side. She took a moment to compose herself, her shoulders rising as she took a deep breath, then looked up at Robin, smiling an unforgettable smile.

"My name is Pim. Perhaps you are looking for me. Please, have a seat," she said, her English, stilted but perfect, clicking in the back of Mark's mind.

"Thanks," Robin said, sliding in tight against the far wall. "I'm Robin, this is my friend, Mark."

"It is a pleasure to meet you," Pim said, shaking first Robin's hand, then Mark's with a firm and practiced three-beat business grip. "You are drinking Leo beer? Please, allow me to get you Heinekens." She made a slight waving motion to catch the barmaid's eye, then turned back to Robin. "So what brings you to Thailand? Business or pleasure?"

"Pleasure," Mark said, cutting in before Robin could say otherwise.

"You have picked a good place for that," Pim said, watching the barmaid sprint across the room. She lifted the Heinekens off the tray, dismissed the barmaid with a nod and set the beers in front of them. "Here is to new friends." She held up her can of Coke Lite. The beer was shockingly cold and Mark drained half the bottle in three gulps.

Pim dabbed the corners of her mouth with a napkin and looked across to Robin. "I think people tell you all the time that you are a very attractive woman."

"Don't joke like that when I'm drinking," Robin said, coughing, wiping her mouth with the back of her hand as she set her beer back down, "I might choke to death."

"But it is true," Pim said, turning to Mark for confirmation. "Your pretty hair, your tan…you have a very nice body. Are you an athlete?"

Robin shrugged. "I hit the gym now and then…"

"And you are a very handsome man as well," she said, her fingertips tapping the back of his hand. "Which hotel are you staying at?"

"Near the ocean. Phuket Inn by the Sea."

Pim thought for a moment, her lower lip rolled up between her teeth, the glossy red vibrant against her straight white teeth. "I am sorry, I do not know that hotel."

"Well there's a lot of hotels here," Robin said. "You can't know them all."

Pim smiled. "I just want to make sure that there will not be a problem, that is all."

"A problem?" Robin looked to Mark. "What sort of problem?"

Mark set his beer down and looked at Pim. "I think you have the wrong idea."

"Oh no," Pim said, smiling back at him. "I understand. This is not that uncommon at all. I am just lucky that you are both so attractive."

"Whoa, whoa, whoa," Robin said, her hands off her beer and out in front of her. "What the hell are you talking about here?"

"Oh, she does not know," Pim said, looking at Mark. "You should have told her first. It is best that way."

Mark reached over and held down Robin's wrist. "As much as we are intrigued with the offer—"

"*What?*"

"—we really came to see you for another reason."

Pim's smile dropped, and he could see her jaw tighten. "Who sent you here?"

"A friend at the Super Queen."

"Won," Pim said, her lip curling as she spoke.

"She said you might be able to help us find someone."

"I do not know anyone. Now you excuse me," Pim said, gathering up her word-search magazine and her empty Coke can. Mark's hand shot out so fast she didn't have time to react.

"Sit down," he said, two fingers holding her arm tight.

Pim looked up, her eyes narrowing, her small nostrils flaring. Mark waited, guiding her back into the booth with a twist of his wrist.

"Please," Robin said, leaning in. "I need your help." She said it the same way she had said it back at his room, her eyes rimming with tears.

Pim yanked her arm free and looked at Robin. She let the anger pass. "If you are coming to me for help then it is already too late for you."

"All I need you to do is look at this picture," Robin said, taking the photo out of Mark's shirt pocket. "Just look at the picture and tell me if you've seen him, that's all." She set the photo down, turning it so it faced Pim, and slid it across the table.

With an annoyed sigh, Pim picked up the picture, holding it so Mark couldn't see her reaction. After a long moment she set the picture back down and pushed it back to Robin. Elbows on the table, she interlocked her fingers, tapping her chin with the back of her thumbs as she looked at them.

"They are going to be following you when you leave here," she said, as if pointing out the obvious. "At least two, maybe more. You need to go back to Bang-la Road. Go to the bars, the big ones. Show the bar-beer girls the picture, ask the bartenders if they have seen him."

"We did that," Mark said. "That's how we found you."

"They need to think that you are still looking. And that I did not help you."

"So far you haven't."

Pim lowered her arms, her elbows pushing out along the table-top, her slight fingers intertwined in a tight knot. "Tomorrow is Sunday. There are Christian services at the Holiday Inn. We can talk there." She looked over Mark's shoulder into the dark area at the far end of the room. "You must go now," she said, the smile back in place, bigger than before. "Try to look not happy."

"Just tell me," Robin said as they maneuvered out of the booth. "Do you know the man in the picture?"

"Yes," Pim whispered as she gave a theatrical shrug, shaking her head no. "He is my husband."

Chapter Nine

Mark checked the map in the lobby of the Phuket Inn by the Sea one last time before pushing open the glass door and stepping out to join Robin in the early morning sun.

"Couple hundred yards down the beach road," he said, pointing to the south. "Then left on Ruamjai. JJ said there's a dive shop on the corner."

"That's a big help. There's a dive shop on *every* corner." With both hands, Robin flicked her hair off her shoulders and for reasons he never questioned, Mark found it sexy.

He paused to put on his sunglasses. The sun was still hidden behind the forested hills of the island but, backlit, the trees along the ridge-tops stood out in sharp detail. The sky was powder blue and cloudless. Other than a few restaurants and a Cinnabon, the stores were all closed, heavy metal doors rolled down and padlocked to hasps set deep in the concrete sidewalk, a rare business lull that wouldn't last till ten. At the corner, an elderly Thai woman sipped on a Starbucks coffee as she stood waiting for the bus. Across the street, committed sunbathers staked out their territory, determined to get the most out of the daylight hours, while tuk-tuk drivers in their white shirts and jeans, cigarettes sticking straight up, stretched out on the low wall that separated the beach from the road.

Did it look like this that morning, he wondered. This beautiful, this perfect? Did anyone notice how quiet it was, how the air smelled of orchids and baking bread and cut pineapples? Did anyone notice when the last lapping wave pulled back from the beach, drawn out to deep water by forces miles below the seafloor? And when they saw it coming in, just a black line on the horizon at first, did they know what it was? Did they run for the high ground, hoping to outrace a wave that came in like thunder? Or was it like watching a hand grenade arching through a busted window, the release lever springing free with a tiny metal ting, everything then in slow motion, like running through mud, knowing you'd never get away in time?

"Ready to go—or did you change your mind?" Robin said.

He turned and looked at Robin. "I'm making sure our friends from last night are gone."

"Those two? Don't worry, we lost them at that knock-off Hard Rock Café." She flicked the thought away with the back of her hand.

Mark pointed at the cement bus stop bench across from the hotel. "They sat out there till just before three, then they went up the beach road to that all-night 7-Eleven. The tall guy, the one with the basketball jersey, got a Coke Slurpee, the other one pocketed a couple of candy bars when the clerk wasn't looking. Then they spent ten minutes trying to jimmy open the lock on a scooter on the other side of Bang-la Road and when they got tired of that they went home. The tall guy lives with his parents above a vegetable market, two miles up that way. And when you stand there with your mouth open like that you look pretty stupid."

Robin started to say something, then snapped her mouth shut.

"Let's get going," Mark said, motioning her along. "We don't want to be late for church."

She fell in beside him, careful to watch her step on the uneven sidewalk, risking a glance up at him as she spoke. "Did they see you?"

"Please."

Her eyes grew wide. "But how?"

"Camouflage."

"Like Rambo?"

"Like Ralph Lauren. I changed my shirt, put on a pair of shorts, and stuck a beer in my hand. I looked like every other guy on the streets."

"You shouldn't have told me," she said. "For a moment I was impressed."

Mark shrugged. "The truth's usually disappointing. Sort of like last night."

"Ugh. *Her.*"

"You don't like your new sister-in-law?"

"She's *not* my sister-in-law."

"She seemed pretty sure to me," Mark said, stepping around a mangy dog curled up in front of a dark souvenir shop.

"She's not Shawn's type. He likes girls that are not so... so..."

"Beautiful? Sexy? Hot?" Mark said. "Stop me any time."

Robin glared up at him. "Not so slutty."

"You'd be surprised at the number of guys who'd be able to overlook that."

"That's fine," Robin said, "as long as Shawn's not one of them."

"Whether this Pim is or isn't married to your brother—"

"She definitely isn't."

"—she may know where we can find him. So don't piss her off." Mark gave her tee shirt sleeve a tug, nodding at the dive shop on the corner before turning down Ruamiji Road and into the entrance of the Holiday Inn.

"She's a liar," Robin said, looking into Pim's eyes as she spoke, a cobra staring down a mouse.

It had been easy to find Pim. Although the hotel lobby was filled with Thai women, many of them gorgeous—maids heading into work or higher-end hookers heading home—Mark spotted Pim as soon as they walked through the sliding glass doors. She was dressed conservatively for Patong Beach, a flowered print dress that hung below her knees with a neckline that refused to plunge, her long black hair pulled back in a ponytail, held in place with a large flowered clip, worn leather sandals on her feet. Yet despite her plain appearance—even the uniformed maids were more fashion conscious—there was something about her, something that Mark couldn't explain, something that made her the most attractive woman in the room.

"They let me come here on Sundays. For church," Pim had explained as they found a table at the hotel's indoor café.

"Are there many Thais at the service?" Mark had said, watching as a pew's worth of Nordic-blond tourists asked a bellhop where the Christians were meeting.

"I do not know," Pim had said, no trace of curiosity in her voice. "I have never gone. I spend my hour sitting in the lobby."

And now, not even two minutes into her story, Robin was calling the woman a liar. Mark knew that she might be right, that she might be making it all up as she went, her accent masking her assured command of the language. But he also knew enough about women to know that calling her a liar wouldn't help. He tapped Pim on the forearm until she looked across at him, breaking free of Robin's hooded stare.

"Let's hear it again, this time with some details." He kept his voice soft and tried to smile just enough so that she would trust him.

"Why bother?" Robin said, tossing a balled up napkin down on the hotel café table. "I told you. She's lying."

Mark held onto Pim's gaze a moment longer before turning to Robin. "Take a walk. I'll meet you at the hotel in an hour." He didn't know if it was the way he said it or the look in his eyes as he spoke, but, teeth clenched, Robin stood up and walked out toward the lobby. Mark waited until she passed through the main doors before turning back to Pim.

"As I said," Pim continued, "my husband is alive. And I can take you to him."

"Yeah, that's what you said. Now tell me why I should believe you."

Pim's eyes widened and she rocked back in her chair. "Why would I lie to you?"

"Why would you tell me the truth?"

"I want to find him."

"There's no money in this. Even if you take us right to him, we're not paying you a damn thing."

"I want to find my husband. This is all I want."

This is all I want. Mark leaned back and waited, wondering how many times he had heard that line.

"Yes," she said, shifting in her seat as she spoke. "This is all I want."

He waited, one arm draped over the back of the chair, the other stretched out onto the table, a finger tracing the condensation trails down the side of his iced tea. "What's the catch?"

"The catch?"

"What are you going to tell me after you say but? As in this is all I want, but…"

Her expression changed though her eyes never left his. "It *is* all I want. But it will not be easy."

"Why?"

"It will be hard to leave Phuket."

"Because?"

"They will not let me go."

Chin down, Mark looked up at her. "And *they* are…?"

"Jarin's men."

Mark nodded, flicking water droplets off the glass. "Tell me, Pim, how long does this church thing last?" He motioned toward the meeting room across the lobby.

Pim shrugged her narrow shoulders. "One hour, sometimes more."

"Then we don't have time for me to pull every answer out of you."

She looked at him, and for a moment Mark was sure she was going to storm out. Instead she hitched her chair forward and leaned in.

"Jarin controls this part of Phuket," she said, her voice so small Mark pulled his chair in to join her. "Drugs, gambling, prostitution, smuggling. He controls it all. The police do nothing—he pays them to do nothing—and everyone else is afraid of him. The bar you came to, the Horny Monkey, that is his, but all the bar owners on Patong Beach pay him something."

"All right, so why is he holding you?"

She paused, her lip trembling as she drew in a deep breath, tilting her head back to look up at the ceiling, blinking to fight back the tears that came anyway. She wiped them off with the back of her hand. "I do not know."

"Some local hood is keeping you captive and you don't know why?"

"Yes," she whispered.

Tears didn't mean the truth. He had learned that more than once. And he knew nothing about this girl. Nothing she was saying made sense, but for now he was willing to assume that these tears were real. "How long has this been going on?"

Pim sniffed and caught her breath. "Right after the tsunami. We were living on Koh Phi Phi." She pointed out the hotel doors as if the small tourist island had just pulled up on the curb. "They came looking for Shawn. I thought he was dead and I told them. The next day they brought me here. They told me that I could never leave, that I had to pay them back."

"For what?"

She shook her head. "I do not know. But last night at the bar," she said, eyes still wet but looking deep into his, "you saw how I work for them."

Mark tapped the long spoon in his glass, kicking up a cloud of undiluted sugar and fruity spices that made the iced tea too sweet to drink. That's what happens when you stir things up, he thought. Across the table, Pim added a packet of NutraSweet and an extra mint leaf before sucking her iced tea through a bent-neck straw.

"Last night, when we met you," Mark said. "You thought we were there to hook up with you."

"I thought Jarin had sent you. He sends men to have sex with me. At first it was men he was making a business deal with, foreigners mostly, but sometimes Thai men in the government. Some of the men were kind to me and a few even gave me presents, but Jarin's men took them from me later. Sometimes there were women, too. Now the men are not as nice—men who work for Jarin. They are not supposed to hit me but some of them do, not where you can see." Pim pushed the mint leaves down with her straw as she spoke, her casual tone adding an icy acceptance to her words.

"When you and that pretty girl—Robin?—when you and Robin came to my table I thought that perhaps Jarin had changed. You both looked so kind. No one has been kind to me for a long time."

Watching her as she spoke, seeing the tiny spark in her dark eyes and the wistful smile that appeared as she remembered emotions half forgotten, Mark knew what he would do. Her story made no sense, but for some reason that made it easier.

"When you go to the hotels with the men Jarin sends, do the guards come too?"

Straw in her mouth, Pim shook her head. "No. Jarin's men, they only follow me sometimes."

"Did they follow you here?"

"No, they never do."

"So they're not outside waiting for you?"

She shook her head, her black ponytail bouncing from side to side.

Mark dropped the spoon back into his iced tea. "Do they watch the bus lines, the port area?"

"Perhaps. I do not know."

The wicker and wood chair creaked as he leaned back and wondered if she understood his question. "Have you ever tried to get away, just get on a bus and head out? There's a bridge to the mainland you know."

"Yes, I know. I think it would be easy for me to go that way."

"Do you have family in Thailand, somewhere you can go?"

"Most of my family was killed when the tsunami came." Pim turned to look out the hotel's glass doors. "My parents, my sisters and my brother, my auntie and my two uncles. My grandmother. They are all gone."

It had taken years for Mark to lose his family. It started with a divorce, then a brother running away, a sister moving to Utah to find God, then a gunshot to the head that the police called a self-inflicted hunting accident, a heart attack, an overdose, distant relatives he hardly knew fading away. Long before the war he was alone. Pim had lost them all in an instant. He wanted to tell her how lucky she was but he knew she wouldn't believe him. Instead he said, "Who's left?"

"Ngern. He is my sister's son. And my grandfather…my father's father. They are my family now." She set her iced tea down, folding her hands in front of her on the table. "And they are your catch."

"*My* catch? What does that mean?"

"It means I will take you to my husband," Pim said, smiling for the first time since they had sat down. "But you have to take my family, too."

Chapter Ten

They were wrong.

All *ferangs*? They didn't look alike.

You just had to know what to look for.

You couldn't go by the obvious things. He had seen lots of tall Japanese and short Americans, even short black Americans, so you couldn't go by size. And you couldn't tell them apart by color, either. He had seen French speaking Arabs and Chinese guys from Australia who couldn't speak Chinese, and black Germans and white guys from Kenya.

It was easy to tell them apart when they talked, anybody could do that, although he still got confused when it came to telling Canadians from Americans, but you couldn't say that to a Canadian since they'd tell you they were from America, too. But everybody else knew what it meant.

The real trick? Telling them apart from a distance.

And you couldn't know by looking at one thing either. You had to look at all the parts and put it together. Sometimes one part didn't fit and you had to say okay and toss it out, take a look at all the parts that did fit instead. He had tried to tell them how to do it, how to read the *ferangs*, but they didn't listen to him. They never listened to him.

The first thing you look at is the clothes.

Tight shirts—European.

Tight *silk* shirt, unbuttoned—France or Italy.

Socks with sandals—Germany.

Striped rugby shirts—British or Australians.

Striped rugby shirts with nut-hugging shorts—Australian.

Baseball caps, the front bill curved up like a tube and turned sideways like they just walked into a wall—Americans.

Russians wore lots of jewelry. Canadians had the best sandals. Swedes went barefoot.

Next you looked at hair.

If it was a skinny guy with no shirt and his hair all matted together like a white Bob Marley, he was probably from Finland or Norway—someplace that was cold all the time so that when they came to Thailand they never wanted to go back.

Australians and Americans wore it short on the sides and longer on the top, Brits wore it long all over. Russians parted it on the side and combed it over like James Bond.

And you could tell a lot by how they sat. Europeans crossed their legs at the knees. Americans and Canadians put one foot up on the other leg, making a little triangle table out of their lap. Germans kept both feet on the ground.

Just by looking, you could tell a lot about someone. It made them easy to spot, easy to trail. He could have told them this, too, if they had only listened.

But they never listened. They just made fun of him, picked on him because of his size, because of the way he walked, which wasn't *that* different, his one leg bending out a bit, that's all. But that was enough. One guy had said he walked like a spider; which was stupid because he didn't walk anything like a spider, but it stuck and that's what they all called him now, Spider, nobody calling him by his real name, nobody knowing anything but Spider.

And nobody knew what he was like growing up, none of them coming from his village. They didn't know what he knew, about all the trouble he'd gotten into: the fights, the time he smashed a bottle on that guy's face, the one that laughed at him when he tried to talk to the girl, how his lip never looked right after. How they made him leave when his mother went crazy and had to be taken away, how he was only fifteen when he ended up in Phuket City, and how he lived on the streets for three years, stealing tips off tables and pulling knives on fat drunk tourists who had paid ten bhat to put a hand down his pants. And they didn't know anything about how he sold *ganja* to the tourists and sometimes some opium, too, and *ya ba* and other pills to the truck drivers to keep them awake for days.

And none of them had any idea how good he was with a knife.

He was certainly better than the two guys that were supposed to tail the American couple last night. He had heard that bitch behind the bar tell them to follow the big guy and the blonde, but he knew those two even though they didn't know him, and he knew they'd screw it up, get spotted or lose the couple in the crowds, which should be impossible since the guy was so big. But they could do it. He knew he wouldn't get spotted and he certainly wouldn't lose them, but nobody ever sent him out on a job like that. Nobody sent him out on any job at all. But as he had watched from his dark corner at the bar, he had decided it was time to show them.

The American couple wasn't a minute out the door before those two started out after them. He had slipped out right behind them. Not that anybody noticed. The couple walked them all over Bang-la Road, to all the places the *ferangs* liked to go, with Jarin's men so close behind that the American had to see them. And then how they sat there on the bench across from that hotel, the Inn by the Sea, with the guy coming out, drinking a beer—they never noticed the American, even though he followed them for an hour. And the American never noticed him.

Just like now.

He watched as the American strode out of the Holiday Inn and headed up Ruamjai Road. Best way to spot Americans? Look for the guy who thinks he owns the sidewalk.

He'd stay on this guy, follow him and his girlfriend like those other two were supposed to do. He'd show them all that he belonged, that he was as good as any of them. And then Jarin would hear about it and he'd say what's your name, and he'd tell him and Jarin would call him by his real name and say you want to work for me, and he'd say yes and then no one would dare call him Spider after that. All he had to do was keep an eye on this American and his blonde.

And the best thing? He might get to use his knife again.

Chapter Eleven

"Right, so you're going to give me twenty US to walk in that bar and pick up a hooker?" The big Australian smiled down at Robin before twisting the top off a cold Singha.

The man wore a blue and maroon polo shirt with a fist-sized Brisbane Lions logo and a pair of khaki shorts that only made it halfway down his tree-trunk thighs. He towered over Robin, with shoulders that seemed as wide as she was tall and the bottle of beer disappeared in his calloused hand. His shaved head glowed red, either from the pulsing neon of bar-beers or too much time in the sun. It was coming up on two a.m. on a Sunday night, Bang-la Road still filled with stumbling male tourists and giddy Thai teens.

"You're going to *pretend* to pick her up," Robin said, flicking the cap from her beer into the trashcan, ten feet away. "What you're going to do is walk her out to the beach. I'll be waiting there. I'll see you, don't worry about that. Then you go off and drink yourself stupid."

The Australian tilted the beer back, draining a third of the bottle in one swallow. "Why don't you go in and get her?"

"If I wanted to do it that way, I wouldn't have asked you."

"And I just bring her back out here? To you?"

"See? I knew you'd catch on."

The Australian nodded, a knowing smile crossing his face. "Right. I'll do it, no charge and be happy as Larry...if I can stay and watch."

Robin rolled her eyes heavenward. "What *is* it with you men? You go in, escort her out of the bar, bring her here, I give you twenty bucks, then you go play with your little friends." She nodded at a swarm of bar-beer girls that buzzed around under the lights of the Steady Tiger nightclub. "Got it?"

"Thought you said you had a boyfriend hereabouts. Why not have him do it?"

Robin reached out and took the man's wrist, turning it to see the face of his watch. "Because right now he's busy. And I'm late. So what's it going to be?"

"Cash up front?"

"No."

The Australian stuck his chin out. "I won't be duded."

"I don't even know what that means," she said.

"And if I say piss off?"

"I find another freak of nature and give him the twenty."

The Australian finished his Singha and gave a beery belch. "Right. Let's get started."

The first one was easy.

Mark had stood in the shadows and watched the man roll a joint. He had long, thin fingers and extra-wide papers, but the man lacked the basic skills mastered by kids half his age and had ended up spilling more than he rolled. Between his cheap lighter and the spit-wet paper, it took him twenty tries to get it lit, but when he did he wandered out of the yellow pool of light on the porch and down into the small clearing that served as a yard, inhaling deep, choppy breaths in the warm, dark night, his back to the wall of palm trees and jungle vegetation.

Mark timed his move, catching the man as he blew out the last of the smoke, one arm around his neck, the other hand clamping shut his nose and mouth. The state trooper who had taught him the move said it was too dangerous for law enforcement to use. Maybe, but it was a lot less lethal than anything he had picked up in the Marines. The man only jerked once before slumping, Mark guiding him down amid the flag-sized leaves and tangled roots. He took a roll of duct tape from the cargo pocket of his shorts and bound the man's hands together, stooping down to check his breathing before positioning a short piece over the man's mouth, making sure to leave his nose clear. He needed the guards out of the way but very much alive. It was bad enough as it was—killing someone would only make things a hell of a lot worse.

In the fifty minutes that Mark had been watching the back of the small, Thai-style house—corrugated tin roof, cinderblock walls, and the whole thing propped up two feet off the ground on stubby cement columns—he had seen all three of the Thai guards that JJ had warned him about, and had watched the white-haired old man through the open kitchen window as he washed a stack of dirty dishes; and he had seen the boy, the top of his head anyway, as he crossed the living room to the small corner bedroom. And JJ was right, there were no guard dogs, although there were plenty on the dirt trail that had led to the hillside bungalow, set far off from the cluster of identical homes squeezed in at the intersection of two nameless dirt roads. It was secluded but not hidden. "Everybody knows Jarin's places," JJ had said over a late dinner of prawns and beer. "And everybody stays the hell away."

Mark spun the roll of tape around the man's ankles, twisting each pass through a jumble of roots and vines. He was still out, but the look on his face seemed to suggest that he didn't mind. Squatting low, Mark fought down the rush of adrenaline that was already making the hair on his neck rise, focusing on his breathing and listening to the sounds that came from the house. He could hear the tinny rattle of cheap flatware in the kitchen and the thumping bass and high-pitched whine of a Thai pop star in the main room. He crept through the darkness toward the back of the house, his eyes trained on the building, avoiding the glare of the dim-watt bulbs. Soon the others would notice their friend's absence, and he would lose any slim advantage he might have had. If they hadn't noticed already.

The back porch, railing-less and dark, was littered with empty Singha bottles and Tiger beer cans. Crouching, Mark eased a leg onto the low porch and was shifting his weight up when the screen door swung up, scattering empties and clattering against the concrete wall.

In a single move, Mark slid under the house, scuttling on hands and knees across the slimy ground and behind one of the narrow support posts. He waited for the man to jump down after him but no one came. Above him, he could hear the lazy shuffle of sandals across the wood boards of the porch, and through the uneven gaps he watched as the second guard shook a cigarette up in a pack, drawing it out with his lips. The man moved to the edge of the porch, his toes hanging just inches over Mark's head, and pushed one hand into his pocket, pulling out a flip-top lighter, the other hand pulling down the fly of his jeans. The butane flame sparked to life, a yellow stream arched into the darkness and Mark sprang out, grabbing the man's ankles, diving away from the porch, pulling the man out and down with him, rolling, spinning around in time to see the man's head bounce off the porch, the unlit cigarette still clutched in his mouth. The man leaned up, shaking his head and blinking, reaching back to rub his neck when he saw Mark's fist. It was the last thing he saw that night.

It took three long minutes to drag the man under the house and bind him with tape, the cracking speakers in the stereo masking the noise. And for three minutes Mark expected to hear the ratcheting click of a shotgun shell dropping into place, but other than the thumping remix version of the same, endless song, all he heard was the deep breathing of the unconscious guard and, far down the hill, a pack of motorcycles racing toward the strip. He assumed the last guard would be waiting.

Mark rolled out under the kitchen window, avoiding the rectangle of light that angled down from the bare bulb above the sink. He knew he should duck into the bush, check the windows, the doors, look for movement, establish his target and reassess his options. He also knew he didn't have the time to do it. There were no phone lines to the house but that didn't mean a thing—even the coconut vendors on the beach had cell phones. He bobbed his head around the corner and, seeing nothing, went up the steps and through the spring-less door the guard had flung open.

At the entrance was a short hallway lined with empty shelves and Mark paused. To his right was the kitchen and he could hear the old man stacking plates in the cupboard. Pim had said that she would get word to her grandfather, tell him that a *ferang* would come that night, an American, but that he should tell no one, not even the boy, and that he must not act nervous, not make the guards suspicious. Mark had no way of knowing if the message had been delivered or, if it was, whether or not the grandfather would agree to go, but it was too late to worry about that now.

Across from the kitchen was the main room of the house and beyond that, a pair of bedroom doors. He could see the end of a rattan couch and part of a table, a pile of CD cases next to the stereo, twin columns of LED lights jumping in time with the beat. Mark took a deep breath, and stepped around the corner and into the room. It was empty, nothing but a matching rattan chair, the rest of the table and a dark TV. He angled across the room to the door on the right, faster than he wanted to move but slow enough to be silent. There was no doorknob, just a metal latch that he raised. Foot braced against the bottom, he cracked the door a quarter-inch and peered in.

At first he thought it was empty, just a dirty cot and bare bulb, but then he noticed the small boy sitting on the floor, a box of crayons fanned out in front of a pad of paper. The boy looked up at the crack in the door, his face blank and impossible to read. Mark had pulled the door shut and had just lowered the latch back in place when the man came out from the other bedroom, a bottle of Thai whiskey in his hands.

The man only hesitated a second but it was long enough. Mark lunged across the room, knocking the man back against the wall, ramming his knee up as the man swung the bottle at his head, cheap whiskey pouring over them both, the man grunting but not dropping, bringing the bottle down hard on Mark's shoulder, more whiskey spraying as the thin glass shattered. Mark's hand shot out, clamping tight on the man's forearm, slamming his arm back against the doorframe, pushing the jagged edge away from his face, pushing until he heard the wet pop, the man's elbow bending back, his numb fingers dropping the bottle. Mark gave the arm a twist and saw the color drain from the man's face and without a sound he slipped to the floor.

Mark stepped back, keeping one eye on the dark bedroom, the other on the slumped guard, careful not to step down on the shards of glass. He was reaching into his pocket for the tape when he heard the floor creak behind him, the bamboo pole whistling as it swung in on the side of his head. There was a bright flash of light and a white noise roar filled his head, everything out of focus as he dropped to his knees, turning as he fell forward, his shoulder breaking his fall. He twisted and looked up at the man, a fourth guard he should have fucking expected, flexing his grip on the short bamboo rod, hefting it like it was a baseball bat, turning his hips to get everything into his swing. Mark tried to rise up but the room was spinning too fast, a warm trail of blood washing over his eyes, the man zooming in and out of focus, wanted to bring his arm up to block the blow but not sure how, everything moving so slow. Above him, the man jerked the bamboo higher on his shoulder, then stiffened, his eyes growing wide, mouth dropping open, a half step forward, then another, then falling face first onto the hard wood floor, Mark watching his eyes all the way down, watching them now as they stared sightless across the floor.

Framed by the hallway to the kitchen, the old man stood silent, white hair, white shirt, tattered canvas shorts, a foot-long bloody knife in his hand.

Chapter Twelve

Jarin took one last drag before dropping the stub of his cigarette onto the dead man's back. It stuck to a sticky lump of congealed blood that had pooled in a fold of the shirt, just above his waist, smoldering out.

The man lay face down, his eyes wide, his mouth open, his body already bloating in the mid-morning heat. He had let someone get behind him, someone who knew what he was doing, the long kitchen knife slicing his kidney in two, twisting the blade as the man went into shock, dead before he hit the ground. The idiot.

Jarin knew the kind of men that worked for him. Not their names, of course. Most were like this one, bottom feeders, far down the food chain. He must have dozens just like him on one payroll or another, too stupid or too lazy to work for anyone else. But, obviously, stupid or lazy enough to get themselves killed. Jarin wondered what the book would say about this.

He had picked it up at the airport in Singapore, the first book he ever bought and the only one he could remember ever reading. It took the better part of a month but he'd gotten through it, reading a page or two every morning, squatting over the porcelain hole of the traditional toilet in his twenty-million-bhat home. *Top Dog: The Ten Rules of Pit Bull Leadership.* It was, according to the cover, everything the successful businessman needed to know to turn an under-performing mutt into a Rottweiler success story. And Jarin knew something about both.

As a kid he had trained fighting dogs for Sok Saek, one of Bangkok's most ruthless gunmen. He had learned a lot from the dogs and learned a lot more from Sok Saek. Things were different back then, easier. Everything done on a handshake or at the end of a barrel. Now it was all unilateral agreements and strategic cooperation, multi-national corporations and electronic funds transfers. And fucking lawyers everywhere. It was almost impossible to make a living. That's why he bought the book. The book said it had the answers, all he had to do was follow the rules, starting with Rule Number One.

You can either play with the puppies or run with the big dogs.

He was twenty kilos overweight, he smoked constantly and liked his Mekong whiskey straight, but as he looked at the body on the floor, Jarin knew it was time to run.

And this race would be with Mr. Shawn.

Jarin stepped around the body and walked into the kitchen, a squad of his men scurrying to get out of his way. Propped up on a stool next to the sink, a row of empty Coke bottles behind him, the man with the twisted arm rocked back and forth. His face was pasty white and his teeth clattered together, his lips red and swollen where they had ripped off the tape. His arm rested on his lap, his elbow bending two different ways. Jarin stood in front of the man and lit a fresh cigarette, the man looking up at him, the terror clear in his eyes. Jarin drew in on the cigarette, blowing the smoke out his nose, and said, "Describe him."

The man was shaking now, the legs of the stool knocking against the metal cabinets. He opened his mouth to speak, stuttering, nothing but air coming out. Jarin sighed and shook his head, pointing to the man's arm. "Did he do this to you?"

The man looked down, surprised that Jarin had even noticed, then looked up, his head nodding in jerky movements as Jarin snatched a bottle off the counter and cracked it against the man's elbow. The man screamed and toppled over, his nose catching the rim of the sink as he fell, the blood cascading down his face, down the white metal doors. He squirmed tight against the cabinet, his good arm reaching up to block the next blow, Jarin grabbing the stool and slamming it down once on the man's ankles before throwing it out of the way, stepping forward, the sole of his sandal pressed hard against the man's face.

"*Ferang*," the man shouted, not daring to touch the foot that was crushing his jaw. "He was *ferang*."

Jarin leaned both hands on the counter and dragged his sandal across the man's face and down onto his neck. He could see the man looking up at him, his eyes wild, too afraid to move. Jarin shifted, rising up, all of his weight pressing down on the man's throat. He flexed his knee, bouncing once, twice, holding his foot in place, the man never as much as kicking out.

It took less than a minute.

Jarin lifted his foot and turned his back on the man, running a hand across his head, sweeping his thin hair back in place.

Of course he was *ferang*. The locals couldn't even look at him without cowering, let alone try something like this. Even now his own men looked away, men half his age, stronger, each of them carrying guns. And every one of them puppies.

Then there was Mr. Shawn.

Jarin walked out of the kitchen, through the hallway, the men shuffling behind him. He stepped around the body, saying, "Get rid of them," without turning around, and walked out the front door and onto the porch.

Another morning in Phuket. Another day at the head of the pack. Jarin closed his eyes and drew in a deep breath through his broad, flat and twice-broken nose, clearing his head.

Rule Number Four: Bite 'em on the ass when they least expect it.

The rule had more to do with motivating employees with incentives, shaking up management teams, and surprising competitors with new marketing ideas, but Jarin saw how it applied to his world as well. Mr. Shawn's little adventure last year had cost him a great deal of money, but it was more than just that. And it was more than the fact that Mr. Shawn had put a kink in what had up to that point been a smooth operation, an operation that had taken several years and countless bribes to establish.

This Mr. Shawn, he realized, had just bitten him on the ass. Again.

Jarin didn't need a book to tell him what he had to do.

Mark Rohr wiped the salt spray off his sunglasses and looked across the inlet. Crowded tight along the back of the beach, a row of thatch-roofed huts perched high on bamboo legs, lines of wet laundry flapping like flags across the small fishing village, a dozen long-tail boats moored up on the sand. As their own long-tail had motored north along the west coast of Phuket, Mark had watched hundreds of boats cruise back and forth through the night, fishermen heading out or heading home, pea-green chemical glow-sticks tied around the stubby point on the low bow. Miles from shore, trawlers attracted whole schools of fish with banks of lights that lit the water like a movie set.

It had taken longer to get down to the boat than he had expected. The old man had led the way, taking them down a hillside path that ran parallel to the main road. They had passed close to several houses, people on the porch watching them as they walked past, the old man looking straight ahead, the boy quiet, watching his feet, careful not to trip on the roots that buckled up under the packed dirt. They crossed the beach road at a dark bend and went down to the shore, the long-tail waiting just as JJ had promised. They walked out into ankle-deep water and stepped over the low bow, the old man swinging the boy up and into Pim's arms. The boat's owner pull-started the motor, swinging the ten-foot propeller shaft to the side and into the surf.

"Any problems?" Robin had said.

"None that could be avoided."

"An old man and a kid." She shook her head. It was dark but Mark was sure she was not smiling. "She better not be lying."

Despite its shallow draft and narrow width, the boat proved stable on the open water, but the sea was flat and Mark wondered how stable it would have been with even modest swells. He sat on an ass-wide board at the bow, Robin behind him, settled between their backpacks on the bottom of the boat, her bare feet up over the side, her tribal tattoo anklet visible against her lighter skin. The old man had sat near the center of the boat. He kept his back straight and his hands on his knees, staring ahead the entire trip. Pim had the last seat—the boy, almost as big as her, asleep on her lap. At the rear of the boat, his lean body silhouetted against the night sky, the boat's owner stood on one leg, a heel propped against a bony knee, a lazy hand on the throttle. When the drive chain broke and flew overboard—the engine revving wildly, waking Robin but not the boy—Mark thought they might drift till morning. But the owner pulled a cardboard box from behind the gas cans, drawing out an oily chain that he wound into place, knocking the engine tight with a wooden mallet, all of it done by the faint light of the crescent moon.

He'd known lots of nights just like this one. Hugging some dark shore, sneaking through some mountain pass, bullshitting past a check point, driving all night in a stolen truck. Sailing off Yemen. Crossing the desert in Libya. Hiding in Iran. Lost in Wherethefuckistan. And in the hold or in the trunk or strapped under a coat or fiber-glassed to the fuselage, kilos of Ethiopian qat, cases of AK-47s, barrels of Johnny Walker, blocks of hashish, DVDs of porn. And people. Illegals looking to get in, a different kind of illegal looking to get out. If the pay was good and the odds acceptable, the cargo didn't matter. And if the pay was excellent, nothing mattered. But the pay was never excellent and the odds were always greater than you planned for, and too many times there was no pay at all. The risk of doing business with the kind of people who needed his skills.

And it was always the easy jobs that fell apart. Just drop off the package and you get paid. Get me across the border and it's yours. Bring it in and you get the reward. Find my brother and I'll pay you five grand. He didn't expect anybody to get killed—he never did—but things happen, especially on the easy jobs. A weekend into this one and so far one guy was dead, he had a fat welt on the side of his head; and in addition to a hot blonde with a surprising catty streak, he was hauling around an old man and a little kid because a Thai hooker who claimed to have the information he needed refused to leave them behind.

It was still early but Mark knew that there was a chance this job wasn't always going to be this easy.

"Hey Columbus," Robin said, tapping the seat of his shorts with her painted toenails, "if you see a drive-thru, pull in and get me a tall coffee." She was stretched out along the bottom of the boat, her head propped up on his backpack, her eyes shut behind her sunglasses, cool despite the rising heat and thick, humid air.

"Pim," he said turning around, raising his voice to be heard over the popping motor. "Is this where we stop?" He jerked a thumb over his shoulder at the beachside shacks.

"Yes, we stop here," she said. "For now."

"For now," Robin repeated, just loud enough for Mark to hear. "Lovely. Just fucking lovely."

Chapter Thirteen

"*Sawatdee kaa*," Pim said, placing her palms together as she bowed her head, the tips of her fingers brushing the end of her nose.

"*Sawatdee krup*," the old man responded, bringing his hands up chest high to return the gesture, smiling at the girl. She was well dressed, her jeans and blouse worth more than all the clothes in his home, but her *wâai* showed respect to his advanced age; and as he watched her climb the stairs to the porch, taking off her sandals and stopping at the top step so that her head remained lower than his as he sat on the wooden bench. The old man was glad to see that some parents still taught their children the important things in life.

He had watched as they had climbed out of the boat. The two *ferangs* had jumped out first, sandals in their hands in the knee-deep water. Like all *ferangs*, they had overstuffed backpacks, with straps dangling like ribbons and liter-sized bottles of water lashed to net pouches, carrying more with them than he owned, everywhere they went. The man looked like all *ferangs*, too tall and too big, but the girl was a pleasant surprise, with her long, blonde hair and curvy figure; a welcome change from the black-haired, flat-chested women he was used to seeing. The Thai girl was pretty, dainty but not fragile, her perfect white teeth and smooth skin reminding him of the village girls of his youth. There was an older gentleman in the boat, and he had watched as this man climbed out without assistance. He guessed they would be about the same age, that man and him, and he hoped that they would have time to talk. Stripping off his shirt and shorts, a small boy—no older than his own great-grand children—dove into the water, the *ferang* throwing a coconut far out into the low rolling surf for the boy to retrieve. Few outsiders stopped by the village and the old man tried not to let his curiosity show.

"You have a lovely home, sir, and I am humbled that you have opened your doors to me," Pim said, adding the polite *kâ* ending to her sentence, her Thai light and clear.

"You are welcome," the old man said, motioning for Pim to sit on the palm frond mat at his feet. "What is your name, child?"

"I am Pim."

"And your father?" he said pointing to the boat.

"My father is dead. That is my grandfather."

The old man nodded. "And I am Saai, but you may call me Uncle. You are not from here. What is your village?"

"My ancestors are from Ko Yao Yai but our home was on Ko Phi Phi. Now we live in Patong."

The old man nodded. He had never traveled to any of those places but he had fished for years in the waters off Ko Yao Yai, the long island, and Ko Yao Noi, its smaller sister, and he had heard how Patong had become a wild place, popular with tourists. And he had heard what had happened on Phi Phi. "I hope that your family is happy in Patong," he said, asking about the tsunami without asking anything at all.

Pim bowed her head. "My parents would not have liked Patong very much, and I think my nephew and grandfather miss our old home."

"And the *ferangs*," he said, pausing to watch them approach his home, "where are they from?"

"Somewhere in America," Pim said, glancing back at Mark and Robin as they started up the steps. "Uncle, do you speak English?"

The old man laughed.

"Perhaps that is best," Pim said, speaking more to herself than the old man. On the beach, the boatman pull-started the motor on the long-tail, swinging the ten-foot shaft to the side of the boat to maneuver out to sea. The boy waved at the boat but the man did not look back. On the stairs, the tall *ferang* nodded at the old man, the blonde gave a quick grin.

"You will stay and have something to eat. The fish is fresh and it is good. It may not be as fancy as you are used to in Phuket…"

"That is very kind of you Uncle, but there are five of us."

"I can count, child. Tell your friends that they are welcome."

"Thank you, Uncle." Pim paused and wet her lip, working up the courage to say what needed to be said, now before it was too late. "Uncle, I am embarrassed to ask a favor of you."

"The embarrassment is mine if I am unable to help."

Pim took the photo from her shirt pocket but held it behind her hands. Behind her, the steps creaked as Mark and Robin leaned forward. "The *ferangs* have come very far. They are looking for a man. He may have traveled past here not long ago."

"Not many people stop here."

"I know this, Uncle. Now please, if you will, I will show you the picture and if you have seen the man, I would be grateful if you would tell me all about it." The old man reached out a gnarled hand but Pim held the photo close. "And Uncle, if you have not seen the man, if he did not come by this way," she said, taking time to swallow, "I ask you to please point to the south."

The old man glared at Pim and she looked down at the mat.

"This is the favor you need of me? To help you deceive the *ferangs*? To lie to them? Is this what you ask me to do?"

Pim drew in a deep breath and lowered her head. "Yes, Uncle."

He looked past her to the *ferangs*, the couple smiling at him. The old man looked back at Pim, running a hand through his thick white hair before reaching out his hand again. Pim hesitated, then gave him the photo.

The man in the picture was a *ferang*, with the muscular build of a kick-boxer and a smile like the toothpaste ads that they showed on satellite TV. The man was on a beach but it didn't look like any beach he knew. It was missing green islands on the horizon and the long-tail boats in the water and the sand was a different color. But it was a good beach, wide and flat, with plenty of places to moor a boat. Maybe the picture was taken in America—but if they had beaches like this, he wondered, why would they bother to come all the way to Thailand? He knew that there were beaches that were far prettier than the one on which he had spent his whole life. But life wasn't about finding a beautiful place to move to. It was about being moved by the beauty in the place you already lived.

The old man looked a moment longer, a broad grin cracking along his weathered face. "I hope you find what you are looking for," he said, raising his arm, pointing a bony finger to the south.

"I've been in Thailand, what, four days?" Robin said, looking up as if the answer were written along the eaves of the old man's hut. "I think all I've eaten is rice."

"It is served with every meal," Pim said, scooping up a ball of sticky rice and fish off the square mat with the tips of her fingers. Cut from a single banana leaf, the mat folded under the pressure, making it easier for her to gather the stray grains. "It plays a similar role to bread in your country."

"Thank you, Martha Stewart," Robin said, the leaf mat buckling in her hand, spilling half the white rice onto her lap as she spoke.

They were sitting on the old man's porch, Robin and Mark together in the shade, Pim, her grandfather, and the boy leaning against the porch railing, their feet tucked under their legs, hidden from view. A large bowl of rice divided the groups, and a series of small plates—the pungent spices stronger than the smell of boiled fish—dotted the woven bamboo floor covering. The old man lay curled up in a droopy hammock. He had seen to it that the women of the household prepared a proper meal for his guests; and now, with the sound of pots being cleaned in the home, he drifted off on a well-deserved nap.

The fish was filled with pin-sized bones and after two bites, Robin gave up, doubling up on the rice. Across the porch, Pim and her family seemed to race through the meal, shoveling mounds of rice into their mouths, spitting the little bones under the railing. Mark made quick work of the meal as well, his fingers long adept at mastering rice and curry. He could taste the subtle flavors in the simple meal: the coconut milk broth and the diced chilies, the earthy lemongrass and sweet tamarind sauce. The tea was weak but the old man had added two scoops of clumpy sugar, which helped explain his toothless grin. It was a good meal and Mark sensed that it was better than the old man and his family usually ate.

"I want to give him something for the food," Mark said to Pim as he sipped at his tea.

Pim frowned. "Please, this is not necessary."

"We ate a lot. It's the least we could do."

"If you do, if you give him money, you will insult him." Pim shook her head, mumbling something to herself in Thai.

"What was that?" Robin said, raising her chin as she spoke.

"I said that Americans can not understand, that is all."

Robin chuckled. "Americans know a thing or two about generosity, or have you forgotten all those aid shipments already?"

"We can never forget," she said, her voice changing, the words sounding less like a promise and more like a command. "That was a great kindness. That kind of kindness Americans know well. But they don't know the small kindness. They don't know *náam-jai*," she said, the others looking over when they heard the familiar Thai word. "The juice of the heart."

"Yeah, kindness. Okay, big deal. I get it."

"No, Miss, you do not," Pim said, countering Robin's sarcasm with a gentle smile. "This man, he invited us to eat, not because he is kind but because we were hungry. If he did not feed us his neighbors would think less of him, and his family would be ashamed."

"They'd lose face," Mark said.

"Yes, but it is even more than that. The way he feels about himself—the way all Thais feel about themselves—it is all based on *náam-jai*. You can not feel good about yourself if you have not helped others who are in need."

Robin nudged Mark with her elbow, raising an eyebrow. "You buying any of this?"

"Excuse me, Miss," Pim said, waiting for Robin to look at her before she continued. "I have only known you for a short time but I can tell that you are a daring woman. I have met many American women and they are like this, too. Being daring, it is important where you are from; it is the way you were raised. You do not think about being daring. You *are* daring. Here, in Thailand, we do not think about being generous, we just do what we have been taught to do."

"Well Mark, it seems we've stumbled onto paradise, a little slice of heaven where everyone does kind and good things and no one is unhappy; and tourists don't get overcharged just because they're tourists, and bad men don't lock up young women and force them to be hookers to cover somebody else's debts. Nope, everything is just peachy-keen here in Thailand."

Pim's shoulders drooped and Mark could hear her sigh over the old man's snoring. She opened her mouth to speak but said nothing, looking down at the banana leaf mat, pushing a stray grain of rice to the center with her painted fingernail. Out of the corner of his eye, Mark could see the smirk on Robin's face. He pinched a piece of fish and a scoop of rice between his fingers, sliding it into his mouth, washing it down with the over-sweet tea, coughing once to clear his throat before he spoke, startling the old man from his nap.

"This was an *excellent* meal." He said the words slowly and clearly, his tone matching his broad grin, patting his firm, flat stomach with both hands. "Pim, please tell this gentleman that this was the finest fish I have ever tasted." He looked up at the man as he gestured to the pile of fish bones on the mat. "And tell him that I hope to repay his kindness someday."

Pim sat up, her smile bright against her dark skin and ink-black hair. She looked first at Mark, then turned and spoke to the old man, repeating what she said when he cupped a hand behind his ear. There was a whiney, piercing quality to the language, a high-pitched and nasal tone that was drawn out with every long A and hyper-extended syllable, a shrewish tongue that did not match the angelic face. He knew he wasn't supposed to think that way, that it made him, as a former Bengali girlfriend had pointed out, a "culturally insensitive jackass." But he also knew that he preferred it when Pim spoke English.

"I told him the first part, about how much you liked the fish. You made him very happy," Pim said as the old man grinned his toothless grin.

"What about my offer to help him?"

Pim kept her smile as she shook her head. "There is no need. It's *náam-jai.* He knows that you will not forget and one day you may help him, too. This is what people do."

"Well you better hurry up and do something nice for him soon," Robin said, wiping her hands off on an extra banana leaf mat. "You said the old man told you Shawn went to the south, and in case you forgot, that's why we're here."

"Pim, those boats," Mark pointed, under the railing and out to the row of long-tails on the beach, "can we rent one, get somebody to take us down to…wherever?"

As she exchanged bursts of rapid-fire Thai with the old man, two girls, no older than Pim's nephew, cleared away the remaining food, rolling up the bamboo mat and sweeping the porch with stubby homemade brooms. The girls giggled when Mark winked at them, and they darted in and out of the open door, peeking around the old man's swaying hammock. Robin snagged one of the quick-moving girls as she sped past, setting the girl on her lap, tickling her sides till they were both breathless from laughter. She could turn it on and turn it off just like that, he thought. Sweet and innocent one minute, a smart-mouthed bitch the next and back again, all in the same breath. She looked good in a tank top and shorts, probably better in less, but all that changed when the claws came out. Then there was Pim.

"Uncle says that one of the fishermen will take us to Krabi," Pim said. "One of the big towns on the mainland, but it is a long way and he will lose two days fishing."

"We'll pay him for his time," Mark said.

"Sure," Robin said, shaking her down over her face, making the little girl squeal with laughter. "Unless of course he's got that nama gee thing going."

"The fishermen are asleep now, but Uncle says in an hour he will wake his youngest son and we can go. But he wants you to know that we are also welcome to spend the night here, as his guests."

"Naturally," Robin said, letting the young girl squirm free, only to pull her back, laughing.

"Uncle says that it is a long ride, but that we should be there by sunset," Pim said, translating as the man spoke. "There should be no problem with *sà-lât*."

Mark had been looking out over her grandfather's shoulder to the fluid line where the turquoise shallows met the navy blue channel as Pim spoke. At the Thai word the man's eyes became alert and he saw the muscles in his scrawny neck tighten.

"*Sà-lât* are sea robbers," Pim explained. "But I don't think they will be a problem."

"Sea robbers? You mean like pirates?" Robin let go and the girl squirmed free again.

"Yes, but we will be there before it is dark. There should be no problem."

Mark sipped his still warm, still sickeningly sweet tea. "We were on the water all night. You should have told us there might be a problem."

"Where we were last night, on the west of Phuket, all that are there are fishermen. Here on this side, between Phuket and the mainland, there are many boats transporting goods and there are more *ferang*—more foreigners with their own sailboats."

"But it's just going to be us," Robin said, "so there should be no problem, right?"

"Yes, no problem," Pim said, pausing too long, then adding, "I think."

Chapter Fourteen

Jarin pushed in the clutch and downshifted around a sharp bend in the beach-hugging road, thirty kilometers over the posted speed limit. In the rearview mirror he saw the two bodyguards lean against the curve, while in the passenger seat, Laang—the man hired a year ago to be his driver—braced a knee against the dashboard, straining not to slide into his boss' space. In Bangkok he would have had a string of black Hummers or at least an Escalade, not driving himself around in a four door Honda. But that was Bangkok and this was Phuket, and here he didn't need a flashy car to stand out since everybody who mattered knew who he was. Besides, he liked to drive.

His earliest memory was of watching his mother pray in front of the shrine in the family's one-room home, not much bigger than the parking space it bordered. She would kneel in front of the painted wooden alcove that held the postcard picture of a seated Buddha—a wispy flame fluttering over his head—her face shrouded in a veil of smoke from the joss sticks held between her pressed palms. When he was old enough to imitate her movements, she had him kneel beside her, watching the candles burn on the altar as his mother whispered prayers. Once he asked her what she was saying, and she told him that her prayer was that one day he would grow up to become a taxi driver. From that day on he doubled his devotions, kneeling alongside his mother, praying that his mother's prayers would not be answered. But as the engine redlined and he popped the car up a gear, he was glad that some of her prayers had gotten through.

It was a twelve-kilometer drive from his home near Surin Beach down to Patong, but in many ways it was a much longer journey. At his home he was Jarin the successful businessman, dutiful husband and loving father to his six adoring children—the eldest just finishing her first year at the private international high school. He could relax at home, enjoy the panoramic view of the ocean on the rustic patio—the hidden AC vents blowing out chilled air—or soak in one of the Jacuzzis, listening to the water splash down the eight-step waterfall. Home was his sanctuary and no one was stupid enough to bother him there.

But in Patong or Kathu or Ra Wai or Phuket City—anyplace outside the walled compound of his estate—he was *Sua noi*, the Tiger, demanding head of an army of criminals, source of millions in bribes to government officials; the man to see if you wanted something that laws prevented you from getting. And every day the list of people who needed him grew.

That was in the book, too. Rule Number Seven: Offer the right bone and the meanest dog will sit up and beg.

Supply and demand, that's all it was. His gift was knowing how to bring them together. And no one did it better than he did. Until Mr. Shawn and his men interfered. Wasn't it enough that he had to deal with reformist politicians and muckraking journalists, trying to pull him down so they could build themselves up? They should be going after the terrorists down in the south, the ones looking to overthrow the government and start some Islamic state. If the press knew how much of his own money he had spent killing off those terrorists they would treat him like a hero instead of a crooked businessman with shadowy connections. The terrorists were the real threat to Thailand, not him. They wanted to disrupt tourism and trade; he promoted it. He needed everything to stay just as it was—a corrupt and inefficient government enabling a tourist trade based on sex and alcohol. Business was better that way.

Jarin sped around an overloaded mini-bus—a snub-nosed pickup truck with a pair of benches in the back—and continued in the passing lane until he got around a Toyota sedan and a knot of motor scooters. He heard the non-driving driver suck in his breath, and in the rearview mirror, the two guards' eyes widened at the blind curve pass. That's why he liked to drive—there was never any doubt about who was in control.

He took the car down the last sloping hill, slowing down enough to make the turn in front of the police station, down-shifting hard as he went past Par Pom Sri Na, its gold leaf statue gleaming in the sun. Built to bring good luck and prosperity to Patong, it was one of the first things destroyed by the wave. At the base of the white stone podium, between a pair of waist-high stone elephants, an altar was covered in fresh garlands of yellow flowers, unlit candles, and green coconuts; tops lopped off, offering up their bittersweet milk. When the community leaders were rebuilding the shrine they had asked local business-men for donations, and although Jarin had already given almost a million bhat toward the recovery, he sent a check for twenty thousand more. He had lost four bar-beers that day and a year on he was still running well behind in revenues. Par Pom Sri Na reminded him how easily he could lose the rest.

He drove up the slight incline of Phrabarami Road, past the government bank, past the mosque, up to Nanai Road, a half a kilometer from the beach. The wave had reached this far before sliding back out to sea, leaving a barricade of debris and bodies at the fork in the road to mark the high water point. He had been home that morning, smoking his first cigarette of the day, enjoying a few hours of solitude before his family awoke, when the wave arrived, lapping up against the lower patio like the wake from a passing power boat; not so much as knocking the fold-ing chair off the dock. The scientists said that it had to do with the sharp slope of the sea floor around Surin Beach, the energy of the wave absorbed by the undersea geography before it even reached land. The same drop off, that created an undertow so strong his children were forbidden to swim past the dock, had saved his home and spared his family.

At Kamala Beach, a mile away, it was a different story. When the tide pulled out—impossibly far out, farther out than he would let his oldest son drive the jet ski, three, four hundred meters at least—the locals rushed with their plastic buckets and their palm-leaf baskets, collecting fish that were flopping about on the sand. They filled their baskets and brought them up to the beach road, rushing back out onto the wide sand and mud plain with anything they could find, laughing and waving and shouting to their children to hurry and help with the unexpected harvest, too busy to notice the wall of water on the horizon coming in as fast as a fighter jet. And there were tourists out there as well, heads down, looking for shells. Backs to the ocean, they never saw it coming, and if they did it wouldn't have made a difference. More people died on that one stretch of beach than the rest of Phuket combined; but at his house, just around the rocky outcrop of Laem Mai Phai, the wave that killed a hundred thousand rinsed the sand off his children's flip-flops.

Jarin turned the car down Nanai Road, slowing down on the busy commercial street. There were no souvenir shops here, just wholesalers and restaurants only the locals ate at; car repair shops and two-story warehouses that supplied the hundreds of hotels and guesthouses that were the heart of the island economy. He turned down a narrow road that took him farther from the beach, pulling up behind a row of warehouses he had bought a week after the tsunami, giving the grieving widow and her family more than he would have paid her husband, but still far below its actual value. Business, after all, was business.

Laang and the bodyguards jumped out of the car before he even had it parked, falling over themselves to open his door, pounding on the steel door of the warehouse like impatient children, the door swinging open, the men inside and the men outside arguing over who was more irresponsible, neither group watching as Jarin stepped out of the car and climbed up the wooden staircase to the second floor offices. It was cool, even cold in the office, the AC units humming louder than the police scanner on the desk. The men sat up as he came in, trying to look busier and more important than they really were. He passed through the room without giving them a glance, heading down the central hallway and through the door marked Private.

Taped to a folding chair—a golf ball-sized welt growing under his left eye, his lower lip swollen and split—JJ looked up as Jarin entered the room.

"That was a smart idea, putting them up in that other hotel," Robin said as they crossed the street and climbed the steps of the City Hotel, the glass doors sliding open, the chilled air blowing out to greet them. "All three of them in one room for eight bucks. That's a hell of a lot less expensive than having them all stay *here*. Besides, for them that hotel's probably like staying at the Hilton."

A step ahead, Mark looked back at Robin as she pulled her long hair through a fat rubber band. She didn't notice him shake his head. "I wasn't thinking about the cost. It's safer if we split up. There can't be too many American couples traveling around with a Thai woman, her nephew, and her grandfather."

"Safe? You're not worried about that gangster guy, are you? So you snuck out with one of his hookers, big deal. I'm sure there are plenty more where that came from."

Mark grunted. It had been a good day, no sense on ruining it with information that would tie her to a homicide; Thai laws about accessory after the fact probably just as picky as the ones in the States.

They had set out from the fishing village an hour after lunch, the old man coming down to the beach to see them off, helping push his son's long-tail out into the surf, handing Pim a basket of fruits and a bottle of water for the trip. Without a compass or a map on board, the fisherman pointed the bow of the boat toward the southeast and gunned the four-cylinder engine.

There were enough clouds in the sky to break up the all-blue monotony, and in every direction Mark could see green islands shooting straight up out of the water. The fisherman's course brought them close to one island, the sheer limestone cliffs undercut by the current, creating massive overhangs and hidden grottos, everything topped with arm-thick vines and jungle vegetation. He had seen some spectacular natural landscapes in his travels—Kashmir valleys with waterfalls as cold and clear as glacier ice, African lakes turned pink from all the flamingos—and he had seen some dull landscapes turned spectacular with horizon-wide oil fires and crisscrossing tracers. Maybe it was the warm sun or the sound of the water sluicing along the wooden hull, but somehow he knew that he'd try to hold on to this view longer than the rest.

Without thinking, they had taken the same seats on this long-tail that they had during their late night trip, with Mark at the bow, Pim and her nephew in front of the engine at the rear, and Robin and the grandfather in the middle. From the moment they set out, the boy could not stop grinning, and the fisherman, through words and gestures, asked him if he wanted to steer. The boy jumped up and grabbed hold of the steering bar, eyes front, watching the sea for sudden squalls or pirates on the starboard bow, never noticing how his great-grandfather beamed or how the fisherman kept the boat on course, readjusting the propeller shaft with his foot.

An hour out they passed between two large islands.

"That is Ko Yao Yai, home of my ancestors," Pim said, pointing to the larger island to the south, breaking the restful silence. "And that is Ko Yao Noi." She pointed to the north. "Perhaps that is where Shawn and I will live one day."

"I wouldn't bet on it," Robin said, shorts again rolled up high on her thighs, the strings of her bikini top dangling to the side as she lay on her back. She dropped her arm over the low hull and let her fingers cut a sharp wake in the flat water alongside the boat.

"Miss, you have very lovely rings. Very sparkly."

Robin sighed but said nothing.

"I would hate to see you lose your lovely rings."

Robin sighed again, louder. "Don't worry, they're not going to fall off."

"Of course not, Miss," Pim said, smiling at Mark as she spoke. "The barracudas will take the whole finger."

Robin sat up, her hand flying out of the water, the other trying to catch her falling top. Mark hadn't laughed that hard in months.

The sun was setting when they motored up the swift-moving river toward the Chao Fa Pier; but once ashore, the fisherman paid and tipped, it hadn't taken Pim long to find a cheap hotel and for Robin to find a better one. Thirsty, sun-baked, and sticky with sea-salt and sweat, they waited as the hotel clerk apologized to the guest in 311 who was not pleased with the poor selection of pay-per-view movies.

"Just one room," Robin said as she handed the clerk her credit card. "But two beds."

Chapter Fifteen

He was late but he was still surprised to find her waiting for him in the lobby.

"Where is Miss Robin?" Pim asked. If she was pleased or disappointed that he had come alone, Mark didn't hear it in her words.

"The sun kicked her ass. She fell asleep as soon as she hit the bed."

"Ngern, too." She noticed Mark's expression and added, "My nephew. My grandfather even looked tired."

"How about you? How you doing?"

"I have been waiting for this for more than a year. I am ready."

He gave a slight bow and waved his hand, allowing her to lead the way through the lobby and out into the humid night.

Across the street, strings of bright bulbs lit up the night market, and a slow-moving crowd brought traffic to a standstill. There were markets like this in every corner of the world, all of them alike, all of them different. Some were deadend mazes of filthy stalls; some, like this one, were orderly and, if not clean, at least not as bad as they could have been. The tourists always went looking for monkey heads and skewered rats roasting over hot coals, disappointed when they found pizza stands and ice cream vendors. Mark and Pim passed stalls of fresh fruits and vegetables, some he knew, some he couldn't identify, and they cut down a fragrant row that sold nothing but flowers. There were few tourists in the crowd and he towered over the shoppers, ducking to avoid the extension cords and speaker wires that passed from booth to booth. He couldn't understand a word but he knew what was being said as the shoppers haggled for the best deal, positive that they and they alone were being ripped off, paying top bhat for second-rate goods, every shop owner insisting just as passionately that they were losing money on the sale. They stopped to eat, Pim inhaling a bowl of rice and fish, Mark downing three Thai-sized hamburgers and a quart of Pepsi.

"I do not think Miss Robin likes me," Pim said as they ate.

Mark shrugged. "I'm not so sure she's fond of me."

She stopped eating and held her pose, her chopsticks steady above the plastic bowl. "Is it right for a sister to be jealous of her brother's happiness?"

Mark said nothing, ignoring the question, hoping she wouldn't repeat it.

"If my brother was married, I know that I would be happy for him and would make his wife feel welcome. I would not be mean to her or say cruel things, and I would not turn my eyes when she spoke to me. I would want to know about her and become her friend. She is the one who makes my brother happy, so I would want her to be happy."

"She doesn't know you, that's all."

"If my brother was married, I would want to get to know his wife. It would make me happy." She sat still a moment longer, then shook her head, the idea falling apart. "But my brother is dead so it does not matter."

Mark set down his burger, wiping his hands clean on his khaki shorts. "Robin's got a stack of pictures. I don't think she'll miss one." He pulled a photo out of his shirt pocket and dropped it on the picnic table, careful to miss the splatters of ketchup and green spices. Pim set down her empty bowl and with both hands she lifted the picture. She stared at the image, different from the one he had given her before—a close-up of Shawn, shirtless, grinning for the camera, his shoulder raised and his arm angled in like he had taken the picture himself. Mark watched as she studied the photo, saw the light that sparked behind her eyes and the watery line that formed below her eyes.

"I was working at my father's clinic when we met. He had been rock climbing near the beach and had lost his footing. He slid and cut his leg badly but he was fortunate and nothing was broken. His friends had brought him to the clinic, but my father had taken the ferry to Phuket that day and would not be back for hours. His friends wanted to take him to Dr. Stubbs, the Australian, but Shawn told them no, he wanted me to take care of him. I explained that we were not doctors, that my father was just a pharmacist and that I was still in university, but he said that it didn't matter, that anyone with such beautiful eyes had to be an angel." She looked up and smiled. "I know. It is a silly thing, but it worked."

Mark could tell her that it wasn't just her eyes, that this Shawn guy was a lucky bastard for having met her and an idiot for leaving her behind. But he knew enough to say nothing.

"He came back the next day," she continued, "and my father replaced his bandages. He asked my father if he could take me to dinner. I was *so* embarrassed."

"Sounds like a gentleman to me."

"For you, perhaps. But that is not how it is here. For us, such formalities mean that the man and woman are ready to be married. My father pretended not to hear. Shawn thought that this meant no, but that night we ate at the Two Palms restaurant on the beach. It was the best restaurant on the island. It is gone now." She took a last look at the photo and handed it back to Mark. "Thank you, but I do not need more pictures to remember."

Mark hesitated a moment before taking the photo. "If you change your mind…"

"Why are you here?" She was still smiling, but the words were firm.

Mark slid the photo back into his pocket. "I didn't want you to go snooping around alone. I know this is your country but there are—"

"No, Mr. Mark," she said. "Why are you here in Thailand? Why are you helping Miss Robin?"

"She hired me to find her brother, that's all."

"Was she a friend of yours?"

"No. I didn't know her."

"So why did she come to you?"

"A friend of mine sent her to me."

"You do not sound pleased."

"Let's just say that me and this friend are now even."

Mark finished off his hamburger, washing it down with the last of the Pepsi. She waited till he was done wadding up the wrappers and tossing them the ten feet into the open barrel, then said, "What do you do, your job?"

"Little of this, little of that. Lot of nothing." She nodded, but he doubted that she understood.

"When you were young—like Ngern," she said, hesitating before she continued. "Is this what you thought your life would be like? This and that and nothing?"

"No." He laughed as he said it. "I sortta woke up one day and there I was."

Pim looked down at her hands and nodded. "Me too."

"Come on, let's get started," Mark said, picking up Pim's empty rice bowl, standing as he spoke. "I don't want to be up all night."

They continued through the stalls, coming out at the far end of the market, the bars and hotels on this side lacking the bright neon and familiar names that pulled in the foreigners. There were fewer people walking around, and the ones that leaned against the concrete walls of the empty shops or sat along the curb watched them approach: street corner toughs, cigarettes dangling from their lower lips, slack-jawed teens in dirty shirts and bare feet, pinpricks for pupils, old men in baggy clothes, gums chomping on air, a few women who called to him from the shadows, staying out of the revealing arc lighting of the street lamps, a few others who didn't give a damn what they looked like, walking right up to them as they passed, telling Mark the things he could do to them for five hundred bhat. Pim reached out for Mark's hand and he guided her along the street, holding open the door of one of the smaller bars on the strip.

There was no bowling alley, no Odenbach beer sign, no jukebox loaded with 70s rock CDs; and none of the bartenders had on a flannel shirt, but there was something about the nameless bar that reminded Mark of bars back home. It wasn't the low-hanging cloudbank of cigarette smoke—New York was smoke-free now anyway he heard—and it wasn't the four bottles of Thai whiskey that sat on the otherwise empty shelf behind the bar, but there was something about the place, a deadend vibe that decades on a bar stool had taught him to recognize. There was a handful of patrons, none of them looking up as Mark and Pim took a seat at an open table, enough problems of their own that they didn't need any more from this big *ferang* and his whore. The men were hunched over their Chang beers, straining their will power, trying to make one bottle last the night. The women—all four of them—were tired versions of bar-beer girls, worn out on the tourist trade, hanging on to the only career they knew. Mark scanned the crowd, wondering which pair of drooping shoulders belonged to the Thai version of himself.

"It would be best if you stay here while I ask questions," Pim said, standing. "Please, may I have the photograph?"

He took the photo of Shawn from his pocket and held it out to her. "Do you recognize anyone here?"

"I have never been to this place," Pim said. "But places like this are all the same. Someone here will have the information or they will know the person who does. It may cost money."

He took a stack of bhat from his wallet and handed it to her. "You learned a lot at the Horny Monkey."

"Yes," she said, turning to leave. "Things I never wanted to know."

The fourth beer was awful—as bad as the first three—but he drank it anyway, more out of habit than desire. What he really wanted was a cigar, not because he liked cigars, but it would mask the second-hand smoke from the low-grade Chinese cigarettes. He could ask at the bar but didn't feel like being sociable, and he could cut back to that all-night 7-Eleven across the street from the hotel, but that would mean leaving Pim alone in the bar. Not that she needed him. The lights were dim but he could see her in the far corner, sipping her can of Pepsi through a bent-neck straw. She leaned forward as she spoke to the man, and now and then he could make out her high-pitched giggle. The tip to the bartender got her introduced to the bouncer, and after fifteen-minutes of small talk and another tip, she was escorted past the men playing pool to the wobbly table near a propped-open fire exit where a potbellied man in rose-tinted aviator glasses sat with his back to the wall, chain smoking Thai cigarettes.

Mark knew the type. Middle-aged guys who saw themselves as players even though they were never in the game, guys who quoted Tony Soprano and dressed like they stepped out of *Scarface*, guys with Welsh-Irish surnames who said *mingia* and *forgetaboutit* like they grew up in Little Italy, who were too scared to cheat on their taxes but who hinted at back-alley deals and bodies in trunks. But they stayed on top of the real local mob scene, dropping names as if they were old *compagnos*, collecting scraps of information like they were baseball cards. And if you could sit through their bullshit, they'd tell you what they knew. As he watched the guy light up another cigarette, he hoped Pim knew the difference.

One thing Mark knew for certain, this guy, Robin's brother, Pim's husband, he didn't want to be found.

Maybe it went something like this. He's working at a dive shop in a true tropical paradise, screwing the occasional tourist girl out looking for an island romance and, despite what his sister thinks, keeping himself happily stoned. One day he meets a beautiful Thai girl, who, coincidentally, has access to prescription-level drugs. Whether or not he meant to, the next thing he knows he's married. It's fun for a month or two but soon it starts getting dull—he's making next to nothing, he's got a new wife to support, the strongest thing his dad-in-law's pharmacy carries is cold pills and his old life of quick sex and blissful highs tugs at him all night long. He knows the tourists, knows their appetites, and decides he can make some big money supplying their needs. But he needs a bankroll to make it happen, so he sees Jarin. Before he can pay him back, Mother Nature steps in. He sees a once-in-a-lifetime opportunity to disappear, to start over somewhere else with no ties. And he takes it. The gangster holds his bride hostage, waiting for him to pay back what he owes. Maybe he's got the money, maybe it got washed away like the rest of the island, but in either case he's not coming back. It made perfect sense.

But at the same time it made no sense at all.

Pim had said that Jarin controlled Patong and some of that rang true—a hideout in the hills, four men to guard a little kid and an old man, the power to force a Thai bride into prostitution until the money was repaid. But how much would a loan shark have risked on a foreigner who worked at a dive shop? And even at Thai rates, holding three people captive for over a year had to be expensive. No, there was something going on, something besides money, and either Pim knew and wasn't saying, or there was a lot she didn't know about her husband.

And as Mark watched Pim laugh, bringing her hand up to cover her perfect smile, he thought about how little he knew her.

Mark was glad when he saw the third man step out from the shallow alcove of the fire exit and into the narrow alley.

It was long after midnight, and they had just left yet another nameless bar when Mark noticed they were being followed. The bar had been noisy, more rowdy than the others, mostly guys under twenty, slamming beers and punching each other in the shoulder, all piss and vinegar, sound and fury. See the one-eyed Chinaman, they had told Pim, not telling her which one of the four they had meant. But Mark hadn't even finished his beer when she told him it was time to go, leading the way out the door and onto the deserted street.

They were almost to the end of the block when the two men came out of the bar. Ahead, on the other side of the street, he could make out four men leaning against a dark gray wall, looking their way. If it was six, then no way.

Coming up on his right, a black alley led back to the night market. Mark rubbed his palms dry on his shirt, not listening as Pim explained what one of the one-eyed men had to say. He took her by the elbow and made a quick turn down the alley. When the man stepped out in front of him, Mark knew it would only be three and he knew he had to work fast.

Holding tight to Pim's arm, he moved up the alley, Pim's sandals scuffing along the dirty concrete as she tried to keep pace. It was not what the man had expected, the *ferang* coming up on him so quickly, his friends just now rounding the corner, the whole plan falling apart. The man held up both his hands, palms open, smiling, letting Mark know he didn't mean any trouble, glancing out toward the street, watching his friends running down the alley, glancing back at Mark in time to see a fist arching around at his head, too late to do a damn thing about it. Mark stepped in with the punch and the man stumbled back, falling over empty cardboard boxes and busted cinder blocks, his forehead clipping the steel doorframe before he went down.

Shoving Pim behind him, Mark turned to face the others.

One was tall and thin, the other short but with a stocky fighter's build. They had seen what he had done to their man, stopping just out of Mark's reach, too proud to back off but too scared to move in, both men cocking their arms, fists loose, leaning their weight back on one leg, the other coiled, ready to strike, self-taught Bruce Lees waiting for their opening.

Mark made it easy for them.

He dropped his hands to his side and stepped up. As if on cue, the tall man lunged forward, snapping a kick at Mark's crotch, not realizing that Mark had given him the target for a reason. The man was in mid-air when Mark angled his hips, the kick catching his thigh. Mark snatched hold of the man's leg, raising it up over his head as he stepped forward, his heel coming down hard on the side of the man's knee, picking the man up before he collapsed and throwing him against the dumpster with an echoing thump. The second man hit him from behind, both arms up around his neck, twisting, trying to pull Mark down as he pounded his knee into Mark's back. Mark reached up and grabbed the man by the hair, bending his legs then diving forward, tucking his head down as far as he could, his body folding, the weight of the other man flipping around, Mark coming down on top, his shoulder driving into the man's chest, Mark jabbing an elbow down under the man's ribs. The man let go, his arms flailing as he fought to catch his breath. Mark rolled to the side and jumped up. "Let's go," he said. Wrapping an arm around Pim's waist, he pulled her down the alley.

As she ran, Pim turned away from Mark to look back over her shoulder. In the darkness, she smiled.

Chapter Sixteen

"I don't know why I waste my time," Robin said, flicking off the hotel's blow-dryer with her thumb, her other hand pulling a comb through her hair. "I'm going to be sweating so much I'm just going to look like hell anyway."

Stretched out on the bed, Mark could see her as she stood topless in front of the large mirror that hung above the dressing table, a hotel towel wrapped around her waist. He thought it was strange her feeling that comfortable with a man she hardly knew, but he wasn't about to complain. There was a white scar on the side of her knee and an unfinished chain tattoo around her left ankle, but those were the only flaws he could spot. Her curves were smooth and even, and if he ran a hand up the back of her thigh or across her flat stomach he knew it would be firm and warm. And she had been right, despite her blond hair—her natural color, revealed when she had adjusted the towel, the mirror lower than she thought—she tanned a golden bronze. His back was stiff, his ears were still ringing from the tinny speakers in the last bar, he had a finger-shaped bump on the side of his head where he had been hit with a bamboo pole, and there was a fist-sized knot welling up where he'd been kicked, but it could have been worse. And besides, with her standing there like that, he hardly noticed.

"So you and the dragon lady last night, huh?" Balanced on the balls of her feet, Robin leaned into the mirror as she applied her mascara. For a moment Mark considered telling Robin how Pim felt, telling her, too, what he thought about the way she treated the others, but the moment passed as he watched her cross the room to get her bikini top off the balcony railing. "Thank you for not bringing her back here."

Mark let it slide. "After the tsunami, your brother spent some time here in Krabi."

"How do you know?" she said, ducking behind the bathroom door with a pair of shorts and a black thong.

"A couple people recognized his picture, knew his name. They knew he had been living on Phi Phi Island. One guy even knew about his run-in with Jarin."

"That guy from Phuket? Interesting."

"Apparently he made some enemies here, too," he said as Robin, now dressed, sat down in the center of her bed, crossing her legs and leaning back on her arms. "Everybody knew about that but nobody would talk."

"Where is he now? Any idea?"

Mark shrugged. "Somewhere south. They know he went to Koh Lanta—it's a big island about three hours south of here."

"Ugh. Three *hours?*"

"Not in a long-tail. There's ferry service between Krabi and Koh Lanta—a regular boat."

"Thank God. So did they tell you where to look on this island?"

"They might have." Mark pulled himself up, leaning against the headboard. The frame of the bed creaked with every movement, the joints worn weak from years of hard riding. "I'll ask Pim what they said."

Robin rocked forward, crossing her arms, her elbows coming down on her knees. "*You* didn't talk to these people?"

"I don't speak Thai, remember?"

"So this is just stuff that *she* told you, you didn't hear it yourself?"

"I heard it," Mark said, trying not to smile. "I just didn't understand it."

With a loud and dramatic sigh, Robin fell sideways, burying her face in one of the fat pillows.

Mark turned back the covers and swung his legs out of the groaning bed. A red and purple bruise as big as his palm peeked out from under his boxers. He grit his teeth as he stood, bracing for the pain he knew he would feel, his hip throbbing already, a four Advil morning. He'd stretch it out in the shower, the hot water not helping the swelling but it would feel good anyway.

Fifteen minutes later, shaved and dressed, his baggy shorts covering the mark, he came out of the bathroom to find that Robin hadn't moved, her face still buried, her legs still crossed.

"There's a restaurant next door, the sign out front says they serve American breakfasts." He stood at the edge of the bed and waited till she rolled her head and looked up at him. "The ferry doesn't leave until after lunch. I'll find somebody who speaks English, confirm what she told me."

"And if you can't," Robin said, the words muffled by the pillow, "we leave them here."

The people in Krabi? They weren't like the people in Phuket.

They didn't stare when he walked down the road and none of the kids he passed pointed or fell in behind him, faking a limp, swinging their leg out with every step. And the people on the bus? They were helpful, telling him that it was an easy walk to the pier from where the bus would drop them off; and they had seen him get on the bus, too, so they saw the way he walked, nobody telling him that he couldn't make it there on his own. He liked that.

Maybe it was because there were too many *ferangs* in Phuket, the Thais and the Chinese all trying to act all cool so the *ferangs* would buy stuff from them. But the *ferangs*, they never made fun of him. They were always polite, even the drunk ones. And some of the *ferang* women sometimes would smile at him, but he knew it wouldn't go anywhere, the women always going with the kind of guys who made fun of him the most. He could never understand that. They already had everything girls liked, why did they need to pick on him?

But in Krabi it seemed different. There were *ferangs* here, sure, they were everywhere, but there wasn't any beach nearby so it was a different kind of *ferang*, the kind with the cameras and the backpacks, the ones who seemed out of place in the bar-beers of Patong, not everybody looking to get drunk or get laid. The businesses were different here, only a few souvenir places and no dive shops, the clothing stores selling things Thais liked, not just tee shirts and baggy shorts. There were car part stores and furniture stores and hardware stores—things tourists never had to buy. And the temples he saw were crowded, all day long.

After the tsunami, people in Patong started praying more, buying garlands of white flowers for their Buddhas; and every morning he woke up to the heavy scent of incense, his neighbors burning joss sticks by the armful. Some of the old people said that the wave was sent to wash away the bad karma and he heard a few of the Christians say it was their god's punishment for all the sin, but that was stupid since everybody knew it was from an earthquake. He had been up at the country club that morning, hoping one of the *ferangs* would hire him as a caddie. It was almost four kilometers from the beach, up in the hills, but you could hear that something was happening. By the time he got down to Patong, the ocean had already pulled back, and there was everything, just pushed up on the streets, and buildings gone and people crying or walking around, not saying anything, and sand and mud everywhere.

He saw his first body near the Patong Beach Hotel, wedged up between a palm tree and the top half of a charter fishing boat, the hull ripped away, and he watched as bodies floated up from the underground parking garage of the Ocean Plaza shopping center. The more he looked around, the more bodies he saw. Thais, *ferangs*, some naked, the wave pulling off their clothes; others laying there by the road like they just fell asleep. The next day the bodies started to swell; and that week the tide brought some in from the bay, all of them bloated and black so you couldn't even tell what sex they were, just whether they were adults or children. He didn't have anybody to lose, but for weeks afterward he felt sad all the time. And now? A few people still had their altars, but when the tourists started returning, everything went back to the way it was before and he didn't feel as sad anymore.

He wiped the sleep from his eyes and took another sip of tea, shifting his weight on the low windowsill of the 7-Eleven that served as his seat. Across the street, at a table near the open window, the big American and his girlfriend were finishing their breakfast.

Yesterday he had watched them as they climbed out of the long-tail at Chao Fa Pier, these two, Jarin's whore Pim, an old man and a boy. It was already past sunset when they arrived and he tried to imagine spending so many hours on such an uncomfortable boat. He never liked the long-tails. They were loud and they rocked too much. Besides, it was so much faster to take the bus.

Back in Phuket, he had watched the American talking with the man at the hotel, the *ferang* with the stupid-looking dreadlocks. And when the American went up the stairs to the rooms, the hotel man had walked straight out and down to the beach, walking right by him like he wasn't there. He watched as the hotel man talked first to one long-tail captain, then another, then another. The hotel man talked to the last one for a long time, pointing up the beach and then bending over to draw something in the sand, the boat captain squatting down next to him, nodding.

When the hotel man left, he walked over to the long-tail and asked the boat captain if he had seen the kick-boxing match the other night, knowing he hadn't. It was four-hundred bhat to get in the door, more than the captain would make in two days. But it got them talking. They talked about fishing and football and how the tourists were finally returning before he brought up the hotel man, nervous that the captain would be suspicious. But no, the captain told him all about it, how he was going to be taking a couple of *ferangs* around Phuket that night, how the hotel man had wanted the captain to take them all the way to Krabi but there was no way he was going that far. He'd drop them off at a fishing village on the mainland, up near Laem Som probably, and from there they could get another boat to take them the rest of the way.

He had talked to the captain a while longer, then walked to the rooming house where he'd been staying to get his hidden stash of hashish and *ya ba* pills. He had it all sold before midnight. Five thousand bhat—almost one hundred and thirty American dollars. And the money? It was an investment, like buying a kilo of Thai weed. You paid up front, but you made more later. The next morning he took a bus to Krabi, a three-hour ride, and he had the seat to himself. That made him wonder why the American would want to go by long-tail with all those hours in the sun. But that afternoon, when he saw the whore get out of the boat with the American couple, he knew that something wasn't right. And he knew that somehow his investment would pay off.

Chapter Seventeen

As he walked up the sloping street, away from the small cafés that were clustered near the pier, Mark remembered what JJ had said about mornings making everything seem possible. Last night he hadn't thought it necessary to confirm the things Pim had said, but then Robin planted a seed. He still believed that Pim had told him the truth, but it was something he felt in his gut, not something he could guarantee. And his gut had been wrong before. When he told Robin he would ask around, confirm the things that Pim had said, it sounded easy enough, but that was an hour ago and, just as JJ had predicted, he was starting to wonder if he'd get anything done at all.

The people in the cafés had been friendly, sitting with him as he explained to those who spoke English how he was looking for a friend who might have passed through. Had they seen him? Yes, he had been by, nice man, very kind. When? Oh, a while ago. A week? A month? Yes, something like that. South? Yes, that sounds right. His name? Well, I am not good with names…enjoy your visit, have a nice day. The Noble Lie, served with a broad smile and cup of Chinese white tea on the side.

The street branched off at the top of the incline, one road circling back to the center of town and the intersection with strange statues mounted on marble pillars—cavemen carrying luggage?—the other road, narrow and in need of repaving, passed between a pair of cinderblock warehouses, leading to the backside of the night market and the late-night dives they had visited. He set off down the warehouse road, an hour to get a real answer before making up a Noble Lie of his own.

In the morning light, the area around the bars lost its menacing feel, the hookers and the street toughs replaced by small kids in school uniforms and even smaller old women toting plastic bags of fresh produce. The bars themselves seemed to disappear, the windowless fronts and nondescript doors blending in with the walls as if they were seldom-used side entrances to elaborate shops that opened on wider streets. In Patong the bars never seemed to close but on this stretch in Krabi they looked as if it had been years since they had been open. He jiggled the handles on a few of the doors but they were locked. Behind one, an argument in shouted Thai stopped suddenly when he knocked; behind another he could hear the heavy hum of machinery that hadn't been there the night before. He passed the opening twice before recognizing the alley.

The walls were cleaner than he remembered and there wasn't as much trash, but the bloodstain on the doorframe, brown and faded, and the larger one at the foot of the dumpster let him know that he'd been down this path before. He kicked some of the cardboard boxes out of the way, checking the ground for the weapon he was sure they had hidden but never got a chance to use, when the police cruiser started down the alley.

It moved toward him slowly, not as intimidating as a Crown Victoria but the banana-clip machine guns in the rack behind the two solemn-faced cops made up for the car's subcompact size. Mark turned and watched the car approach, smiling his best lost-tourist smile. He could see the driver speaking into the radio's handset, the springy black cord looping on the dashboard. The passenger stepped out of the car, adjusting his white belt, smoothing out non-existent wrinkles in his polyester uniform shirt. He ran a finger up the ridge of his nose to push his mirrored aviator glasses tight against his face. It was only when the cop gave a two-finger wave that Mark noticed a second police car pulling up behind him.

Mark widened his smile as he walked toward the policeman. "I'm glad to see you. Can you tell me how to get to the City Hotel from here? I seem to have—"

"Shut up," the officer snapped. He strode up to Mark, his fists balanced on his hips, his thin arms and bony elbows sticking out like a set of wings. Mark was a foot taller and eighty pounds heavier, but they both knew that that meant nothing now. "Why are you here for?" the cop shouted.

"Like I said, I was walking around and got lost—"

The cop stretched up and slapped him hard across the face. "You lie." Without thinking, Mark clenched his fists, an unseen cop behind him responding with a sharp jab in the back from the end of a nightstick, the cop in front of him stepping closer, daring him to do something. "Why you here?"

This time Mark said nothing, not even flinching when the cop slapped him a second time. There were two cops behind him now and they pulled his arms back, rapping the cuffs down hard on his wrists and ratcheting them tight. Mark did not resist but they shoved him down on the hood of the car anyway, kicking his legs out wide to pat him down. He let them push him into the backseat of the car and he didn't sit up until they had backed out of the alley.

It was hot and airless, with a thick taxi-style Plexiglas divider keeping the AC to the front of the car. He leaned back and closed his eyes. He had been in the back of enough police cars to know how to use his time. It would be a short ride and he needed to clear his mind. It could be nothing—a couple of corrupt cops shaking down a lone tourist, taking their frustrations out on someone twice their size. It could be everything—a clear link to a body found in a hillside shack on Phuket.

He focused on his breathing.

No matter what was waiting at the end of the ride, he knew he needed to be ready.

◇◇◇

"Can I get you something cold to drink? A Pepsi, maybe? Or a Thai iced tea?" The police captain leaned back in his chair and pushed a button on the window-mounted air condition-ing unit. It gave a shudder, the metallic hum stepping up an octave. Mark could feel the cool air blowing on his sweaty face. He would have liked to run a hand across his forehead, wipe the sweat away from his eyes, but the handcuffs kept his arms locked behind his back.

"I'm going to get you the iced tea," the officer said, turning back to face his prisoner across his paper-strewn desk. "It's not like the iced tea you're used to, but you really should try it." He picked up the phone on his desk and punched in three quick numbers. He smiled across at Mark as he waited, then spoke in Thai to the person at the other end. "Do you like your tea sweet?" he said, tilting the receiver away from his face. He raised his eyebrows, smiling warmly the full forty seconds it took Mark to respond.

"Not too sweet," Mark said. His lip was swollen where one of the cops had elbowed him as he got out of the car, not hard enough to break the skin but enough to make his words sound fat and slurred.

"Good idea," the captain said, "I'll tell them to make it two."

The office was on the second floor of the police station, past a warren of cubicles, across from a dust-covered photocopier and far away from the row of small holding cells where Mark had sat for the last three hours. Other than a stained porcelain drain that served as an open toilet, the ten by ten foot cell had been empty. In the twin cell to his right, fifteen Thai men spent their time watching Mark as he sat on the concrete floor, asking him questions in Thai, laughing at jokes they knew he could not understand. They had fallen silent when the guards came down the row, stepping away from the bars, looking down at their own bare feet as the guards unlocked Mark's cell. Mark was trying to stand up when the guards entered, shoving him back on the ground then shouting for him to get up, hoping he'd give them a reason to pull out their nightsticks. But Mark had had time and he was ready. They could knock him down and make him stand all day. They'd get bored before he'd snap, a high tolerance for physical harassment and general bullshit one of the benefits of being a Marine. They let him stand on his thirty-third attempt, then walked him to the captain's office without a single shove.

The captain wore old-style army fatigues, dark brown, tailored to match his lean frame. The sleeves were rolled up high on his arms, tight against his biceps. He was no larger than the other cops, but stronger, the muscles in his forearms twisting like cables. A multi-colored patch showed his unit and twin bars on his collars denoted his rank, his name embroidered in black Thai script above his right chest pocket. His black hair was freshly trimmed and his face glowed from a close shave. He was handsome and his smile and bright eyes made it hard for Mark to guess his age or his intentions. The tea ordered, he leaned back in his chair, interlacing his fingers behind his head. "So, Mr. Rohr…may I call you Mark? Great. My name is Jimmy—"

Mark felt himself smirk.

"Okay, it's not my real name, but it's easier for foreigners to say than Kanjorngiat Niratpattanasai. Hell, get a few Singhas in me and *I* can't say it right." He chuckled, swiveling his chair from side to side. "So tell me, Mark, are you enjoying your visit to Krabi?"

Mark considered several answers before saying, "I haven't been here long enough to form an opinion."

Jimmy nodded. "Sure, sure. Okay, first impressions then—what do you think?"

Mark ran his tongue along his swollen lip. "It seems like a nice place."

"It is, isn't it? The people are generally honest…okay, *most* are, but if it weren't for the others I'd be out of a job, right?" He chuckled at his own joke. "It's not a big city, but then it's not some little village up in the hills. And—no offense—there's not as many tourists as, say, Patong or Koh Samui." He paused a long beat. "Have you been to Patong Beach, Mark?"

It was Mark's turn to smile. The bigger the lie, the more truth you needed to support it. "That's where we came from yesterday."

"Yes, yes, of course," Jimmy said. "You and your girlfriend."

"And the Thai family—a girl named Pim, her nephew and her grandfather. They're with us, too. I'm sorry, I can't remember their names." The officer continued to smile and nod, and Mark couldn't tell if he was confirming what the man already knew or surprising him with revelations that would mean trouble later.

The door to the office opened behind Mark and the cop who had slapped him walked to the desk carrying their drinks on a round plastic tray. He set one glass down on a coaster in front of the officer, the other he set in front of Mark.

"Ah, just in time," Jimmy said, lifting his drink from the desk. "You're going to enjoy this." He poked a straw in the drink, shifting the ice and mixing the light, frothy top with the creamy middle and dark liquid at the bottom of the glass. He took a long pull on his straw before he noticed that Mark hadn't moved. Laughing he said, "Go ahead, Mark, it's not poisoned."

Mark raised his shoulders, tilting his body to show off the handcuffs.

"Oh, I forgot." Jimmy snapped his fingers and said something to the street cop, who reached over and placed an unwrapped straw in Mark's glass before leaving the office. Mark looked across at Jimmy as he leaned forward and worked the straw into his mouth. It had a strong tea taste with hints of cinnamon and vanilla. But it was cold and wet and Mark drained a third of the glass before sitting back in the chair.

"It's better if you mix it up first," Jimmy said, pumping his straw in his glass to illustrate what he meant. "Maybe next time." He set his glass back on his coaster. "So Mark, tell me, what were you doing in that alley last night?"

"Which alley is that?"

Jimmy raised a finger. "Good point. We may not have as many alleys as, say, Canajoharie, but we have a few. No, the alley I mean is the one where you were jumped by those three guys. Ring a bell?"

"If you know about the alley," Mark said, ignoring the casual reference to his hometown, "then you know I was just walking through and that they jumped me."

"Hello? Isn't that what I said?" Jimmy shook his head as a show of disappointment. "Is that where you got the fat lip?"

The fat lip twitched as Mark smiled. "Actually, I got that from one of your men."

"Ouch," Jimmy said, bringing his hand up to rub his own lip in sympathy. "Well, they can be a bit rough. Not like in the States, huh? Yeah, I was a cop down in Maryland for a few years, the Gaithersburg area. Been there? You should check it out, very pretty. This was after the military. I was ninety-five B...Army talk for an MP. You're a jarhead, right?"

"Ex."

Jimmy laughed. "No such thing as an ex-Marine, Mark, you know that. And a Gulf War vet, too. What did you do to get that Bronze Star?"

"I didn't do anything."

Jimmy waved his hand, dismissing the question. "Sure, sure. They just give those things away."

"Were you in the war?"

"Me? *Hell* no. I did my three years and got out. Ended up here when my father died and my family moved back. Started as a patrolman and bought my way on up. Pay's not as nice but when you add in the bribes it's been a good living."

"Is that what this is about?" Mark said.

"Bribes? Come on, Mark, you're a tourist. How much money are you going to have on you? Enough to bribe a street cop, maybe even a sergeant, but I'm a captain. It takes more than you've got to buy me." He was still smiling but the humor was fading from his voice. He glanced up at the clock that hung above the map of Krabi. "Look, Mark, I'm going to make this easy for you and fast for me. I've landed a position with a special maritime police unit based out of Phuket City—smuggling intervention, illegal immigration, piracy prevention, that sort of thing. It cost me a small fortune but the kickbacks and the potential for serious bribe money is enormous."

"Serve, guide and protect, huh?"

"Don't get all self-righteous on me, Mark, or I'll turn you over to Jarin."

Mark dropped the sarcastic smile and held his breath.

"His offer is the best one on the table right now. Not a lot, but more than the other, and enough to get my attention." Jimmy reached out for his glass, stirring the ice around with the straw before taking a drink. His throat was dry, but Mark had lost interest in the spicy tea.

"Fortunately for you, Mark, I plan on doing a lot of business with this man. If I turn you over to him now, he'll think that he can get me for, well, let's just say far less than I'm worth. There's the other offer, but I don't trust it. Sadly, all that 'honor among thieves' stuff is crap. Which brings me back to you." Jimmy set down his empty glass and picked up the phone. "And you, Mark Rohr, you are an inconvenient distraction."

He said something into the phone, something short and curt, and Mark could hear booted footsteps coming up the stairs.

Chapter Eighteen

It had been a busy day.

It started with a phone call, one of his mid-level minions calling to tell him that a shipment had arrived the night before, as expected. The man was professional and business-like and as meekly subservient as the rest, and Jarin had thanked him, certain that the man was just trying to be efficient and responsible.

But the man had broken the main rule.

He had brought business into his home.

It was only a phone call and he had been discreet and polite, but that was not the point. The man had defiled his home, his sanctuary, and would have to be dealt with. He had to set an example for the rest. The *Top Dog* book understood. Rule Number Three: Your bark and your bite are the same thing. He felt sorry for the man and would tell him so, resolving to make it fast and painless.

The day then continued with a recital at his daughter's pre-school. They sang the same old traditional Thai songs he had sung his few years in school; they forgot half the words, mixed up the rest and they were off key and none of them clapped in time to the music. For the money he was spending they should have been more than just adorable.

Of course the headmaster had spotted him, ambushing him as he left the auditorium. On and on about how it was always an honor to have Mr. Jarin stop by, and how he was such an important businessman and role model, not just for the children and the teachers but for the entire community as well. It was embarrassing, the headmaster fawning on him like some bar-beer whore buttering up a fat German tourist. This time it was a new computer classroom with his name on the door. Jarin knew what would come next. The headmaster—'*what* a coincidence!'—just happening to bump into him in Patong, maybe a note sent home with his daughter or a visit by a couple of her teachers, the pattern repeating until he paid up. And he knew he'd pay, too. It was the same technique he had been using for twenty years and it never failed, although he doubted the school would break his legs if he didn't send a check. Rule Number Six: Bite down and don't let go. That was in the book, too, but there were some things that didn't have to be written down to be true.

At his office he reviewed the disbursement details and sales figures for an amphetamine shipment, made a courtesy call to the out-going chief of the maritime police, arranged for an inconvenient fire at the computer store owned by a man whose son had racked up a six-figure gambling debt, and approved a bootleg-movie deal with a new connection in Hanoi. He had spent some time after lunch meeting with accountants and attorneys from his construction company about prospective government contracts—all legitimate and by the book—then stopped by the beach home of an elected official to go over the sealed bids of his competitors.

It had been a busy day and he still had one last stop to make.

Jarin turned down Bang-la Road. It was still early—it would be a couple hours before the police blocked off both ends of the street for the nightly dusk-till-dawn party. He pulled the Honda up in front of the Super Queen, the two bodyguards and Laang, the non-driving driver, jumping out before he had the engine off. He had told them many times to carry themselves like they were his business associates, not armed guards, but there they were, putting on their Ray-Bans and scanning the rooftops like there were nests of snipers on every corner. In all the time he had run Patong, no one had so much as sneered at him, but he knew that part of it was because he had bodyguards. And he had bodyguards so that no one would so much as sneer at him. Zen-like balance, or a dog chasing its tail, all the same thing.

It was still early but there were already fifty tourists scattered around the vast space—nothing but a fancy tin roof and glittery lights that you couldn't see in the daytime. But it wasn't the décor that brought them in, had them sleepy drunk at three in the afternoon. It was the small army of small women, all big smiles like they actually wanted to be here. In their black and yellow striped rugby shirts they swarmed around the balding, middle-aged men like cute little bees, flirty and sweet until you tried to leave without spending what they thought was enough. Then the stingers came out and they turned into foul-mouthed tramps, armed with memorized phrases in every language that shattered the spell they had cast, reminding the tourists what they looked like and what was really going on.

Most of the bouncers and a few of the bartenders recognized him—hell, they probably worked for him—and he could tell by the way they shifted their feet that they were shocked he was here, paralyzed between slinking into what anonymous little shadows they could find and stepping forward in case he should need their help. The bar manager was gone, probably halfway down the coast by now, unable to imagine a good reason why Mr. Jarin would visit the club in the middle of the day. As for the bar-beer girls, most were from up-country, the mountains above Bangkok, and all of them too young to care who he was. To them he was just some fat local businessman, old enough to be their father. Well, he couldn't blame them. That was the image he projected, the one even those who knew better pretended to be true.

Jarin cut across the empty dance floor, the speakers thumping out the crap that passed for music these days. With a flick of his wrist he waved off his entourage. They fanned out around the bar, watching the crowd and covering his back. Despite their occasional screw up, like that screw up at the warehouse the day before, they were efficient, self-taught professionals, good enough at what they did. There was something in the book about that,

Rule Eight or Nine, something like 'pat them on the head when they do well'. It was stupid advice. You never pat a pit bull on the head unless you want your hand ripped off. And you never tell a bodyguard he's doing a good job. They get lazy that way, start thinking for themselves. Either way, dogs or people, rewarding expected behavior was dangerous.

It had been months since he had visited the Super Queen but not much had changed. All the tourists cared about was the size of the bar and the number of girls, and the Super Queen had the longest and the most. Some of the other bar-beer owners sunk thousands of bhat in smoke machines and fish tanks or laser-lit bar-backs and self-flushing urinals. But no guy came to Bang-la Road to see high-tech toilets. They came to get fucked—well and cheap. The Super Queen would be here long after the smoke and laser bars were gone.

He walked past the last tables to the booths that ran along the back wall, spotting her fire-red hair in the dim light. She sat alone, lighting a fresh cigarette, the breeze of an unseen fan creating a jet stream of smoke across the tops of the empty booths. When she saw him approach she clapped her hands once, cackling as she gripped the cigarette with her thin lips.

"*Four*-time, *Four*-time," Won shouted, pointing a bony finger at him, her dangling earlobes bobbing as she laughed.

Jarin smiled a rare smile at the sound of his old nickname, earned after an evening with some bar-beer girls, word getting back to Won about his bedroom performance. That was twenty-five years ago. They were older now—Won looking a hell of a lot older—but he was glad that over all that time, over all those changes, it was still the same between them.

"*Sawatdee krup*, you old bitch," Jarin said, bringing his palms together and bowing his head slightly as he slid into the booth across from her.

"*Sawatdee kaa*, little dick," Won said, smiling so hard her voice was an octave higher. She took a drag on her cigarette as she looked at him, her head nodding.

"Little dick? I'm Mr. Four-time, remember?"

"Well they got Viagra now," she said, switching to Thai. "Everybody's Mr. Four-time." She held out her hand, snapping her fingers, starting the game they played every time he visited. Jarin took a pack of Marlboros from his shirt pocket, ran a thumbnail across the front, tearing the cellophane off the box. He knocked a cigarette up and offered it to her. She reached over and took the whole pack. "So I hear you lost your whore."

"She wasn't my whore. She was bait. And he took it."

Won lit a fresh cigarette and handed it to Jarin. "You think he was behind it?"

"Who else would it be?"

Won shrugged, flicking ash onto the tabletop.

"No, it was him," Jarin said. "And you know more than you're telling me."

"I haven't told you anything."

Jarin nodded and for a few minutes they sat, smoking their cigarettes, enjoying the comfortable silence. He was counting the ceiling fans, wondering why they had them on when there was such a good breeze coming off the water, when Won tapped his arm. "Who was that guy, the one that used to own the Playpen?"

"That's going back," Jarin said, smiling as he rubbed his chin. "Tray. Tran. Something like that. Why?"

"The place had that funny entranceway. You came in and had to make a hard right then back again, remember? Well this guy…Tong, that was his name. Anyway Tong decides to fix the entrance, make it easier to get in. Everyone told him to leave it alone, but no, he had to make it better. He goes in with his own crew and they knock out a wall, the one with the mirror on it. They're cutting the last poles when there's this big crack and the whole corner of the bar drops down five feet. Nobody got hurt but he had to close until he got it fixed. Cost him a bundle and when it was done it still had that funny entrance."

"And the moral of the story is I shouldn't go after Shawn."

Won finished her cigarette, crushing it out in the full ash-tray.

"I need your help, Won."

She smiled but much of the humor had drained away. "That's what JJ said. Got the shit beat out of him." She waited, but he didn't say anything, rolling his cigarette in his fingers as he watched the smoke rise. "I want your word you won't hurt Pim."

"Fine," he said.

"And the old man and the kid. You leave them alone, too."

He nodded.

"That American couple. They're not part of this."

He looked across at her but said nothing, the look in his eyes saying it all.

"It's Shawn you want, not them."

Jarin leaned back and slung an arm across the back of the bench seat. "Just tell me what you know, Won."

Chapter Nineteen

There was one guard ahead of him on the stairs, two behind, with a third joining them as they passed the second floor landing. At first Mark thought they would start at the top floor and give him a push, one of those unfortunate accidents that tended to happen in the stairwells of certain police stations, but they seemed content to let him walk down on his own. He wondered if they were taking him back to the holding cell, but that was on the other side of the building and this was not the way they had come.

The lead guard stopped at the bottom landing and pushed open the crash bar on the fire exit, everyone squinting at the blinding white light of the afternoon sun, the blast furnace heat of the blacktop parking lot rushing in, sucking the cool air out of their lungs. There were five white patrol cars in the lot, the whole thing surrounded by a high wooden fence and an even higher row of palm trees. The guards spoke to each other in Thai, and between the words Mark heard a heart-stopping, metal-on-metal click, either the safety release on a police issue automatic or a tiny handcuff key lining up lock tumblers. A lifetime later, he felt the cuffs come off and, slowly, brought his hands from behind his back. He rubbed his wrists just like he did every time he had cuffs removed and stepped outside.

"*Haaeng nee,*" one of the guards said, tapping him on the shoulder. Mark turned and the guard handed him a clear plastic bag. Inside Mark could see his wallet, passport, and sandals.

Without another word, they pulled the door shut, leaving Mark to hop from foot to foot on the sun-baked blacktop. He slipped on his sandals and thumbed to the picture in the passport to be sure it was his. All the money in the wallet—bhat and dollars—was still there, another surprise courtesy of the Thai Police. He stuffed the wallet and passport in the cargo pocket of his shorts along with the wadded up plastic bag and started across the parking lot toward a latched gate at the end of a sidewalk. He was passing between a pair of parked cruisers when the passenger door opened and blocked his path.

Mark stopped and took a deep breath of humid, sauna-hot air. He should have known it wouldn't be that easy. He bent down to look in the patrol car, expecting to see Captain Jimmy sipping on a tall Thai iced tea. Instead he saw a small, dark-skinned policeman with oversized mirrored sunglasses and a patchy mustache. "Seat," the man said, waving Mark in, snapping his fingers for Mark to shut the door behind him.

He wore the same uniform as the others, the same flat arrogant smile, no idea how ridiculous the giant-sized aviator glasses made him look. His right arm was stretched out and draped over the top of the steering wheel and, although the seat was so far back the toes of his polished boots just touched the pedals, Mark's bended knees were wedged tight against the dashboard. The cop stared out the front of the car as if Mark wasn't there. Eyes level, he turned his head left and right like a slow moving camera scanning the parking lot. He said something in Thai and by the inflection in his voice Mark assumed it was a question.

"I don't speak Thai," Mark said, realizing after he said it that no matter what the cop asked, it was a stupid answer, either obvious or irrelevant. It didn't make a difference, the cop kept talking, his words as steady as his gaze. Hands on his knees, Mark said nothing.

Back in his office, before the guards had taken Mark away, Captain Jimmy had told him that he was to leave Krabi by the next ferry. "If I ever see you again," the captain had said, "I'll make up a reason to lock you up." It was all very John Wayne, the captain's voice dropping to a whisper, his dark eyes looking out from under his brow, but Mark didn't doubt that he'd do it. As he sat in the car, the sweat starting to roll down his back, he wondered if missing the ferry was part of the plan.

The cop stopped talking and turned his head until Mark could see himself in the cop's mirrored lenses. The cop waited a full minute, then said, "Shawn."

Mark felt his eyes widen, the cop nodding at his involuntary reaction. "Shawn," the cop said a second time, this time drawing the word out as he turned back to scan the parking lot.

"Yes," Mark said, "Shawn Keller. Do you know Shawn?"

The cop smiled. "Shawn."

"Listen. I'm trying to find Shawn Keller, his sister—"

The cop snapped out a sharp reprimand in Thai, and Mark stopped talking. Mumbling, the cop did a quick left right scan before turning back to Mark. He held up an index finger. "He she drink."

There was a pause, then Mark heard himself say, "What?"

"He. She. Drink."

"Great. What the hell does that mean?"

"He she drink, he she drink." The cop's voice was rising, his finger shaking at Mark.

"Is this about taking that girl to the bars last night, because I already told—"

"Shawn. He she drink."

Mark turned his palms up as he shrugged, wondering how the gesture translated. "Shawn he she drink?"

"*Krup, krup.* He she drink. Shawn."

"Wait a second," Mark said, his expression matching his disbelief. "Are you saying Shawn is a lady-boy? A, uh, what's the word...a *katoey?*"

The cop grit his teeth and slapped at Mark's head, his short reach landing the blows on Mark's shoulder. "*Gwonteen,*" the cop spat out the syllables in time with his slaps. Mark turned his head away and tried not to flinch. The cop grabbed his upper arm and shook it. "Shawn. *Krup?*"

"Yes. Shawn. *Krup.*"

The cop shook his arm again but he seemed pleased with Mark's response. "He she drink. *Krup?*"

"He she drink. *Krup.*" Mark nodded, but that didn't make it any clearer.

"*Krup, krup.* He she drink." The cop let go of Mark's arm and patted him once on the shoulder. He pointed at the door. Mark stepped out, his knees cracking as he stretched his legs. The cop reached over and pulled the door shut.

Mark crossed the parking lot in ten quick strides. He raised the latch and swung the gate open and looked back. The patrol car was empty.

A woman's voice came over the PA system and although she spoke in Thai, Mark could tell by the reaction of the others in the waiting area that she was announcing that the afternoon ferry to Koh Lanta was ready to board. He nudged Robin awake and stood up, Pim and her grandfather stepping up behind him, the boy busy making his final selection at the bank of gumball machines. There were thirty or so people in line, most of them tourists, and although the monitors listed a dozen ferry runs that would leave before nightfall, when the ferry to Koh Lanta pulled from the dock, the open-aired terminal would be empty. A plaque near the entrance said that the terminal was less than a year old. Mark wondered what it replaced.

They handed the security guard their tickets and joined the line of passengers that weaved back and forth through open rows of handrails like they were all heading for the same unpopular amusement park ride. Although it was no larger than a pair of city busses parked side by side, compared to the long-tail they had arrived on, the ferry was a huge and seaworthy vessel. The tourists clambered topside to work on their tans, all the Thais ducking below, sliding into the fast food restaurant style booths that butted against the large open windows. It was like his first week in Kuwait, when American troops ran around in their tee shirts and gym shorts while the Arabs, fully dressed, just smiled. He ducked his head and stepped down into the boat.

The Thai passengers had all filled the portside tables which told Mark that even though he had brought them below, they'd have some of the afternoon sun anyway. There were a couple of family groups, a booth of twenty-somethings with backpacks, and few passengers traveling alone—an old woman in a flowery print dress, an orange-robed monk, a soldier on leave, and a young guy with a bum leg who pulled out a newspaper and held it up in front of him the whole trip. Mark tossed his backpack in an empty booth, Robin sliding in across from him, Pim and her family filling the booth behind them. Robin dug in her backpack and pulled out a bag of trail mix she had bought in the terminal and set it on the table. She also palmed a fat Snickers bar and Mark pretended not to watch as she stretched her arm out along the back of the booth, yawning, dropping the candy into the boy's lap. "So one more time, what'd that Australian guy tell you?" she said, ignoring the excited giggling erupting behind her.

"He said that your brother came to Krabi shortly after the Tsunami, maybe mid-January. He had lost some weight and was still pretty banged up, but he was healthy. This guy says that Shawn was at every party he went to, but that he never saw him smoking. Anything. Anyway, he said Shawn stayed in Krabi for a few months, then decided to move to Koh Lanta, try to get a job with a dive shop. The last this guy heard, he was still there." Mark untied the plastic bag and scooped up a handful of strange nuts and unfamiliar dried fruit.

"And what about her?" Robin said, jerking a thumb back at Pim.

"He didn't mention her one way or the other."

"Who? This guy or Shawn?"

Mark thought a moment. "Shawn." He watched her face light up. She leaned back in the plastic booth, as happy as she had been since he met her. Maybe there was something to this Noble Lie business after all.

Outside, the harbor chugged past. The port was small and the only cargo ships docked were old style tramp steamers, right from the pages of a Conrad story, rust-buckets that oozed oil and diesel fuel and god knows what else into the fish tank-clear waters. Flying above paint-chipped names and ports of registry were the earth tone tri-color flags of third-world banana republics he couldn't have found with a map. The high-pitched roar of long-tails' engines competed with the high-pitched whine of the Thais' conversation; proximity giving the edge to his fellow passengers. The Arabic he had learned in Egypt and the Gulf had been deep and guttural, the patois in Jamaica almost lyrical. Thai was all nasal. He wondered what they would say about English, what sounds they made up when they were pretending to talk like an American. Did they notice the differences between a Brooklyn and a Boston accent, could they tell a Californian from a Canadian, or were the inflections too subtle? What about a Texas drawl and a Scottish brogue—were they broad enough to hear? The fact that they would know it was English at all would have impressed him. He wasn't even sure they were speaking Thai.

Robin swung her legs up on the bench seat, propping her back against the window frame. It was one thing to be attractive on a tropical beach or standing naked in an air conditioned hotel room, it was another to be just as good looking, just as sexy, with sea-spray matted hair and your face glistening with sweat like a glazed ham. She noticed him looking at her, "What?" she said, raising an eyebrow.

He leaned sideways to rest an elbow in the open window. "What's so special about your brother?"

She paused, looking at him, then shrugged. "What do you mean?"

"I just think it's strange for someone to travel halfway around the world to look for a relative who is old enough to take care of himself."

"You have any brothers or sisters?" she said.

It was his turn to pause and shrug. "I suppose I do."

"And if they were missing, you wouldn't try to find them?"

"There's a difference between missing and hiding."

"*Whatever*," she said. "You know what I meant. You wouldn't look for them?"

"Not particularly."

"Now see, I find *that* strange." She smiled. "And I think that says more about you than about me."

Mark saw his opening. "So tell me more about yourself."

"I'm not the mysterious loner here." She scooped up more of the trail mix.

"Where you from in the States?"

"A small town in Ohio. You wouldn't know it."

Mark nodded, conceding the point. "When did you decide you needed somebody to help you in Thailand?"

"At your friend Frankie's bar, when I realized that I was a chicken shit."

"Don't you have any friends back home that would have come with you?"

She looked away. "No. Next question."

"So you just walked into Frankie's and said I'm looking to hire somebody to find my brother, who you got?"

She pursed her lips and thought a moment. "Yup. That's pretty much it," she said, nodding, "except I was bawling my eyes out and hyperventilating so it probably didn't come out so clear." She tossed a couple peanuts in her mouth. "Frankie told me all about you."

"Obviously not," Mark said.

Robin dug in the plastic bag, pulling out a wafer-thin dried banana slice. "You were a Marine in the First Gulf War."

"Operation Desert Storm," he said, like the Great War veterans who couldn't have conceived of a sequel.

"I was in fourth grade. We made cards in art class for the soldiers. Did you ever get mine?"

"Crayon drawing of stick figures under a smiling sun? About ten thousand of them? Yeah, they arrived."

She picked up the bag and gave it a shake, forcing more fruit to the surface. "She said you were a hero."

Here it comes, he thought. "She's wrong."

"She said you got a Bronze Star."

Mark took a fistful of nuts from the bag, avoiding the dried fruit.

"She showed me this thing she printed out from the Internet. Nice write-up. Not a lot of details—something about you and some Saudi troops coming up on a bunch of Republican Guards…" She waited, but the silence didn't bother him.

"There was a picture of you. Didn't print too well." She looked at him, studying his face. "You really changed a lot in fifteen years."

Mark bit down on a macadamia nut. Tell me about it, he thought.

"She told me about what you did in Mali."

It was Malawi, but he didn't correct her.

"That guy, was it Mahmoud?" she asked, "Frankie says you saved his life."

"Her memory's not so good," Mark said.

"Anyway, I think what you did was amazing. But I have to ask you," she said, holding up a shriveled yellow cube. "Is this pineapple?"

"Yeah. It's pretty good, so don't eat it all," Mark said, bringing the other conversation to an end as a tall, thin man in his twenties—the tallest Thai Mark had seen—came and stood at end of the booth.

"Excuse me, where are you going?" the man said. He wore round, rose-tinted sunglasses that matched his shaggy Lennon-esque hairstyle, and a baggy white tee shirt that said something in Spanish. He was holding a thick three-ring binder under his arm.

"Is there a problem?" Mark said.

The man smiled and bobbed his head, pointing at the bench on Robin's side table. "May I?"

Robin swung her legs clear, sitting up. She pulled the trail mix toward her.

"My name is Ton." He held out a long, bony hand until Mark shook it. "We are with the Koh Lanta tourist association. We are here to help you find the right resort for your stay on the island." He motioned to a table of Thais who were busy pulling similar binders from their bags and heading topside. He slid the binder in front of Mark, opening the cover to reveal a high-gloss booklet for the Paradise Resortel tucked in a plastic page protector.

"Wow, those have gotta be expensive," Robin said as Mark flipped the pages to look at other full-color brochures and pre-printed rate sheets.

"We have many types of hotels at all different price ranges," Ton said. "And if you book with us we can promise a special reduced rate not available anywhere else. There are hotels and…" he reached across and turned over a stack of plastic pages until He reached a cardboard divider. "There are also beach huts. Bungalows. Very inexpensive."

Mark turned the pages, the back section all template brochures and tenth-generation photocopies. The names were different but each of them featuring the same bullet points; individual bamboo huts, café, a beach-side bar, shuttle into town and something called a fire dance, all of them noting that, whatever this fire dance thing was, theirs was the best on the island. He was nearing the back of the binder when he stopped at one brochure.

"It is still high season and it is difficult to get a room without a reservation," Ton said, pushing his long hair behind his large ears. "We can book everything for you right here."

"I'm sure you can," Robin said, "but I think we'll find something ourselves, thanks."

"Can you get us in here?" Mark said, tapping the brochure he had been reading.

Ton turned his head to see the name word-processed across the top of the brochure in seventy-two point, Comic Sans font. "Lanta Merry Huts? Yes, no problem."

"What are you doing?" Robin said, looking over at Mark.

"I'm going to need three huts. They're traveling with us as well." Mark pointed past Ton to Pim's table.

"Three? Yes, no problem, no problem. How many days?"

"Let's start with a week, take it from there," Mark said as Ton tugged a blank registration form from the front of the binder.

"What the hell are you doing?" Robin said, staring at Mark. "I'm paying the bills, I pick where we stay. In case you've forgotten, this isn't some holiday for you and your little friends."

Ton held his pen above the form and glanced up at Mark.

"Book it," Mark said. He reached over and put his hand on top of Robin's balled up fist. "Trust me on this." And then he smiled.

Chapter Twenty

There were no problems checking in at Lanta Merry Huts. The owner, an attractive woman nearing forty, insisted they have a glass of pineapple juice and something to eat before heading to their huts, three thatch-roofed, one-room bungalows straight out of Gilligan's Island. They ate on the covered patio that doubled as the lobby, the beach twenty steps from their table. The tide was out, revealing the rugged moonscape of rocks that lay just below the surface, the owner telling them that they could find crabs hidden in the rocks, that she could cook the crabs, mix them in with the breakfast meal, that it would be good. The old man and the boy were out there already, poking around the rocks with short sticks, Robin asking the owner if she had any Corn Flakes.

The owner pointed out the hotel bar, a dark clump of trees at the edge of the beach, a darker lean-to in the center ringed by high stools. There was a sign tacked to one of the trees, impossible to read in the twilight. She told them that it was closed for the night, that it would be open tomorrow, for sure maybe. She pointed to a speck of light a mile down the beach, telling them that it was the Monkey Bar and that it was open if they wanted a beer or a drink or maybe something else, bringing a pantomimed joint up to her lips so fast it was easy to miss. Robin said she could go for a beer, Mark saying that it sounded good. They agreed to meet back at the lobby in an hour, just relax a bit in their rooms, Mark saying he was going to lie down for a few minutes, waking up eight hours later, the call of some unseen tropical bird as cutting as an alarm clock.

He caught a ride into town in the back of a pickup truck and spent the morning showing Shawn's picture around the dive shops that lined Saladan Pier, all of them with the same looped Go Dive! videos, the posters showing the fishes of the Andaman Sea, the stack of current dive magazines, with glossy photos of lionfish, moray eels, whale sharks and corals tacked up next to nautical charts, the dive sites obliterated by thousands of sun-screened fingertips, the bigger shops flying the red flag with the white diagonal slash that meant there was a diver below. The dive boats had left for the morning before he had arrived, but the in-shop sales staff—usually a stunning Thai girl or golden-tanned European in a bikini—invited him in to their open-air offices, offering him a complimentary bottle of water before launching into their laidback sales pitches. With every shop offering the same thing at the same price, it came down to who told the better story. Or who looked better telling it. He tried to explain why he was there, that he wasn't looking to dive, just seeing if anyone knew this guy in the picture, but once they got rolling, started that slow, easy talk about the morays and the soft corals, about the beach over at Maya Bay or the currents at Hin Huang, they didn't know how to turn it off.

They'd ask if he was certified and he'd tell them that he was, Advanced Open Water with about two hundred dives, some in the Caribbean, some in South Africa, some in the Red Sea. Then they'd jump ahead in the script, ask him if he ever thought about getting his Divemaster certification, thinking about the hefty commission the three-week course would bring. When he said no, they'd retrace their way back to the break-even day trips, giving up when he showed them the picture for the fourth time. They'd look at the photo, the waist-up beach shot Robin had showed him that first day, and go on about how they would definitely remember having met this guy or how they wish they had seen him, a couple of women making the kind of comments that would get a guy's face slapped.

"You're gonna want to check with Fiona over at F and A," one sleepy-eyed Swede said as she stared at Shawn's smiling, tanned face.

"She hire on many instructors?"

"Nope," she said, handing him back the picture. "But she fucks a lot of hot guys."

It was the little things that let Mark know that on a street of interchangeable dive shops, F&A Divers was a step below the rest. There was a TV and VCR but instead of running the same souvenir dive video, it showed a bootleg copy of a Hindi movie musical, the color all wrong, the sound turned off or not working at all. There were magazines on the homemade bamboo coffee table, year-old *Cosmos* and fashion glossies in French, and instead of Bob Marley, the stereo blared out Robbie Williams. Out front, in a wooden crate below a sign that said We Rent Equipment, frayed weight belt straps and taped-up snorkels were mixed in with cracked masks and ripped fins, the kind of gear other dive shops threw away. Competition was tough for good dive shops. Mark wondered what kept F&A in business. He kicked off his sandals and went inside. The floor was gritty and warm. He rang the bell on the counter, waited a few minutes and rang it again. He was looking at a faded poster listing the 1998 Premier League schedule when she stepped through the beaded curtain, and it was then that Mark knew why F&A was still open.

She wasn't the most beautiful woman he had seen that morning. She lacked Pim's dainty features, she didn't have Robin's flawless complexion, and compared to the girls in the other dive shops on the street, she was ten pounds too heavy and ten years too old. Her hair was short and choppy, like she did it herself with a pair of scissors and no mirror. It was road-sign yellow and gelled to give it that just out of bed look. There were several shades of dried paint on her tank top, the swooping armholes and low neckline revealing most of her breasts. She wore a pair of men's madras shorts, the plaid faded and bleached with a denim patch sewn on the ass. A ring of keys dangled from a leather lanyard tied around her wrist and an unfinished tattoo of a dolphin leapt up her calf. She looked at him and smiled, an uneven smirk. She had it. That look, that vibe, that unmistakable something. Women called it slutty and would ask their husbands if guys *honestly* thought that it looked sexy, the men pretending they didn't understand the question, busy fantasizing about things they'd never ask their wives to do. Convincing guys to sign up with F&A? Nothing to it.

"Sorry," she said, her Canadian accent evident in one word. "I was smoking a bowl out back, didn't hear you ring. Been waiting long?" She opened a cooler behind the counter and held out a Singha.

"Just got here," Mark said, taking the bottle, popping the top off with a coin in his palm, another trick he had picked up in the Marines. "Are you Fiona?"

She smiled again, a different smile but it had the same effect. "I'm Erin. *Fiona*," she said, making air quotes around the word, "is the name that came with the job. F and A. That was Andy's idea. Yeah, real clever guy."

"So it's not your shop?"

"Might as well be. I book the divers, I make all the arrangements for the boats, I schedule the instructors, I pay off the cops, I skim money from the till." She looked up at him and winked. "But no, this is all Andy's. Till a shark gets him anyways."

"There a problem with sharks here?"

"No, but a girl can dream. Speaking of dreams," she said, climbing into the hammock that ran along the back wall of the shop, "how can I make your dreams come true?"

"Scuba diving dreams?"

"Those too, sure."

"I'm afraid I lost my dive card," Mark said.

"Cards? We don't need no stinking cards." She laughed. "I love when I get to say that. No, if you want to dive, mister..."

"Mark. Mark Rohr."

"Well if you want to dive, Mark Mark Rohr, you just let me know. Your word—and your cash, up front—is good enough for me."

"Not afraid to lose your license?"

"If we had one, maybe. But you're not interested in diving, are you Mark Mark Rohr?"

He pulled the picture from his shirt pocket and stepped over to the hammock. "Ever see this guy before?"

Erin switched her beer to her other hand, wiping her fingers dry on her shorts. "Shawn Keller. What the fuck are you carrying around a picture of this asshole for?"

"His sister hired me to find him. He's been missing since the tsunami and his family thought he was dead."

"And they want him *back*?" She looked back down at the picture. "He was a cutie, I'll give him that."

"Was?"

"He used to come around a lot, him and Andy working some deal or something, I don't know. Anyway, we hook up one night, next morning…" She shrugged her shoulders.

"He's gone and you feel used."

Erin looked up at him. "Please. I'm not *that* kind of girl. Anyway, the next morning I'm sneaking out of his place, trying not to wake him up. It's not easy getting dressed in the dark when you can't tell whose shorts are whose. All of a sudden he springs up out of bed, *tackles* me, slams my head into the floor a couple of times and sticks a gun in my face. Oh, he said he was sorry, that I *startled* him, but come on, how many people get *that* startled? And with a gun? I told him I had enough nut cases in my life already, that he'd better stay the hell away from me. Since then I haven't seen him, but I hear he's still around."

"When was this?"

"Let's see, it was right after Andreas went back to Sweden, Fredrick was still here, but this was before Ola got his tattoo." She smiled at the memories. "Oh yeah. *Ola…*"

"So this was…?

"Sorry. About four weeks back."

"How'd he look?"

Erin handed back the picture. "Like this. Tanner, maybe."

"Healthy?"

"*Very.*"

Mark put the picture back in his pocket and sat down on the edge of the coffee table. The beer was already warm but he drank it anyway. Swinging on the hammock, Erin bobbed her foot in time with the music. He waited for the song to end—something about a monkey with a gun—before saying, "I need to find him."

"You need to talk to Andy," she said, foot still bobbing. She leaned up to see the Tiger Beer clock on the wall. "The dive boat won't be in for another two hours. I was gonna close up till then."

"Won't you be missing out on new business?"

Erin laughed. "There's only so many suckers out there." She sipped her beer and looked at him. "So. Wanna come back to my place, grab a bite?"

"I'm not really hungry," Mark said, finishing his Singha.

"That's funny," she said, and downed the rest of her beer. "Neither am I."

The dive shop boat revved its twin engines as it eased up against the row of tires that protected both the dock and the hull of the boat. On board, fifteen sun-whipped divers rocked unsteadily as they waited to get back on dry land. The captain kept the engines running as one of the dive instructors leapt onto the dock and tied off the boat at both ends. He gunned the engines one last time before shutting them down.

"Gear first, then divers," the captain said, barking it out as if they were sandbagging crewmembers and not paying customers, his harsh British accent putting a sharper edge on his words. The trip over and now non-refundable, he could afford to drop the happy skipper role.

"God *damn* it, watch it with those tanks. And get those weight belts away from the edge unless you want to go in after them." The captain was lean and hard, nut-brown with bleached out, scraggly hair and a hawk nose. True to type, there was a swirling tribal tattoo on his arm and a cigarette butt hanging on his lower lip, the uniform of the non-conformist beach bum turned entrepreneur.

"Bloody hell, watch the damn regulators."

The divers, all guys, shuffled past, each lugging a pair of empty tanks to the waiting pickup truck, glancing worried looks back at their mesh bags of personal gear the captain was tossing onto the dock. Some of them still had the pink-red line of their dive masks running across their foreheads and circling down onto their cheeks. It was a rookie mistake, not clearing your mask at depth, one that Mark had made a few times himself. The second trip they carried their BCDs and regulators—the inflatable vests and tangle of breathing hoses that dive shops rented as if they had to buy new ones every week. It was a standard two-tank dive, with each dive shop offering identically priced excursions to the same dive sites, but Mark knew how these divers got lured into signing with F&A.

"Don't wave that dive book at me," the captain said through his teeth, the nervous passenger stepping backward off the boat as if he expected to get hit. The captain watched as the passengers piled on the back of the mini-pickup for the short ride to the dive shop, glancing at each other but no one looking back at the boat. "And I don't sign off on a single one of you until *all* the gear is accounted for," he shouted as the driver popped the clutch, kicking up dirt. It was just Mark on the dock now, the captain still in the boat, glaring at him, flicking his cigarette butt into the water. "What the fuck you looking at?"

Mark kept his hands in his pockets and didn't bother to smile. "A guy named Andy who knows Shawn Keller."

He watched Andy's eyes, a split second of surprise then the same hard stare. "Don't know him." He gathered his mask and snorkel and stuffed them in his dive bag along with his black split-tail fins and the rest of his gear.

Mark looked out to the horizon, the perfect blue water, the cloudless sky, the dark green shapes that someone had said were the Phi Phi Islands. "I need to find Shawn Keller."

Andy stepped out onto the dock, tossing the extra lengths of guide rope back into the boat. He dug a hand into his pocket, pulling out a pack of smokes and a clear plastic lighter, shaking loose a cigarette, drawing it out with his lips, cupping his hands around the end as he got it lit. He reached over and pulled his dive bag from the captain's seat and slung it over his shoulder and started down the pier.

"I said I need to find Shawn Keller." Mark watched as Andy approached, the man looking past him.

"And I said I don't know him, right, so piss off." Andy looking at him now, all attitude.

Mark stepped sideways into his path, his eyes level with the top of Andy's head. "One more time. I need to find Shawn Keller." He waited for the man to say something, push past him, watching as the man's lips twitched and his neck muscles tightened, but the man did nothing and it was over.

"Shawn Keller?" Mark said.

The man took a half step back, smirking, playing it off. "Right, and who the fuck are you?"

"A friend."

"Bullshit. Keller has no friends."

"Then you do know him."

Andy drew on his cigarette, twisting his mouth so that he blew the smoke to the side. "I've heard of him, sure. But I don't know him."

"Erin tells me you and Shawn were working on a business deal."

"Stupid bitch," Andy muttered.

Mark leaned forward. "I wouldn't say that again if I were you."

Andy looked up at him. "You're an American?"

Mark nodded.

"Right, thought so. It's that whole American thing, think you can go anywhere, stick your nose where it don't belong. Fine, I might know Keller. And I might have done a bit a business with him, too. What I don't see is what business it is of yours."

"It's not my business. I don't care what you do. You're not part of this. I just need to find Shawn Keller."

"I tell you, take you to him, you leave me out of it?"

"That's what I'm saying."

Andy sighed, took one last drag and dropped the just-lit cigarette to the cement pier, grinding it under his leather sandal. "Right then." He shifted the strap of his dive bag and nodded up toward the road. "Let's go."

At the end of the pier, miniature Toyota pickups and snout-nosed three-wheelers waited for the last of the dive boats to return. In the street-side bars he could hear divers one-upping each other's stories, while in the shops, instructors shook their heads as they recounted the ass-backward screw-ups they had to deal with on the dive. Andy stayed a stride ahead, his left hand keeping the dripping dive bag on his shoulder, the right swinging wide with every step.

"This way," Andy said, turning down a dirt and mud path that cut between a pair of souvenir shops to join the narrow access alley that snaked behind the storefronts. It was too narrow for dumpsters but there were bikes and scooters chained up to wire-heavy utility poles and a few bags of trash piled up behind the closed service doors of the restaurants. Mark watched as Andy shifted the dive bag so it was in front of him, hidden from Mark's view, his left hand lower now, probably feeling for the zipper, his right hand crossing in front of him, digging around in the bag.

Mark wondered how he'd do it. Would he stop suddenly, letting Mark walk into him, then turn quick, pulling the dive knife out of the bag, sticking it under Mark's chin and force him up against one of the cinderblock walls? Or would he drop the bag off his shoulder, thinking that Mark would look down at the bag, then turn with the knife? He could swing the bag at him, then step in with the knife, but only if he was trying to kill him and Mark was sure it was just going to be talk, the stay-the-fuck-away speech or the who-the-fuck-are-you drill. He heard the scratch of the Velcro strap and Mark could picture the man easing the knife from the ankle sheath, figuring Andy for the kind of guy who'd carry the double-edged dagger type instead of the more practical utility knife with the blade on one side and saw-tooth edge on the other. He could see Andy tensing up so he took a breath to relax, letting it out as he watched Andy slip his thumb under the strap and lift it off his shoulder.

"*Right*," Andy said as the bag hit the ground, spinning around to see Mark smiling, Mark's left hand already locked tight around his wrist, pulling him forward, Mark turning now, keeping the knife away from his body, the arm stretched out straight, Mark's right hand coming up hard on his back, Andy stumbling over the bag at his feet, going down, face first into the dirt path, his arm still held up, his wrist bent back, the knife slipping free. With his thumb pressed into the back of Andy's hand and the man's elbow locked against his leg, Mark picked up the knife. It had a titanium blade with both a sharp edge and a low ridge of rounded serrations, a deep-notched line cutter near the handle. Expensive and top of the line. He held it by the tip and tested its balance before flicking it up toward the roof of the shop, the knife sticking with a solid thud into the center of a two by four that braced a small satellite dish, twenty feet off the ground. It was a lucky shot, one in a hundred, but he wasn't going to tell Andy that.

"Right, that wasn't mine, you bastard," Andy said, jumping up when Mark let go of his arm. He was rubbing his wrist and flexing his fingers and there was dirt on his face and dots of blood where his cheek had hit the path. They stood there a moment, looking up at the knife, the bass of a bar stereo thumping through the wall. "Bastard," Andy said again, snatching up his dive bag and walking away, turning back when he was ten yards away, shouting, "you'll pay for that, you bastard."

Mark smiled and waved. "Say hi to Shawn for me."

Chapter Twenty-one

"Here's to cheap drinks," Robin said, tapping the rim of her third gin and tonic against the side of Mark's fifth Singha.

A hazy cloudbank on the horizon had obscured the sunset, but the light breeze and the heavy scent of wild orchids made it a beautiful evening. They had eaten on the beach, the owner of the Lanta Merry Huts setting out a picnic style meal, a mix of seafood and rice, a Thai-style stew that even Robin enjoyed. Pim was eager to help in the kitchen, the owner just as happy to let her. The old man and the boy had borrowed a pair of long fishing poles and spent the day on the rocks at the point. Mark was sure that even though they caught the fish and Pim had cleaned and cooked it, the full price of the meal would be added to their bill. Robin had walked the beach all day, checking at all the bungalow hotels, everyone so helpful and nobody telling her a thing. Now, with the sky turning blue-black, Pim and her family talking with the owner and her staff—their high-pitched voices cutting though the night air—Robin and Mark sat at the beach-side bar, Bob Marley's *Exodus* CD starting up for the fourth time.

They were the only patrons at the bar, the bartender sitting in the sand to the side, close enough to refill their drinks but far enough away to give them privacy. The bar itself was a plank propped up on bamboo stakes and gnarly driftwood, and an orange extension cord ran from the four-way plug behind the dorm fridge back across the clearing to the registration desk. On the back bar was one bottle each of gin, vodka, whiskey, and rum, and the bar napkins advertised chain hotels on other islands.

"How's this one?" Mark said, pointing to Robin's drink.

"Better than the last. The tonic's flat and there's still no ice, but he's doubled-up on the gin. Your beer warm?"

"Toasty." He didn't know if it was the heat or if they brewed their beers stronger in Thailand, but he was feeling that buzz that usually hit after a couple six packs of American beer.

She squeezed the lime into the glass. "We could walk down to the other hotel, that Monkey Bar."

"I like this place," Mark said, looking around, nodding in approval. "Good tunes, good company, a crack wait staff—"

"Stupid bar name."

Mark put his hand to his heart, "Stupid? The name is why I picked this place. As soon as I saw it in that guy's binder, the one on the boat, I knew we'd stay here. Besides, it came highly recommended."

"By who?"

"A kindly police office in Krabi," Mark said, remembering the parking lot encounter. "It's prophetic."

"It's not prophetic, it's pathetic. What the hell does that mean, He She Drink?"

"He—that's me—she—that's you—drink. And that's what we're doing."

Robin used the swizzle stick in her drink to mash the lime wedge into the bottom of her glass. "We can drink tonight, but you better remember why we're here."

"To find your brother, I know. And like I told you at dinner, we'll find him this week or we won't find him at all."

"I can take that either way, you know—like you're confident or like it's a lost cause."

"I'm confident. But that doesn't mean it's not a lost cause."

A shrill laugh erupted from the covered porch at the reception desk, the owner howling at something that had been said. Mark could see them in the tiki torchlight, Pim, her grandfather and nephew, the owner, and a few of her employees, all of them sitting close around a picnic table, Pim's bright white smile flashing as she spoke. "It looks like Pim's keeping them all entertained."

"Good," Robin said without looking back. "Maybe they'll give her a job."

He started to say something and stopped, then thought, what the hell, and said, "Why do you have to ride her like that?"

Robin said nothing, licking lime pulp from the plastic swizzle stick.

"She's a good woman and she's helped us out."

"I've paid all her bills. Ferry tickets, hotels, food…" she said, tapping out the words with a fingernail against her glass. "Not just for her but for all of them."

"Yeah, well it wouldn't kill you to be nicer to them, too." He took a long pull on his beer.

"You sure about that?" Robin said, her head propped up in the palm of her hand.

"You could at least be more friendly."

"Really?" Robin looked up at the palm fronds of the bar's droopy awning. "So tell me, Mister Congeniality, what are their names?"

"Their names?"

"Old man, about a hundred, sits real straight? Cute kid, loves chocolate? Sound familiar?"

Mark wet his lips and rubbed his chin with his thumb. He hadn't shaved that morning and the stubble felt like fine sandpaper. He'd have to shave in the morning if he could find some hot water. He took another sip of his beer and wet his lips again.

"Well?"

"The old man is Pim-san, that's where Pim got her name. The boy's name is Timmy."

"Nice try," Robin said. "I'll give you points for that Pim-san thing. Very creative."

"How do you know I'm not right?"

"Because the old man's name is Kiao. Pim calls him *Bpuu*, it's a Thai term for your grandfather on your father's side. And the boy's name is NamNgern but they call him Ngern. Sometimes she calls him *lor*. I think it means cutie or handsome, something like that. By the way, Pim's just a nickname. Her real name is Prisana."

"And you know this because…"

"Because I asked." She downed her drink and stood up, wiggling her toes into her flip-flops. "Thought you had me all figured out, didn't you? Guess I fooled you." She turned and started toward her bungalow. "Don't forget to sign for the drinks," she said over her shoulder. "And be sure you give the nice man a big tip."

Mark smiled as he watched her walk away, her hips swaying with a reggae beat.

"If you have get more like this," the man said, holding up to the light three sticks of Golden Thai, the potent strain of marijuana the *ferangs* loved, "you may can stay as long as you wished."

He smiled. The ones from Europe? The ones with the blue eyes and thin hair? They were the best *ferangs*. They were the easiest to get along with and they never got mad, no matter what. And their English? It was no better than his, so there were no funny looks and they never raised their voices when they talked to him, as if they said it louder he'd understand.

"This is good. This is much good," the man said to him, examining the buds. It should be, he thought to himself. The Chinese kid who tried to sell it to him wanted four thousand bhat for it, which was crazy because it was only worth five or six hundred, tops. But even if the kid had said three hundred, it would have ended the same. He couldn't spare even that much, and anyway he didn't know the kid, a huffer who sold weed to tourists so he could buy his cans of spray paint. He had to spend a full hour digging a hole for the kid, dragging his dead ass deeper into the tree line, digging with his hands, breaking his long pinky nail when he hit a root. The way he saw it, he lost money on the deal.

The blue-eyed guy? He spent the day smoking bowl after bowl and he even offered to share, and he didn't once try to touch him, even at night. He had first seen this *ferang* when he was hanging out at the pier, watching the big American waiting for the dive boats to come in, the big guy never noticing him. On the ferry from Krabi he had sat not five meters from the American, peeping through the tiny hole he had poked in the newspaper. He had watched as the tout from the tourist board signed him up for a hotel, the tout—a tall guy with floppy ears—bragging to the others that he had booked three bungalows at the Lanta Merry Huts and charged the *ferang* for four. And he watched as the late afternoon sun angled into the starboard windows, the big American and his tan girlfriend falling asleep. It would have been so easy to walk over, slip his knife down the man's collarbone. He could never get away, sure, but he could have done it. Besides, he needed them alive.

When the ferry arrived at the port, the American had hired a tuk-tuk to take him and his people to the hotel. It was only ten kilometers or so down the beach and he knew they wouldn't be going anywhere since, according to the tuk-tuk drivers he spoke with, there wasn't anyplace to go. It was a good walk, and he got there just as the sun was setting, the blue-eyed *ferang* approaching him as he sat on the beach, a hundred meters from the Lanta Merry Huts, watching the big American and his group as they ate in the twilight. It had taken ten minutes of bullshit but the guy finally got around to asking him if he had any Thai stick to sell. He didn't, but he knew he could get it easy enough from any of the tuk-tuk drivers, so they came to an agreement, swapping a safe supply of weed for a spot on the floor of the guy's less pricey hut down the beach.

That night the American stayed in his hut. Alone. That had surprised him since, when he had crept up to the hut and peeked through the open slats of the bamboo shutters, he had expected to see the American woman in there with him, too, or at least the Thai whore. But he had been alone. The Thai family all slept on the same bed. And the blonde girl, the one with the tan? He had seen her sleeping, sprawled naked face down on the bed, her tight white ass glowing in the moonlight.

The next morning he caught a ride to town on the back of a delivery truck. He needed to score enough *gencha* to keep the *ferang* happy without having to spend any more of his money. That's when he had spotted the huffer with his cans of spray paint and plastic bag out near the dump.

He was standing on line at a noodle shop, his pockets bulging with baggies of Thai stick, when he saw the American going to the dive shops, showing around that same picture he had flashed at all the bar-beers in Phuket.

This is what he knew. The American was looking for the guy in the picture and somehow Jarin was involved. The next night the American gets Jarin's whore and her family and they all leave together on a long-tail, ending up in Krabi late the next day. The American was still looking for the guy in the picture. And when he saw two of Jarin's men get off the ferry that morning, he knew that Jarin was still looking for the American.

Now, as he stood in the *ferang's* hut watching as the man inspected each of the bud-heavy shoots, he formed a plan.

He'd stay close to the big American, wait for him to find the guy he was looking for, then capture them both and take them to Jarin himself, and Jarin would be impressed and would hire him on, right there, make him part of the gang, something like his assistant since he would know he could trust him with the hard jobs, and then everyone would have to respect him and call him by his name because he was Jarin's man.

Well, maybe not capture. The American was huge and if he was looking for another *ferang*, that guy would be huge, too.

He'd stay close, find out what they were up to and get word to Jarin, let him know where they were and what they were doing.

But how? He'd only made three phone calls in his life and even though he had lived there for four years now, he didn't know anybody to call in Phuket.

Okay. He'd stay close, find out what they were doing and then figure something out. Jarin would like that. He'd say you're a quick thinker, I need smart men like you. Yeah, he'd figure something out.

It was dark, getting close to midnight. The blond *ferang* was happy and that meant he'd have a place to sleep for the next few days. Not that he needed it, he'd lived on the streets for years, but it was still nice and it didn't cost him anything other than offing a huffer who would have been dead in a couple months anyway. He'd take a walk down to the Lanta Merry Huts, wait for the American to go to bed, then come back and get some sleep.

But what if Jarin's men found the American first? They were already here, he had seen them near the pier, two of them, guys he'd seen all the time at the Horny Monkey. What if they got him first? Then everything he'd done would mean nothing and Jarin wouldn't hire him and everyone would still call him Spider. He had to do something, keep Jarin's men from finding the American first, but how? He couldn't talk to them, tell them the American wasn't here—they wouldn't believe him and they'd wonder what he knew, beating it out of him, then killing him. And if he went to the American and told him that Jarin's men were coming for him, the American would want to know how he knew, and he'd get beaten up and probably killed by him instead. He had to think, come up with something. He'd come too far to give up and this was it, his one chance, he knew that more than anything. Screw it up now and that's it, it's over. And then what? Go back to Phuket and get picked on for the rest of his life, or go back home and become a farmer? No, this was it, this was it.

"Hey?" the blond *ferang* said, looking up at him from the bed, his legs crossed in front of piles of buds and stems. "You are all correct? You are looking not good."

The first time he heard the sound he thought it was part of his dream. He had been sitting at the bar in Phuket City, talking with Frankie Corynn, but instead of dark red hair, she was blonde, and then it wasn't Frankie anymore, it was Robin and they were at the Horny Monkey, and the noise was part of the dream, maybe a pool ball hitting the floor. The second time the sound was louder and it woke him up, a stone tossed up against the door, bouncing down onto the planks that served as a porch.

He reached over and thumbed the switch on the lamp cord, remembering when the room stayed dark that the owner cut off the generator at midnight. He got up, slipped on his shorts and peered through a space on the wooden shutters. There was no one on the porch. Robin would have knocked, and Pim would have never come to his room at night. When they were at her apartment—a studio smaller than his bungalow, a street away from the F&A dive shop—he had told Erin where he was staying. She would be the kind of woman who'd show up in the middle of the night, knowing she wouldn't get sent away, so it could be her. But no, it would be Andy, his new knife-wielding friend, wanting him to come out and play. He was strapping the Velcro on his sandals when a third stone clattered on the porch. This time he'd keep the dive knife instead of tossing it away, hoping that Andy had brought the matching sheath with him as well.

Mark undid the hasp and eased the door open. His eyes had adjusted to the darkness in his bungalow but it was lighter outside, making it easier to see the grounds. The trees and bushes were shades of dark green, the flowers gray in the moonlight. He could see down the short row that made up the Lanta Merry Huts, the porches in a line, nothing moving. There were palm trees on either side of his bungalow but too narrow to hide behind, and while the hut was built on short stilts, it was too low to the ground to get under. He stepped off the porch and stood on the crushed shell path that led to the beach, listening. Other than the sound of the tide rolling back in, it was still. His eyes took in the darkness around him, stretching farther out with each pass, scanning the reception area, the picnic tables, the hammocks and lounge chairs, the beach.

And the bar.

There, alone on the center stool, a dark shape waved.

Mark took his time walking over, one eye on the lone figure, the other on the shadows all around him. The path widened as it reached the bar, and Mark stopped. The man was turned to face him, one elbow on the bar the other arm in his lap, his bare feet stretched out in the sand. It was dark, but Mark knew the face, and in a voice just above a whisper, Shawn Keller said, "I hear you're looking for me."

Mark stepped to the bar and took a seat, leaving an empty stool between them. There were no bottles on the shelves, the stereo was gone and there were two padlocks on the fridge. He would have liked a drink. "My name is Mark Rohr. I'm here with your sister. She hired me to find you."

No one spoke for a full minute, the sound of the waves slapping the beach louder in the silence. "My sister, huh?" Shawn said, his voice almost lost in the surf. "What's her name?"

"Robin," Mark said. He could see Shawn nod his head but it was too dark to read his expression.

"She's here now?" Shawn motioned to the row of bungalows.

"Yeah. The hut next to mine."

More nodding. "So she came looking for me."

"She spotted you on CNN, some tsunami anniversary special. Your family thought you were dead."

Shawn sighed but said nothing.

"Something else," Mark said and waited until he saw Shawn's head turn his way. "Pim's with us."

"Oh shit," Shawn said, rolling his head back to look straight up at the night sky.

"I'm sure she's excited to see you again, too," Mark said.

Shawn shook his head. "You don't have a fucking clue what's going on."

"I know that your sister paid me to find you and I did. How it plays out between you is none of my business."

"If Pim's with you," Shawn said, ignoring the comment, "then that means Jarin's not far behind."

It was Mark's turn to shake his head. "We lost them in Phuket."

Shawn laughed. "You think you lost him."

They fell silent again, Shawn looking up at the stars, Mark watching Shawn, planning how he'd do it, how he'd reach over, pull the man from the chair, clock him with a quick left, hold him down as he shouted for Robin and Pim, get it all over with. If he wanted to run off on his wife and sister, disappear, play dead, that was up to him. But before he'd go, Mark would see to it that he spent some quality time with his family. Mark focused on his breathing, slowing down, getting ready when Shawn looked at him. "I'm going to need your help."

Mark let the words hang in the air, sensing something different now. "Go on."

Shawn slid to the open stool between them, Mark watching him as he moved. "I need to meet with you tomorrow. Not here. There's a little fishing village about three miles south of here, right on the beach. Come early. Don't worry, I'll see you." Shawn was closer now and Mark could see his eyes. They were clear and alert, no sign of the drugs that were everywhere in Thailand.

"What's this about?"

"You'll just have to trust me till then."

Mark smiled. "Forgive me if I'm a little skeptical. I'm here with some people you already lied to. Give me a reason to trust you."

"Put it this way. If we do this right, we don't screw this up," Shawn said, his eyes locked on Mark's, "there's a good chance we'll all get off the island alive."

Chapter Twenty-two

Mark had been running for thirty minutes when he decided that it had to be something in his genes.

The last time he had run it had been six months ago in Dahab, the time before that in southern Turkey, and before that it was either Beirut or Oman, whichever place he had met that girl from Osaka. There was no logic behind it, no cultural explanation, but when he saw a long, open stretch of ocean beach, he just started running. His hip would bother him later and he'd walk with a limp for the rest of the day, but there wasn't much he could do. There was a beach and nobody on it so he had to run.

In Phuket there were tanners every few yards and there was something about seeing all those leathery-brown topless retirees that counteracted the otherwise overwhelming urge to kick off his sandals, pick a direction and go. But here, when he stepped out of his bungalow, stretching the early morning stiffness out of his muscles, and saw all that empty sand, that was it.

He ran close to the shoreline, staying to the wave-packed wet sand. It was easier than running in the deep dry sand and there was less chance he'd step on a buried beer bottle or rusty can. In the Corps he had run miles and miles every day, and when they were laid up in Saudi Arabia, bored out of their minds, waiting for the ball to drop, they'd run in the desert just for something to do, the sweat evaporating before it could wet their shirts. And he had run in Kuwait, too, but running was easy when you had somebody shooting at you.

The beach narrowed as he ran south. There were a few stray bungalows on this section and no bars so few tourists made it this far. Ahead, he could see some long-tails pulled up on the sand and a handful of tin-roofed plywood huts, with kids and mangy dogs playing in the low surf. He spotted Shawn sitting alone under a stand of palm trees and angled toward him, slowing to a walk.

"Admit it," Shawn said as Mark stripped off his sweat-soaked tee shirt. "You didn't think I'd be here."

"I had my doubts."

"What made you decide to trust me?"

"Who said I do?"

"Ouch. Okay, then, why'd you let me go last night?"

"I didn't." Mark sat down in the shade, his shirt over his lap. He leaned back on his hands and looked out to the sea. "I followed you back here, watched you go in that crappy bungalow up there." He pointed over Shawn's head to the cluster of buildings up the beach. "You had a beer on the porch then went inside and fell asleep."

Shawn's smile drooped.

"When you came back here and went to sleep," Mark said, "I knew you weren't planning to run off. If you did you would have gotten started right away. So I figured you'd be here this morning. If it was just me and your sister, I would've kept you at the bar."

Shawn chuckled. "Well, you would have tried."

"Nah," Mark said, without looking over. "I would have kept you there. But when you brought up Jarin I had to think about the kid."

"Pim?" Shawn said. "Pim's no kid. She can take care of herself."

Mark nodded, wanting to say something about how he should know, running off on her, leaving her behind, knowing damn well what would happen to her, but instead said, "I wasn't talking about Pim. I was talking about Ngern."

"Who?"

"Her nephew. About ten or so."

"She has a *kid* with her?"

"Yeah," Mark said, enjoying this for some reason. "Him and Kiao. Her grandfather."

Shawn fell backwards into the sand. "I don't believe this." He stared up at the swaying palm fronds. "Why'd you let her bring them along?"

"Had to. Pim said she wouldn't take us to you if we didn't."

Shawn hissed out a sigh. "She played you, Mark. She had no idea where I was."

Mark shrugged his shoulders. "I'm sitting next to you, aren't I?" He was tempted to tell Shawn about the Thai cop, the one in the parking lot with the cryptic He She Drink message, but held off, waiting to see how this played out. For ten minutes, neither man said a word. Mark watched as a fisherman dropped the long propeller shaft off a beached long-tail, dragging it prop first up behind one of the huts where a hammer knocked out a steady metal on metal beat. Shawn broke their silence.

"What did Robin tell you about me?"

"She said that you used to have a problem with drugs but that you seem to have kicked it."

"That's fair, I guess. She tell you why I was in Thailand?"

"She said that you liked to test yourself, go to places where drugs were cheap and easy to get to see if you can just say no."

"Do you believe that?"

Mark shrugged. "It's not the stupidest thing I've ever heard."

"But I bet it's close." Shawn sat up, brushing the sand off his shoulders. "That's the way she sees the world. A series of temptations to say no to."

"So there's no truth to it?"

"Some, I guess," Shawn said. "But does anybody really know why they do the shit they do? I'm sure you've come up with a good reason why you're here that has nothing to do with the truth."

Mark looked out at the waves hitting the shore. It wasn't a question so he didn't feel he needed to respond.

"Robin doesn't know what I'm up to. She *thinks* she does—she *always* thinks she does—but she doesn't."

"Is that why you don't want to see her?"

Shawn shook his head. "No, I want to see her. But it's too dangerous right now."

"Because of what you're really up to."

Shawn grunted. "You've got no idea either."

"Maybe not, but I've got a pretty good guess."

"Let's hear it."

"All right," Mark said. "You don't use drugs but you know a lot of people who do. You've put your experiences as a user to work and set up shop here in Thailand, small stuff at first to meet expenses, moving up to bigger deals to get rich. But that meant doing business with Jarin. About a year ago you were in to him deep—money or product, it doesn't make a difference, you owed him a lot. When the tsunami hit, you saw a chance to disappear. Except he wasn't fooled. Now he's pissed and he's still looking for you. Sound right so far?"

"Not even close," Shawn said.

"Jarin had Pim kidnapped and held her out as bait, assuming you'd do the honorable thing and try to rescue her."

Shawn laughed. "Honorable? Try suicidal. Do you have any idea how hard that would be?"

It was Mark's turn to laugh. "Yes."

"He wasn't expecting you. If I came anywhere near Phuket it would have been completely different; and she'd be dead now, and so would her family. Look, I know this sounds cold but she was better off without me."

"I agree," Mark said.

"Fuck you, okay?" Shawn said, no passion in his voice. "You got no idea what's going on."

Mark turned his head to look at Shawn. "So tell me."

Shawn raised his legs up and rested his elbows on his knees. He closed his eyes and took a loud, deep breath, letting it out in a long, silent whistle. "Ever hear of the IMP?"

"Should I have?"

"Not really. It's post nine-eleven. Back when all the good guys were on the same team. IMP is International Maritime Police."

"Sounds impressive."

"At least it's got that going for it. Looks good on paper, too. But it's UN so what do you expect."

Mark had heard the UN was blamed for everything from Iraq to lite beer but assumed that there was enough blame to go around, and in Kuwait and Cyprus and Lebanon he had seen soldiers from the world's armies with only those stupid sky-blue helmets in common, directing traffic or watching as the real troops got the work done.

"I suppose it was somebody's brilliant idea," Shawn continued. "Small teams, pretty much independent, supposed to protect the high seas by stopping the terrorists and pirates and jaywalkers before they got started, all covert and shit. What it is is two hundred lame-dick agents and sixty-four million square miles of ocean. No boats, no training, and no real authority. And zero help from the local governments. Still, they go around like they're on some mission to save the world."

"Let me guess," Mark said, still watching the waves. "You're in some sort of trouble with this IMP."

"I'll say," Shawn said, and laughed so loud the stray dogs by the water looked their way. "I'm in charge of the Thailand team."

Mark tilted his head, looking over the top of his sunglasses, waiting for the punch line. Shawn stared down at his fingers, pulling fibrous strands from a piece of coconut husk.

"If we had the funding and the manpower, and if the people we did have were well trained and could be trusted not to sell us out, and if the governments weren't part of the problem in the first place, we might be able to do some good. We poke around here and there, try to stop what we can." Shawn tossed the husk in the sand and met Mark's gaze. "It beats flipping burgers."

"And you're telling me this because…?"

"Because I'm an idiot," Shawn said without humor. "And because there's a ship coming up from Singapore, docking in Langkawi day after tomorrow, then going on to Chennai, up in

India. East coast. We lost this ship about six months ago, just found it last week."

"How do you lose a whole ship?" Mark said, trying to keep the growing interest out of his voice. "They gotta have those GPS things on them, find them anywhere in the world."

"New ships, yeah, and big ones, definitely. But this is neither. It's under five thousand tons, built back in the early eighties. Should have been scrapped years ago. It's what they call a Death Ship. The owners keep them afloat, keep them insured, have them hauling worthless crap through rough waters hoping they go down. Ships like this, they disappear every day. I thought this one was lost off Madagascar, but I guess not."

"Couldn't you just go after the owner, find out where the ship was supposed to be?"

"If they played by the rules, maybe, sure. But nobody does. Why do you think all these ships are registered out of Liberia and Somalia and shit? Nobody's watching what's going on. There's so many layers of ownership and holding companies and fronts. Hell, *al-Qaeda* owns ships and the US government can't figure out which ones." Shawn ran his hands through his hair. "If people had any idea what it's like out there…"

Mark remembered catching snippets of some BBC broadcast, an oh-so-earnest interviewer tossing softball questions to a stern-faced admiral. There was a report from Spain about an oil tanker that had split in two a few years back, shots of the coastline knee-deep in sludge and frustrated investigators who couldn't uncover the ship's real owner. He didn't recall any mention about the IMP, surprised that he had remembered any of it at all. "What makes this ship so special?"

"Nothing. It's the crew we're interested in. I don't want to get into the details," Shawn said, looking straight at Mark now, "but this is where you come in."

Mark turned away and looked at the horizon. "Forget it."

"I made some calls last night before I stopped by. You were a Marine in the Gulf War, got a Bronze Star and everything. This would be simple for you."

"No thanks." Mark stood and slapped the sand off his shorts.

Shawn looked up at him. "You don't really have a lot of choice here."

Mark pulled his still-wet tee shirt over his head. "That so?"

"I made some calls last night—"

"Yeah, you said that already. You found out I was a Marine, so what?"

Shawn rose and stood next to him. He was taller than Mark but not by much, with shoulders that were just as wide. "I also found out that two of Jarin's men were killed up in Phuket. Oh, it wasn't in the papers, the police probably don't know too much about it either. Yet. But word gets out, you know how it is."

"I wasn't there," he lied, knowing that the place was covered in his prints.

"Mark, come on, you should know by now that that doesn't mean a thing here."

Hands on his hips, Mark watched the waves break on the sand.

"I don't want to be a bastard," Shawn said, "but I've got a job to do. And now," he said as he smiled at Mark, "so do you."

Chapter Twenty-three

Robin sat cross-legged on the beach towel and watched as Ngern built a sandcastle just beyond reach of the low-rolling surf. She could hear him talking to himself as he excavated tunnels and mounded up sloping walls, his voice dropping down as the imaginary foreman dictated last-second design changes, calling for more scoops of the wet stuff. She was too far away to hear clearly and it was all in Thai, but he was a kid playing in the sand. She didn't need it translated to know what he said. Ten yards out, with his baggy trousers rolled up to his knees, the grandfather poked around in the exposed rock with a stick, pulling out the occasional crab and dropping it in the plastic bag he had tied to a belt loop. Out of the corner of her eye Robin could see Pim walking toward her and pretended not to notice.

"Excuse me? Miss Robin?" Pim said, edging forward.

Robin turned and looked up at her.

"I want to thank you again for the clothings," Pim said, touching first the white DKNY tee shirt, then the blue shorts that hung below.

Robin shrugged. "Yeah, no big deal." She turned to look back at the water.

"The short pants fit very good, but the shirt is loose. I think you have much bigger titties than me."

Robin laughed. She didn't want to but couldn't help herself. Pim looked at her nervously. "What the hell, have a seat," Robin said, making room on the oversized towel.

Pim hesitated, then sat on the corner of the towel, making herself as small as possible. For ten minutes they said nothing and watched the construction site and the pointy-stick fisherman beyond. Pim sat with her arms wrapped around her legs, her heels tight against her ass, and Robin noticed that she rocked back and forth as slow as the waves. "He's a cute kid," Robin said, surprised by the sound of her own voice.

"Yes," Pim said. "He looks much like my sister."

"He plays well by himself, too. Keeps himself entertained."

Pim nodded—quick little head bobs that made her long hair bounce. "It has been a long time since he has had anyone to play with. I hope he will know how to make friends again." She paused and wet her lips. "They would let me visit him on Sundays after I went to church, but he did not want to play then. We would lie together on his sleeping mat and he would hold on to me. I would listen to him breathing and rub his back. He would fall asleep and I would watch him as he slept. Then they would make me go back to town." She watched the boy add a ring of shells to the seawall.

"He's a tough kid. He'll do all right." Robin leaned forward and brushed the sand off her hands. "Look, I gotta ask you something. And I don't want any bullshit, either. You know what that means, bullshit?"

"Yes. You want me to tell you the truth."

Robin took in a deep breath. "Yeah, that's it. I want to hear the truth." Elbows on her knees, she ran her fingers up under her sunglasses and rubbed her eyes, then propped her chin up in her hands. "Do you love Shawn?"

Pim stopped rocking and tilted her head to the side. She chewed on her lower lip for a moment then nodded. "Yes," she said. "I will."

Robin looked over at her. "*You will?* What the hell does *that* mean? Do you love him or not?"

"We had only been married a short while before the tsunami, and then he was gone. I think that if we had been together all this time that I would by now perhaps come to love him."

"Whoa, hold on," Robin said, sitting up. "You saying you don't love him right now?"

Pim wrinkled her nose. "It is hard to say. I do not really know him."

"You don't know him? You're frickin' *married* to him."

"Of course," Pim said, "how else would I get to know him?"

Robin looked at her wide-eyed. "You date him; you don't go and marry him."

"We dated for two months," Pim said, holding up her fingers. "He bought me many things, so I knew that I should marry him."

"*What?*"

"He bought a TV and a DVD player for my parents and he bought my sister a stereo and he bought me many nice things all the time. He bought a laptop computer for my father's pharmacy even though my father did not need one. He showed great *ndam-jai*. This is how I knew that he liked me."

"That 'juice of the heart' shit again? Listen." Robin moved closer. "You don't show someone you love them by buying them things."

Pim blinked. "Yes," she said. "If you love someone and you have money, you buy them things."

"No, no, you don't," Robin said, the frustration building in her voice. "If you love someone you don't have to buy them anything, okay? You just tell them you love them and that's enough. Buying them shit doesn't prove a thing."

"Yes, it shows that you want to support them. Anyone can say words, but buying nice things…" She waved her hands as she let the sentence trail off.

Robin rubbed her temples. "All right. Let's go back to Shawn. Does he know he got married to you or is this some secret Thai thing you spring on him later?"

"Of course he knows," Pim said and laughed, bringing her hand up to cover her perfect smile. "He had promised to pay my parents four hundred thousand bhat dowry. That is ten thousand American dollars."

"He *bought* you?"

"No, Miss," Pim said, shocked. "That is what he and my parents decided on. It showed great *náam-jai*."

"Oh I'm sure it did."

"Yes, my father told *everyone* at the wedding. He was very proud and I was proud of Shawn, too. He showed how much he cared."

"By paying your father money to marry you?"

"Yes, of course, Miss."

Robin leaned back. "I don't frickin' believe it."

"But it is true, Miss."

They sat silent for several minutes, then Robin said, "Why do you want to find him?"

"Miss?"

"Shawn. Why do you want to find him?"

"Miss, I don't understand…"

"He ran off on you, Pim. He left you behind for that Jarin guy. He's been gone a *year*. Trust me, him buying you shit doesn't mean he loves you. And you just said yourself that you don't even love him."

"Maybe, Miss. I do not know."

"Then what the hell do you want to find him for?" Robin said, her voice hot and harsh.

Pim looked at Robin and swallowed, then looked away, hugging her legs, staring at her toes. Robin sat quietly and watched as a fat tear rolled down Pim's cheek and dropped into the folds of the baggy white tee shirt.

In a voice tiny and muffled, Pim said, "He is my husband."

Mark sprinted the last fifty yards, crossing an imaginary line in the sand that ran from the first bar stool of the He She Drink bar to the water's edge. He slowed to a jog, then a walk. Off to his left the old man poked around in the exposed reef while straight ahead, Ngern watched as the sea reclaimed all that he had built. Further up the beach, in the shadow cast by a trio of palm trees, Pim sat on a beach towel, her chin resting on her bent knees. He stretched his arms above his head and pulled in deep gulps of humid air and watched Robin walk toward him. The blonde hair, the tan, the low-rise bikini—Mark felt familiar stirrings and wondered what had taken so long.

"How was your run?" Robin said, stopping in front of him.

"Good," Mark panted. "You two have a nice chat?"

Robin looked back over her shoulder. "Who was it that said that it'd take a lifetime to figure out Thais?"

"You mean JJ? The guy at the hotel?"

"Well he underestimated it." She watched Pim a moment longer then turned back to face him, crossing her arms. "The cook said that last night he was in town and there were some guys asking about an American couple traveling with a Thai family. The cook said the guys weren't from here so he didn't say anything."

"He told you this?"

"No, he told Pim." She paused. "At least that's what *she* says he said."

Mark stepped into the surf. He knelt down and splashed water over his head.

"I was thinking that today we should catch a ride across the island and check out Lanta Town," Robin said. "There's a post office there and maybe Shawn has a mail box or something."

Mark cupped water in his hands and poured it down the back of his neck, running his hands through his hair. "We're going to stay right here for now. After lunch we send Pim, the old man and the kid up to the pier and have them wait for us there. We'll follow about an hour later. Then we'll catch a ferry to Langkawi."

"Ferry?" Robin said.

"We've got to get to Langkawi by tonight."

Robin stepped toward him, her hands on her hips. "What the hell are you talking about? I thought you said we had to stay here for a week?"

"We need to go today." He stood up and wiped the salt water from his eyes with the sleeve of his tee shirt.

"Oh really?" she said, her foot tapping in the sand as she spoke. "When did you decide this?"

"I didn't," Mark said. "It was decided for me."

"It was decided for you? What the hell is that supposed to mean?"

Mark looked into her eyes. "Can you just trust me on this?"

"No," she said, leaning forward as she said it. "I'm sick of this. You have me buying tickets and renting boats and paying for hotels and what have I got for it? A chick who *says* she's married to Shawn and some bullshit stories that people tell you when I'm conveniently not around. And now you want to go to some other island—what's the matter, you don't like the view from your hut—the hut that *I'm* paying for?" Robin paused, looked at him and shook her head. "No, it's over. We're done here. You can take Pim and the kid and the old man and go where you want, I'm done with you. You haven't found shit since we've been here and now you want me to run off to the next stop on your little tour. Well let's see how far you get when I'm not paying the bills." She gave a disgusted laugh. "You know, I actually believed that bartender. Mark's a hell of guy," she said, dropping her voice and imitating Frankie's easy cadence, "he won't let you down. Well fuck you, Mark Rohr." She turned and strode off. Mark waited until she had taken a few steps before he spoke.

"Afghanistan bananastand."

Robin froze in mid-stride, one foot hovering inches above the sand. She set her foot down and turned slowly to look at him, her mouth open, a strange look in her eyes. "What did you say?"

Mark took a step toward her and smiled. Shawn had been right. "Afghanistan bananastand," he said, hitting every rhythmic syllable.

Robin ran to him and threw her arms around his neck, jumping off the ground to wrap her legs around his hips. "Oh my God, you found him," she shouted in his ear, and he staggered to get his balance. "He's alive. He's alive and you found him," she said, her voice dropping to a whisper, and he could hear sobs mixed in with her words. He held her tight for a few minutes, the waves lapping at his ankles. She lowered her legs and kissed him once on the neck before stepping back, brushing the hair from her tear-streaked face.

"You going to tell me what it means?" Mark said. "Afghanistan bananastand?"

She laughed as she sniffed and ran her hand under her nose. "It's a line from some movie—it's stupid, just something we'd say."

"He told me it would get your attention."

She laughed again. "Yeah, well, it worked." She looked down the beach, back in the direction he had run. "Where is he?"

"He's going to meet us in Langkawi."

"Did he say anything about me?"

"He said he wanted to see you," Mark said, leaving off the bit about it being too dangerous right now.

"Did he say anything about her?" Robin tilted her head in Pim's direction.

Mark looked across the beach to where Pim sat alone. With her knees pulled up to her chest she looked even smaller. "He said she should come with us. Her and the others," Mark said, revising Shawn's plan as he spoke. "Jarin has men looking for us here. It's not safe."

"Did he say anything about them being married?"

"I don't remember," Mark said, thinking about the question. "He just said to be sure we got them to Langkawi with us."

Robin lowered her head and sighed. "All right."

"Talk to the owner, ask her if she can get us a ride to the pier. Give her an extra twenty bucks so she'll keep it quiet. And we're going to need two trips. They'll go early, we'll go late. If we time it right we won't be at the pier for long."

She nodded. "What are you going to do?"

"Get something to eat, grab a shower," he said. "But first I'm going to talk to Pim."

Kiao leaned on his stick and watched as the man walked toward him, one leg swinging out wide with each step, catching the water at a funny angle and sending up a fantail spray. It looked awkward, maybe even painful, but the man kept a big smile on his face.

"Good afternoon, sir," the man said, stopping twenty feet away, the water just touching his rolled-up pant legs. "How is the fishing today?"

The old man grinned. The stranger spoke Thai with a bit of a lisp but had used the respectful forms of address that many young people seemed to forget these days. He had seen this young man before, on the beach with a tall, blond foreigner, and before that, on the ferry from Krabi, he had sat at a nearby table, holding a newspaper the whole trip. He looked to be his granddaughter's age, but he could have been younger, too. The old man knew that a hard life could make you age faster, and with a twisted leg and a fat tongue the young man's life could not have been easy. "It is a good day for the fish and a bad day for the fisherman," the old man said.

"The rocks around here? People tell me you can find lots of crabs in them."

The old man patted the plastic bag at his side. "That's what I'm finding out. I'm too slow to get the fish but the crabs are kind enough to stay put while I grab them."

"Tomorrow night? There's a full moon. The tides will be even further out and you'll find even more crabs."

"More good news for the crabs," the old man said as he poked his stick into a crevice. "My granddaughter just told me that we are leaving for Langkawi on the afternoon ferry."

The old man stooped down to examine a promising niche and didn't notice the look of surprise that flashed across the young man's face. By the time he determined that no crabs hid in the rock, the young man's smile had returned.

"I give the crabs to the cook at the hotel where we are staying," the old man said, gesturing toward the shore. "The cook is Chinese but he is very good. He takes the crabs and cooks them up with some curry paste and coconut milk and a whole head of bok choy and a kilo of snow peas."

The young man nodded his head, not hearing a word. Langkawi was in Malaysia, the first big island just south of the border. He didn't have a passport or even an ID card. He'd have to find a way to get past the customs check at the pier. It would be tricky but he had done things that were even harder. He had planned to steal back all of the un-smoked drugs he had sold to the blond *ferang* as well as the *ferang's* money, but if he was going to Malaysia he couldn't risk it. He'd leave the drugs and take the money, maybe take the Walkman, too.

"My wife used to make the best steamed catfish. She made them in banana leaves with fish sauce and fresh *bai makroot.* When she would send me out to the morning market for banana leaves, I always knew what we would have for dinner."

He was picturing a map. Phuket was to the west, maybe eighty kilometers. Langkawi was south, twice as far at least. The ferry? It wouldn't be one of those open boats they had taken from Krabi. It would be bigger, all enclosed. It would cost more, too, but that wasn't the problem. He'd have to make sure they didn't see him again, especially this old man. He remembered that the old man had sat and stared out the window the whole ride from Krabi so maybe he'd do the same on this trip. Still, he would be sure they didn't see him.

"...a piece of tuna steak about this big, chopped up in cubes. You put it in with the noodles and let it cook about two minutes..."

He could tell Jarin's men where the American was, but then they would take all the credit, probably not even mention his name. No, he had come this far, he would find a way to tell Jarin himself. Besides, fate was on his side. Why else did he come out to talk to the old man? It was just something he did, no reason, but now he knew their plan. He wasn't sure how yet, but he had been waiting his whole life for this chance and he wasn't going to stop now.

"...right out of the shell. Tastes like chicken. Very good with relish, too."

"I will remember that, sir," the young man said. "Enjoy you time in Langkawi. Goodbye, sir."

Kiao smiled as he watched the young man walk back to shore, his leg kicking up a splash with every step. He had wished the man had stayed longer, very polite and respectful. Pim should have met a man like that, he thought, a good Thai with traditional values. Marrying an American wouldn't work out, but he had told her that.

Chapter Twenty-four

When he thought about the job so far—the hunt for Pim in Phuket, the "incident" at the shack in the hills, the night-long ride to the fishing village, his little chat with Captain Jimmy, taking the knife away from Andy, the midnight meeting with Shawn—the ferry ride to Langkawi had been the easiest part. The owner of the Lanta Merry Huts arranged for everything, even sending someone to buy the tickets in advance. He and Robin arrived at the pier just in time to get aboard the ferry—a sleek, high-speed job with airline seats and frigid AC. They were the last to board, and the ferry was a kilometer out of port before they found a pair of empty seats near the restrooms at the back of the boat.

It was a long ride—three hours—and with the hum of the engine and the even rocking, he was asleep in ten minutes. He woke to the sound of Robin's laughter and the scratchy audio of the in-cruise video, a Thai comedy without subtitles.

"It's hilarious," Robin said, holding her sides as the movie's hero made a Jackie Chan leap from a moving train. "Just like the Stooges."

"You like the Three Stooges?"

"I may be a bitch," she said without turning from the screen, "but I know genius when I see it."

They docked in Langkawi and made their way through the immigration pavilion. Mark watched as Pim and her family cleared customs, their Thai IDs enough to get them in the country for weekend visits. They were stamping Robin's passport when he overheard the Malaysian official berate the dockworkers for allowing one of the passengers to get past customs unchecked. They met up outside and took a cab to the no-star hotel Shawn had told him about, the last no-name independent in the area that would rent rooms by the hour. Robin booked three rooms—one for Pim and the others, one for Mark, and one for herself—spreading them out over the hotel's three floors.

The neighborhood was filled with brightly lit stores, none of them selling tourist crap, and the only non-Asians he saw were uniformed sailors hitting the duty free shops, stocking up on liquor and cigarettes. Robin joined him for dinner at a burger place in a nearby mall, Pim and the others happy with the hotel's noodle shop.

"What's the plan?" Robin said, all smiles since he had uttered Shawn's ridiculous magic phrase.

"We wait for your brother to contact us," he said, then sighed and added, "It's his show."

"It usually is," Robin said, dipping a limp fry in tamarind sauce.

They walked the streets for an hour, window-shopping at the electronics stores and jewelers, splitting a fat ice cream sandwich on their way back to the hotel. No sooner had Mark shut the door of his room than the phone rang, the night manager telling him there was a note waiting for him at the front desk.

"There's a bar at the Bay View Hotel," the note read. "Meet me there at midnight. Come alone." Mark reread the note and laughed to himself, hoping the melodrama was intentional.

It was a short cab ride to the Bay View, a western-style hotel that towered over the busy commercial district. There was the requisite grand entrance, with floodlit fountains and strings of colored lights in the trees, and eight uniformed doormen manning the sliding glass doors. He found the bar—The Woodpecker Lounge—on the mezzanine level, the house band working through a medley of Madonna covers. He spotted

Shawn watching him from a corner booth, his back to the wall, the man sitting next to Shawn glaring at Mark over the top of his pint of Guinness.

"Glad to see you could make it," Shawn said as Mark pulled out the lone empty chair. "And I believe you know Agent Cooper…"

His scraggly hair pulled back into a short ponytail, a cigarette dangling from his lower lip, Andy raised his glass an inch as a welcome.

"*Agent* Cooper?" Mark said as he sat down, remembering the last time they chatted and wondering if Andy ever got the knife back. "I hope he's not your martial arts expert."

They both smiled at Mark but only Shawn's was a friendly smile. "This is a UN operation. Andy, he's the British contingent. He's our boat man."

"A sailor, huh?" Mark said. "That explains a lot."

"Right, fuck you, you bastard."

"Well, now that we're through with the introductions," Shawn said, "shall we get down to business? What are you drinking, Mark?" He flagged down a passing waitress, her short skirt distracting all three men.

"I'll take a Singha."

"Gone native on us, have you? Suit yourself. Again with these." Shawn pointed to the two dark stouts on the table. "And, because he doesn't know better, a Singha." They watched her turn and walk off, the tension dissipating in her wake.

Shawn turned back to the table. "Let's see, what's the least I can tell you and still make this all happen?"

"You're going to have to give me more than that. I'm not going to walk into something unless I know what it's all about."

Andy grunted. "You don't have to know shit."

"Obviously not," Mark said, watching the insult fly over Andy's head, "but you need me more than I need you. We're in Malaysia now. I doubt the cops would care what might have happened up in Phuket. You want my help, you tell me what's going on."

"What about Robin? You told her you'd find me? You don't help, you can't deliver."

Mark shrugged. "Won't be the first job I screwed up."

Shawn drained the last of his Guinness, licking the tan foam off his upper lip. After a long pause he said, "All right, here it is."

"What the fuckin' hell?" Andy said, spitting the words out, both hands coming up in disgust.

"It's my call," Shawn said, his eyes locked on Andy's until, with a grunt, Andy slumped back in his chair. Shawn turned to Mark, his eyes hard. "Like I told you on the beach, the ship we're following is the *Morning Star*, an old wreck waiting to happen. Six months ago it was due to dock in Dar Es Salaam but it never showed. That's why I thought it went down off Madagascar. Last week we get word that it was spotted in Singapore, except now it goes by the romantic name of *AIS-3267*. That happens, ships change owners, change names, no big deal. But this time our man in Singapore spots the captain, a Ukrainian guy, ex-Russian Navy. Now he's a pirate."

Mark's head snapped up at the word.

"I see I have your attention," Shawn said, holding up his hand as the waitress returned to their table with their drinks, flirting with her as she cleared away the empties. He waited until she was gone before continuing. "You say pirate today and people think CDs and designer jeans, but I'm telling you, it's huge. And it's never been easier, either. With those big tankers, everything's automated. All you need is a crew of, what, twenty-five, thirty?"

"If that," Andy said, looking into his beer. "Remember the *Burnett*? Sixteen. And half of them never shipped before."

"So you've got these third-world shit holes—sorry, *undeveloped nations*—with double-digit unemployment and everybody trying to live on a hundred bucks a year, and you've got these floating department stores as big as the Empire State Building sailing on by, a mile off shore, with a tiny crew and millions in cargo." Shawn sipped his beer. "One man's pirate is another man's opportunist."

Mark pictured the container ships he had seen in port, fifteen stories tall with decks a hundred feet above the water line. "They still have to get on board."

"These are organized gangs. Well-armed, well trained. I've seen as many as fifty on one job. Grappling hooks, scaling ropes, all that shit. Now I'm not saying it's easy. The advantage is definitely with the tankers. They run with these huge blinding spotlights pointed straight down the side, and then take their fire hoses and spray off the side of the ship, full blast, all night long. It's like a waterfall. There's no way you're going to get up that. But you don't have to. There's always some idiot captain who thinks his ship's too big to mess with or some worthless rating who forgets to turn on the lights."

"Or the hoses," Andy said, still looking down at his beer. "Aim 'em too far out or turn 'em off after midnight."

"The shipping companies, they don't want any trouble," Shawn continued. "They all have the exact same policy. Do what you can to keep them from getting on, but if the pirates get aboard, do not fight back. Give them the ship, give them whatever they want."

"Wouldn't that just encourage more pirates?" Mark said.

"Actually it's pretty smart," Shawn said. "They know the pirates are looking for stuff they can haul off. Cash, small electronic shit, porno DVDs the crew might have stashed away. They're not going to be off-loading some eighty-foot container onto their long-tails. So the crew gets roughed up and they lose the petty cash. No big deal."

Andy held up a finger. "Right, petty cash ain't so petty. They got four-hundred thousand US off the *Valiant Carrier*."

Shawn nodded and sipped his Guinness. "True, but what they *don't* want is to have the pirates take over, steal the whole fuckin' ship. They used to do that, steal the whole thing, take it out to the Indian Ocean, paint a new name on the back, whip up some forged papers, then sail right back to port. Here we are, fresh from East Bumfuck with a cargo of whatever," Shawn said, changing his voice to play the role. "We're ready to sell on the cheap, in a big hurry don't you know. What's that? Deliver your cargo to Tokyo? What'd ya know, that's our next stop. Load it on my friend, load it on. It was that easy. They could do this two, three times. Load up, sail off, sell the stuff in another port, all the money wired to some bank account. Then they'd take the ship on one last run, up to the breaking yards in India or Bangladesh. They'd sell it for scrap, pennies on the ton. Six weeks later even the builder wouldn't be able to identify it. A year after that, nothing. GPS changed all that. The big ships have a dozen transmitters on them. They sail five miles off course, some home office in Lisbon is on the radio. The old ships—like the *Morning Star*—well, their GPS systems have a nasty habit of turning off."

Mark took a long pull on his Singha. The place was crowding up. Chinese businessmen in Aloha shirts and naval officers on shore leave were filling the tables of the Woodpecker Lounge, finding extra room for the hotel's version of bar-beer girls who squirmed up close, giggling on cue. He knew he should stand up and walk away, tell Robin and Pim they were on their own, but he knew he wouldn't. Maybe he had spent too many years doing nothing, maybe it was all the testosterone in the room. Didn't matter. Mark still wasn't sure where this was all going, but as he finished his beer and waved for another, he knew what he would do.

"This captain," Mark said, over-tipping the waitress as she handed him a fresh Singha, "if you know he's a pirate, why don't you just raid the ship while it's at port?"

"Give us some credit, Mark. If it was that easy, that's what we'd do. But the minute we get the local cops involved, somebody would tip them off and they'd scatter. If you haven't noticed by now, there's a lot of corruption out here. There are cops in every town that are on the payroll of one gang or another. They get the inside information, act as a lookout for the gang, all while drawing a government paycheck. We work with some of the cops, the ones we can trust, but on the whole, it's best to avoid them."

Mark thought about Captain Jimmy up in Krabi, bragging about his promotion and the graft it would clear, and he thought about the cop in the parking lot, the one who led him to Shawn. Mark had spent most of his adult life avoiding cops in one country or another and saw no reason to change now. "This isn't about petty cash or some insurance payout on lost cargo," Mark said. "You've already said it's worthless, so it's not about the ship. What's the story?"

Shawn and Andy exchanged glances, Andy giving his fingers a flip then focusing back on his beer. Shawn cleared his throat and leaned in.

"You got Malaysia here on the east," Shawn said, folding a bar napkin into a long rectangle. "And you got Indonesia on the west." He stretched out a second napkin and laid it alongside the first. "Right here, this is the Malacca Strait." He ran a fingertip between the napkins. "A mile and a half wide at the narrowest point. It's the busiest shipping lane in the world, from Phuket down to Singapore, thousands of ships every week. A quarter of the world's oil passes through a space no wider than a mall parking lot."

Mark looked down at the thin strip between the napkins as if it were a map. "He could scuttle the ship, close it all down."

"No money in it," Shawn said, shaking his head. "But you've got the idea. We got word—you don't need to know how—that a bunch of terrorists were looking for a ship in these waters. And no, it's not al-Qaeda. Some homegrown separatist group, real small but looking to make a name for itself. And if we don't stop them, they will."

Mark took a drink and thought it through. "This *Morning Star*, what's it loaded with?"

"Last time we heard it was hauling molasses. In shipping, that's the bottom end of the food chain. The next stop is the breakers. But now the *Morning Star* is loaded with bunker fuel. It's a low-grade, heavy oil, not good for much, but it'll burn and it'll make a real mess."

Mark could see how they'd do it. Get the old ship going, dead ahead full, drive it bow first, right through the triple hulls of a supertanker. There'd be an explosion and they'd all be killed, but they'd leave behind an environmental disaster, wiping out the fishing for a generation and killing off the tourist industry. It'd take a year to clear the shipping lane but by then economies would have collapsed and situations would have become so bad that the destitute would line up to join the very group that ruined their lives. You couldn't say it out loud—people always took it the wrong way—but Mark could see that it was a damn good plan.

"The *Morning Star* sails tomorrow on the night tide. We know when they plan on transferring the ship to the terrorists and it'll be a cash deal. We need to let the ship sail from port, then get aboard when it's at sea. We're going to arrest the pirate crew, lock them up, then wait for the terrorists to arrive. It's a small group so we figure their top guys will be there for the handover. They won't stick around of course, they'll let their martyrs have all the fun, but if we're there, we can get them all and nobody gets hurt. Well, none of the good guys anyway."

"What do you need me to do?" Mark said. There was no hesitation in his voice.

"Tomorrow you get to a ticketing office—I'll give you the address—and book passage on the *Morning Star*."

"Passage? I thought it was a tanker?"

"It is, but like most of the older ships they cut the costs and raise the profit margin by renting no-frills rooms. The *Morning Star* has about a dozen or so, and believe me, you get nothing. One meal a day and no shuffleboard."

"What about Robin and Pim and the others?"

"Bring them along. They'll be safer there than they will be here. The crew that's on the *Morning Star* now, they're not going to do anything to mess up their payday. My team will take them out without a shot. The terrorists will be unarmed, that was part of the deal, so they'll be safe on the ship. Besides, once this goes down, Jarin will know where we're at. It'll be easier for us to get away as a group."

Mark finished his second beer and motioned for a refill. "Okay, we get aboard, then what?"

"It's pretty simple. The *Morning Star* will be sailing north. It's slow as shit so there's no hurry. You'll need to get down to the ass end of the ship. Should be no problem. There's a bulkhead door that leads out to a platform off the stern, right above the water line, just like on a dive boat. I think they call it the fantail deck. When the ship's in port the crew uses that door to bring in small supplies, let in fresh air. They bolt it shut when they sail and there's an alarm system that let's the bridge know if the door's been opened. Andy will show you how to get around it."

Andy nodded. "Two-wire bypass. Easy as pie." He flipped over a paper placemat, clicked open a pen and started sketching wires.

"You make sure the door is open by two a.m. Probably best if you stay there and wait for us, just in case someone decides to check the door."

"Not bloody likely," Andy said without looking up from his drawing.

"Still, it's better to play it safe," Shawn said. "Once we're aboard, my team will know what to do. You just stay out of the way."

"I can lend a hand," Mark said.

"My team has been training for this for weeks. They all have a role to play and they know the ship." Shawn looked at Mark and read his eyes. "Taking the ship from the pirates, that's our first mission. After that, we've got a couple hours before the terrorists arrive. We'll get you up to speed by then. You never know, we might just need you."

The waitress arrived with Mark's Singha, setting down a fresh bowl of odd-shaped pretzels. "Thank you, sir," she said as she pocketed the pair of hundred bhat notes. "We have drink special tonight. You have Sex on Beach with me?"

"No, thanks," Mark said, seeing through the sales pitch for the fruity drink with the stupid name. "But tell you what, bring us a round of shots. Make them doubles."

Andy looked up, a wide grin in place. "Right. Now you're talking. I'll have a Bushmills, sweetheart."

"I'll stick with the Guinness," Shawn said, shaking his head.

"And you sir?" the waitress said, her chest pressed against Mark's arm. "What you want to drink? Something special?"

"Yeah," Mark said and smiled. "Tequila."

Chapter Twenty-five

He didn't hear the first set of knocks. The second set—three quick taps delivered a bit harder than the first set—blended into his half-awake, half-asleep dream. The third set of three shook the door casing and rattled the framed room-rate chart on the wall.

"Go away," Mark said, at the same time pulling the pillow tight against his head. He heard the door open, heard the disgusted sigh, and flinched when the door swung shut with a bang.

"Did you get it?" Mark asked, his words muffled by the sweat-soaked pillow.

"Yeah, I got it," Robin said, throwing the plastic bag onto his bed. He listened as she plopped down on the room's matching twin bed, the headboard rapping against the wall.

"That's what that was," Mark said, moving the pillow off his head. He was sprawled, face down, on the small bed, his feet hanging off the end. His shirt was balled up on the dresser but he still had on the khakis he had worn to meet Shawn at the Bay View Hotel.

"That was what?" Robin said, not masking the disappointment in her voice.

"The headboard hitting the wall. That's what I heard all night."

"Ugh. You had some girl in this room?"

Mark tried to shake his head but it lost something lying down. "No," he said. "Next door. All night long."

"Well at least someone in this hotel had a good time." Robin folded over a thin pillow, wedged it behind her back and leaned against the headboard. "I take it you enjoyed yourself."

Mark considered the statement. They had stayed at the Woodpecker Lounge for a few more drinks, then hired a cab to take them to the places that Andy or Shawn knew. Langkawi was in Malaysia; and unlike tolerant, open-minded, Buddhist Thailand, Malaysia was a Muslim country. But that just meant the strip clubs were harder to find. Shawn kept them supplied with low-denomination Malaysian ringgits, and while he and Andy slipped into backrooms with giggling strippers, Mark sat at the bar, catching up on his drinking. Ten years ago it would have been an epic night out. Now, with a thousand nights just like it under his belt, it had already blended into his collective drunken memory. Familiarity didn't breed contempt. It bred boredom.

"You get it?" he asked, his hand feeling around the bed near his knees.

"I told you I did," Robin said as his fingers found the plastic bag. He took a deep breath and slowly, slowly, slowly sat up.

"They didn't have any Sinutab, but the pharmacist gave me some pills, prescription stuff. They're not as tight about that shit here as they are in the US."

Mark took a small one-inch square baggie that held two white, horse-sized pills and a warm can of soda from the bag.

"I couldn't find any Mountain Dew. You'll have to get by with Zam Zam."

Eyes closed, Mark popped the top on the soft drink and washed down the pills. It had a strong cola taste and the sugar made his teeth tingle. He took a second swig and leaned back on the mound of pillows he had created. He knew it was only psychological, that it would take twenty minutes for the pills to take effect and for the caffeine to kick in, but he felt better already. "Did you get the tickets?"

"Yes, I got the tickets. I thought I was running late since the office didn't open till ten and they took their sweet time waiting on me, but I see that your morning hasn't even started yet."

He pinched the bridge of his nose, squeezing his brain back into his skull. "Any problems?"

"I told you I got them, didn't I?" She paused and thought for a moment. "There was this kid though, weasel-faced, kind of creepy. I saw him watching me through the window of the shipping office."

"Think he was following you?"

Robin shrugged. "Probably not. He'd have a hard time keeping up with me. He had this handicapped leg…it's just that he looked at me funny, that's all."

"I thought beautiful women got used to guys staring at them."

"Don't start with me, Mark, okay?" She leaned her head back to rest it against the wall. "We need to be at the dock by four. You think you'll be ready?"

Mark squinted at the red numbers on the alarm clock on the dresser. "Plenty of time. You tell the others?"

"That's your job."

For a long time they said nothing, Robin watching the ceiling fan, Mark looking at the far wall of the room, thinking about what lay ahead. Down the hall a door closed and in the silence the sounds of the traffic drifted up and through the open window in the bathroom. They sat like this—Robin on one bed, Mark on the other, both leaning back, their knees up—long enough for Mark to feel the sinus pressure fade along with the headache.

"Why hasn't he come to see me?" Robin said, her voice no louder than the hum of the fan. "I come looking for him, thousands of miles, all the way from Ohio. He can't even come down the beach to see me. He can go out all night drinking, but can't even fucking call the hotel to say hello?" She let the silence fill the room again before saying, "Why hasn't he come?"

Mark knew he couldn't tell her what he knew. And he knew that anything else he'd tell her would sound like the lie it would have to be. But he knew what brothers were like. He had a sister in Utah, at least that's where he thought she was, but they hadn't talked in fifteen years. Given the choice of spending an evening alone with a family member or out at some seedy dive with a girl paid to be friendly, he knew which he'd pick. "I don't know," he said.

It was well past noon but the unfurled rattan blinds gave the room an early morning feel, the colors washed out and dim. In the other bed he could hear her sniff back tears, hear the heavy swallows, her breath coming in short sobs that she struggled to control. Someone else might have gotten up, laid beside her and held her as she cried, stroked her head and whispered, told her to let it all out or that everything would be fine. But he knew he wasn't that kind of guy. And he knew that there were times when you had to cry alone.

Thirty minutes and an ice cold shower after Robin had left, Mark knocked on Pim's hotel room door and asked if they'd be ready to go in an hour.

"Yes. But we will not be going with you."

It was not the answer he had expected.

She stepped back from the door, allowing him to enter. On one of the two single beds, remote in hand, Ngern sped through the twenty satellite TV channels, flicking between Asian MTV and two episodes of Pokemon. The grandfather—Kiao? Kayto?—arms intertwined behind his back like an apprentice contortionist, stood by the window, watching the midday traffic jam. Mark took a seat at the end of the second bed and patted a space beside him. Pim hesitated a moment, then sat down. Mark said nothing and waited for her to sort out her thoughts.

"We are a burden on Miss Robin," she finally said. "She has taken us very far and we have done nothing to help. Before, in Thailand, I could help, but here I am a stranger."

"That's all right, Pim," Mark said. "You helped us out a lot. You don't owe us anything." He watched as she chewed on her lip. She seemed to grow smaller the longer she sat next to him.

"Mister Mark, you must know this. I did not always tell you the truth."

Mark smiled but she did not notice, busy watching her feet sway an inch above the polished hardwood floor. "Well, I guess we weren't always completely truthful with you, either."

"I did not know where to find Shawn. I heard him talk about Krabi before and told you he was there, but I did not know for sure." She paused and turned to him. "I lied to you."

The way she looked up at him—those soft brown eyes, those pouty lips—he knew he'd have to tell her. He took a breath and looked into her eyes. "I've seen your husband. I've seen Shawn."

She shrugged. "I know. The cook at the Lanta Merry Huts said you were talking to a man late at night. He described him and then I knew. And yesterday, the man here at the front desk told me you received a message to go to the Bay View Hotel. The man has a cousin who works there. He called his cousin and told him what you look like. His cousin said you were sitting with two men. He described both men and I knew that one was Shawn."

Mark felt his shoulders sag.

"I had hoped that my husband would come for me, but it has not happened."

"He's been busy," Mark heard himself saying. "He's involved in…several things. I'm sure he'll explain it all soon."

"Yes, I am sure that is it," she said without conviction. "But it has been a long time, and I have come so far. Now it is time for my family to go home."

"Why? We're close to the end now."

"He does not say it, but my grandfather is nervous. He has never left Thailand before." She leaned forward and looked past Mark to her grandfather, leaning back before the old man noticed. When she spoke again her voice was a whisper. "He is not happy with Shawn. He thinks that Shawn has shown our family a great disrespect. He thinks Shawn should have returned after the tsunami and supported his family. That is his obligation," she said, struggling with the word. "He thinks I should have married a Thai man, someone who shares our ways."

"He said this to you?"

Pim looked surprised. "No. He has said nothing. But I can tell."

On the other bed, his expression as animated as the anime hero's, Ngern watched a mutant yellow cat battle a spinning blue turtle. Mark reached over and covered both of Pim's hands with one of his. "We'll be leaving today, all of us. No one gets left behind. We'll be getting on a boat. Shawn will meet us on the boat, later. I'm sure he'll explain where he has been and why he couldn't come to see you."

"Perhaps," she said, not believing it would happen.

Mark looked around the room. The few extra clothes they had, washed the night before in the hotel sink, were air-drying on the backs of chairs. "You need to pack. We'll be leaving for the dock in an hour."

She nodded. "Where are we going?"

"We'll be going to Phuket Town," he said, leaving off all things that were to happen before they arrived.

"Phuket Town," she said, looking back down to the floor. "Then Jarin will come for me and take me away again; and he will kill my grandfather for what he did to that man in the hut, and he will kill Ngern, too."

"Look at me, Pim," Mark said, raising her chin with his finger till their eyes met. "No one will harm you. I promise."

He heard Pim swallow hard, but her deep, brown eyes were dry. "You can not make such a promise, Mister Mark. That is for fate to decide."

Chapter Twenty-six

They rode to the dock in two cabs, Robin and Mark in one, Pim, Ngern and Kiao in the other. There was no security checkpoint at the port, no passport control to clear, just angry-eyed guards in military-style uniforms and shoulder-slung AK-47s, bored enough to be dangerous.

The cab dropped them off in front of a warehouse—high windowless walls of gray-white aluminum with the words To Ship stenciled in black paint under a droopy spray-painted arrow. They followed the arrow around the corner of the building to a fenced-in walkway that led through the loading area and to the waiting ship. Late-night movies and Louis L'Amour paperbacks had left vivid memories of Far East ports in his mind, but nothing looked familiar. There were no wooden crates marked This End Up or soft-sided bundles held fast with burlap and netting, no sweaty stevedores in coolie hats and wife-beater tee shirts, no banana-eating monkeys or talking parrots, no spice-soaked smells, no oriental flowers with porcelain skin and jet-black spit-curls riding past in open cars and rickshaws, the high band collars of their fiery-red kimonos hidden behind paper fans. Instead there were rows of shipping containers stacked five high and men in light blue jumpsuits and hard hats, scanning barcodes and punching numbers into handheld computers, directing giant rolling cranes to the right coordinates, the loudest sound the high-pitched beep of a forklift in reverse.

Ten stories tall and longer than a football field, the former *Morning Star* loomed above the concrete pier. The hull was painted in thick coats of black marine paint, a dull red stripe running the length of the ship, just below the deck. The ship's superstructure was crowded onto the stern, boxy and industrial, like a factory outbuilding or a French museum. It was painted white but the late afternoon sun gave the whole ship a pink tint. Shawn had said that it was an old ship, already overdue for the breakers, yet from where he stood it looked seaworthy enough. But what did he know about ships? Mark smiled as he remembered the ditty that had kept his grandfather's used car lot in business. A little putty and a little paint, makes it look like what it ain't.

Leaning against the chain-link fence that enclosed the gang-plank, a man in a blue jumpsuit and two dark-skinned sailors chatted with a uniformed guard. The guard sat on a wooden barstool, his weapon laying on its side across his lap, the barrel pointing down the walkway. They watched as Mark and Robin approached, the others following a step or two behind. Without turning his head, the guard said something that made the others laugh, and the way they kept their eyes on Robin, Mark could guess what was said. The guard held out his hand, and Mark handed him the envelope Robin had received from the shipping office. The guard unfolded the bottom three copies of a form, peeling off the top pink copy and handing it to the man in the jumpsuit. Mark wondered if any of them—or all of them—were with the imposter pirate crew. The two sailors bent in to read over his shoulder as the man studied the form, the guard keeping his eyes on Mark. Two minutes later, the man handed the pink copy back to the guard, saying something official sounding while the sailors nodded in agreement, pointing up to the ship. Mark put the envelope in his pocket and started up the gangplank. Behind him, the four men turned to watch Robin walk past.

The air was heavy with petrochemicals—diesel exhaust, oil-based paints, the cloyingly noxious fumes that had to be the low-grade bunker fuel. Mark could feel a headache building with every breath. The guards were on post for hours at a stretch, inhaling the same kind of chemicals that rotted the brains of glue sniffers and paint huffers. He wondered about the long-term health affects the guards faced, and he wondered about the wisdom of giving them machine guns.

At the top of the gangplank, two men leaned against the ship's railing, European, about forty years old. One was heavy-set and doughy, with wavy steel-gray hair, the other was short and thin and wore a baseball cap on his shaved head. They had on matching short-sleeved white shirts, and there were four gold bars stitched on to the epaulets of the big man's shirt. Captain's rank. Mark stepped aboard the ship and the smaller man turned and smiled.

"Welcome aboard," he said. It was an eastern European accent, maybe Russian, maybe Polish, maybe Ukrainian. "You are passengers sailing to India?"

Mark nodded, remembering what Shawn had said about the boat's alleged destination, how the crew wouldn't jeopardize the deal by keeping innocent people off the ship. "That's right. All of us," he said, thankful some shipboard clatter kept Robin from hearing them speak. Mark held out the forms but the man waved them off, pulling a small walkie-talkie from his pants pocket.

"Singh to the gangway, please," the man said, then pointed to a passageway with the radio's stubby antenna. "Through there, to your right. Mr. Singh will meet you. He will show you to your quarters."

Mark thanked him and led the others through the doorway, glancing back at the two men before he turned. Before Oklahoma City, before 9/11, it would have been hard for him to picture two middle-aged men as terrorists. Now it was too easy. But these men were pirates, not terrorists, and their motive was profits, not prophets. Not that that mattered to those they killed. Ahead, a slight Indian in black slacks and a Miami Heat tee shirt came down a spiral staircase. He took the forms from Mark without saying a word and read them as he turned and walked away, assuming that they would follow him down the corridor. He led them up three flights of stairs and down a short hallway lined with doors. It reminded Mark of the dorm-style barracks he had seen in the Corps, only not as well maintained, no gunny sergeant there to ensure that the brass fixtures were shiny enough to shave in.

"Here. And here," Singh said, pointing to two rooms on opposite sides of the hallway. He opened one of the rooms and motioned for Mark to follow. The room was larger than he expected, the size of a one-car garage, but he could reach up and touch the ceiling without straightening his arm. Other than a bunk bed and a single folding chair, the room was empty. There was no window. The mattresses were rolled up at the foot of the beds with the sheets and blankets folded on top. The man pulled the door half shut and tapped a finger on a column of typed papers taped to the back of the door.

"These are rules. You must read. You are lifeboat number two. No smoking." He waited for Mark to acknowledge that he understood, nodded once, then went across to the second room, pointed at the typed list and delivered the same message, this time in Thai.

"I like to be on top," Robin said, brushing close past Mark to claim the upper berth. She turned back and winked seductively before she burst out laughing, cutting through the tension that had been building all afternoon. It was good to see her smile again, and Mark found he was smiling too. "Can you believe this? It's like a frickin' prison cell," she said.

"With a cabin like this what you're really paying for is the view," Mark said, hands on his hips, admiring the blank, off-white wall.

Robin walked back to the door and ran a finger down the list of rules. "It is strictly prohibiting the eating of durians while aboard." She looked over at Mark. "What the hell's a durian?"

"The forbidden fruit. It's got a wicked smell to it. Tastes all right, sort of, if you can get past the stench."

"You've had it before?"

"Last night. Got it from a street vendor outside a—" He stopped himself. He hadn't gone into the brothel but he didn't want to explain why he was waiting there. "Outside some club. At least I think it was a durian."

"It says here that the complimentary dinner is only five ringgits. Well that's a bargain."

"Is there a map of the ship with that list?"

"Yeah, but it doesn't show much. I guess these boxes are our rooms. This must be the door we first came though and these squiggly lines I think are the stairs. If it's any consolation I don't think there's too much to see." She squinted as she read the fine print on the map. "Here's the way to the dining hall—or as it says here, the dinning hull."

Mark walked over and looked at the map. It showed the layout for their section and a similar, smaller section somewhere else on the ship. There was no larger diagram that put their location in perspective. He had a rough idea where they were in relation to the gangplank, but as to the location of the crew's quarters or the bridge, he could only guess. He could find his way to the stern of the ship, but finding the stairway that would take him down to the one door that led out to the fantail deck, well, that was going to be something else. He had a few hours of daylight left, hopefully enough time to get his bearings and make a few sorties below deck. If he bumped into any of the crew he could play the lost passenger bit, but that would only work once. Shawn had assured him that if he stayed toward the back of the ship and kept heading down, he'd find the door he was looking for; and last night, after three beers and four shots of tequila, it sounded easy enough. Maybe Frankie the bartender was right. Maybe tequila really did make him stupid.

"Check this out." Robin stooped over to read the last page, a fifth-generation photocopy of a low-quality fax. "Anti-piracy precautions will be in effect from eighteen-hundred hours to zero-five-thirty hours whenever the ship is sailing within fifty kilometers of land in the waters east of the Andaman Islands to the Philippines and from the Asian mainland as far south as northern Australia." She looked up at Mark. "We're in that area, right?"

"It's a big area," he said, and remembered Shawn's beachside comments about the futility of the IMP's mission. "You could fit the whole US in and have enough room left over for Europe."

"Muster point is in the number 1 deck alleyway," she continued. "Great. It's not even shown on the map."

What could he say? That it was too late, that the precautions didn't work, the pirates are already aboard? That the captain was a killer, about to turn over a massive floating bomb to a bunch of terrorists? And for reasons that now seemed ridiculous, their little group was on that ship? Instead, he said, "I wouldn't worry about it."

"If pirates succeed in boarding—*holy shit*—do not place yourself or others in further jeopardy by resisting or antagonizing them." She stood up and shook her head. "You think Shawn knows about this?"

"Yeah, probably," Mark said, and despite everything he knew already, despite everything he knew was coming, he couldn't resist smiling as he said it.

◇◇◇

The door to Pim's cabin was ajar but Mark still knocked. Their room was larger, with four sets of bunk beds, a couple tall wardrobes, and a writing desk but no chair. Ngern had made a fort of pillows on one of the upper bunks, his head popping up at Mark's knock. He jumped down and ran over to pull the door open, all smiles and giggles, his shyness finally wearing off.

"Hello Mister," the boy said, dragging the words out so that it still sounded Thai.

"Hey Ngern," Mark said, hoping he got the name right, "how ya doing?"

His English exhausted, the boy looked at him and laughed, then ran back and dove onto one of the empty bunks. Mark thought about how exciting this would seem to a kid his age, all the boat rides and the different hotel rooms, and now aboard a huge ship. The kid had seen a lot in the past year, but somehow he still seemed like a normal eight year old. In two days it would all be over and he'd be back in Phuket, his old life gone and the new one uncertain. Maybe that's why the kid was warming up to him—he could sense that they had something in common.

"Mister Mark?" Pim came and stood close to him. She glanced over her shoulder where her grandfather was busy making his bed. "I heard the man say we are going to India," she said, her voice lowered. "Is this true?"

"That's where the boat is supposed to go," Mark said, dropping his to match hers, "but we'll be going to Phuket Town first. But you can't tell anyone this, not even your family." Pim nodded her head, and he continued. "Tonight you must stay in your room. Do not open it for anyone but Robin or me. Or your husband."

"He is here?"

"Not yet, but he will be. After dinner just stay in your room, no matter what. You may hear some stuff going on, you just stay in your room. Got it?"

She nodded again, her eyes wider now but alert.

"It'll all be over soon," he said, hoping it was true.

At one end of the hallway was the stairwell they had used, at the other an open bulkhead door and a passageway that ran left and right. He could see pipes and cables running overhead in the passageway and could hear the distant hum sound of an electric motor. The talkative sailor had led them up three flights from the main deck. Given the size of the ship and the low headroom, he was at least ten stories above the waterline and the fantail deck. He knew where the stairway led—he turned and walked the other way. He passed other cabins—most were empty—but behind one closed door he could hear muffled voices, and from another the steady thump and shrill singing that passed for talent in a Thai pop tune. The door to the last cabin was open and he glanced in as he walked past. Sitting close together on the floor, their bodies twisted so their feet pointed away from each other, five dark-skinned men shared a meal, the curry-rich smells wafting out into the hallway. One of the men looked up and waved, his fingertips coated in sticky rice. Mark gave a nod and continued, but paused just past the open room.

In a few hours IMP agents would be swarming aboard. Shawn said they'd take the ship from the pirates without firing a shot, but who knew what the pirates would do. In all the commotion it would be easy to mistake one of the Indians in the cabin for pirates. He could go back and warn them, tell them to stay in their cabin just like he had warned Pim. But as soon as the idea formed, he dismissed it. One word from them, one nervous look and the whole operation could be ruined and all of it traced back to him. They could well be innocent tourists but they could also be part of the captured crew. They could even be the pirates. He walked on. One way or the other, when the shooting started, they'd know what to do.

Mark stepped through the open bulkhead door and into the passageway. There was a fresh coat of white paint on the walls and exposed pipes, and there was a dull sheen to the linoleum floor. The ship seemed better maintained than he expected but cosmetic repairs were cheap—the real problems would be under the paint. Hands in his pockets like he was out for a stroll, Mark headed toward the humming sound. He could hear voices echoing from somewhere in the ship, the words lost in the ambient noise. Just past a coiled, wall-mounted hose and long-handled fire ax, a stairwell opened on his right. He turned and without a pause, started down the steep steps. He'd only have one chance to claim he was lost, might as well make it count. He moved quickly but made little sound, counting the flights of steps as he went, the engine noises getting louder with each level. Six flights down he heard them, seven flights down he could make out their voices, Thai or Chinese, he didn't know. He thought about ducking out on one of the levels, waiting till the voices passed, but he wasn't sure where they were. He might walk right into them. He slowed up but kept moving down the stairs. He rounded the top of the ninth flight and froze. Two men were sitting in the passageway, their backs to the stairwell. Neither man turned as Mark backed up the steps, the diesel engine masking the sound.

Mark moved into the shadows of the landing. Below, the conversation continued, and he heard someone open a soft drink can. From his angle the passageway looked just like the one he started on, just like every passageway he had passed, down to the fire hose and fresh paint. But there was something different about the one below. Every passageway had the same wall-mounted light fixtures with the same fluorescent bulbs in clear glass casings, the lighting dim and industrial. But below it was different—the warm glow of natural light—and Mark knew he had found the fantail deck and the door he would have to open.

"Fuck you doing here?" a voice shouted, the thick Australian accent loud enough to be heard over the engine's din. Mark turned, his best blank expression on his face. He was a big man with a full beard and small eyes that squinted in the darkness. He was carrying a pipe wrench in one hand, a clipboard in the other. He shifted his grip on the wrench as he hung the clipboard on a peg in the wall.

"I'm looking for the dining hall," Mark said, doing his best to look lost and foolish.

The man stared at him hard, his small eyes narrowing as he spoke. "Rack off the way you came. And don't let me see you down here again."

Mark gave a timid smile and pointed up, still playing his role. "Do you know where the dining hall is?"

"Yeah," the man said, hefting the wrench to his shoulder, not saying another word.

Mark knew he could step over and take the wrench from the man, slap him upside the head with it before the man saw him move. Instead he nodded and looked down, turned and went up the stairs two steps at a time. He was two flights up when he heard a group of men laughing below.

He reached his level and kept going, the stairs running out three flights up. The passageway looked like all the others—he turned to his right and started walking, stepping outside to a narrow deck that looked out toward the open sea. The ship was still at the dock and toward the bow, cranes loaded pallets of last-minute supplies onboard. Open hulled transports chugged past and a few cabin cruisers darted through the port. He was looking out at the water, watching a line of long-tails negotiate the passage, and didn't see the man approach.

"Are you English?" the man in the captain's uniform said, coming toward him, a stack of papers rolled in his hand, the words clipped by his accent or anger, Mark wasn't sure.

"American," Mark said, certain the man already knew the answer.

The captain stepped closer, crowding Mark against the waist-high railing. "Then you will tell me what I need to know."

Mark waited.

The captain unrolled the papers and glanced down. "Tell me, Mister American, what is a four letter word that starts with K?"

Mark looked straight at the man as he shifted his weight off his heels to the balls of his feet, ready now. He said, "Kill?"

The captain leaned forward. "No, mister American, that is not it." He held up the papers in his hand and jabbed a fat finger at an unfinished crossword puzzle. "The last letter must be J."

For a moment, no one said anything.

Mark wet his lips, still watching the man's eyes. "What's the clue?"

The captain pursed his full lips and looked down at the crossword. "Ach, I don't use the clues. I put in any words that fit."

"Isn't that cheating?"

"You think it is *easy?*" the captain said, his voice rising. "Ach. Clues. Anyone can do it with clues. Now you tell me, what is the word?"

"Four letters, starts with a K and ends with a J?" Despite everything, Mark found himself running down lists of words. After a moment he shook his head. "I don't think there is any."

"What about kudj?" the captain said, his eyebrows arching as he waited.

"That's not a real word."

"Perhaps. But it fits," he said, pulling a pen out of his shirt pocket and printing in the letters. When he was finished he took a last look at the papers, then rolled them up and stuffed them in his back pocket. He leaned his forearms on the railing and looked out to sea. "How do you like Malaysia?"

Mark leaned in alongside the man, their elbows almost touching. He hadn't expected to talk with the captain that Shawn had called a filthy pirate, but now saw no reason why he shouldn't. "I didn't see much. Just here in Langkawi."

"Ach, you should get down to Penang. That is a...a picturesque, yes? That is a picturesque city. You can skip KL—Kuala Lumpur—it is not as nice, unless you like big cities, then it is very nice. But now you go to India. Have you been?"

"No," Mark said, looking at the horizon.

"It is different from Malaysia. Very crowded. Good trains, though."

They stood there, leaning for several minutes, watching a sleek cabin cruiser glide past. The boat turned and they could read the name painted in black across the stern. *The Pirate's Curse.*

"Ach, that is a stupid name."

Mark nodded. "Especially in these waters."

"Yes, I suppose that, too. Who would put a curse on their own boat?"

"I heard that there are a lot of pirates around here," Mark said, surprised that the words came out so easily, the hair on the back of his neck dancing.

"Nayah, this is true. Not so much now, but ten years ago, yes, very true. But not for ships like this. Nothing to steal."

"But they could still get aboard," Mark said, pushing it. "They could damage the ship."

The captain pointed along the bow of the ship. "There is the wire," he said, miming razor sharp points. "And at night we put on the hoses and the lights. That is enough."

"Is it?" Mark said, looking over as he smiled.

"Yes, plenty. Still, we have these," he patted an odd-shaped holster on his belt.

"That a gun?"

The captain grunted and reached back with his hand, popping open the snap and drawing the weapon. It had a standard pistol grip but that's all Mark recognized. Instead of a barrel there was a stubby black box capped with a bright yellow plastic cover. Matching yellow hash marks moved down the side of the box ending in a lightning bolt that ran down the grip to the wide base. It reminded Mark of a cordless screwdriver.

"Taser," the captain said. "You know these?"

Instinctively Mark's left hand dropped down and rubbed his side. It was six years ago and there were never any charges filed, but he remembered the first time he saw a taser. The border guard had said he jumped five feet but Mark didn't remember a thing. "Yeah, I know them."

"We all have them. The people on the water, the fishermen, they know it too. They tell others, soon everyone knows. We don't have problems." He holstered the taser and was leaning back on the rail when his radio squawked. He held the radio to his ear.

"If he says he is not a cripple, let him walk," he said into the radio, pausing for the reply. "That is not my problem. Let the Indians worry about that. If he has paid his fare we don't need a passport." He looked at Mark and shook his head. "You ask about pirates? They are easy compared to this, this," he pulled out the papers and glanced down at the crossword puzzle. "This *kudj*. We sail soon. Have a pleasant trip."

Chapter Twenty-seven

Mark lay on the bottom bunk, hands behind his head, eyes open, too dark to see the mattress that was just overhead. There was no clock in their cabin, but there was one in the communal bathroom at the end of the hall. When he had checked it had been eleven, so now it had to be close to midnight. He had to have the door open at two. He couldn't go early and wait, somebody might spot him, and he couldn't open the door and leave, somebody might come by and close it. He needed to be there right on time. It would only take a minute to rig up the alarm bypass. If he screwed it up and the alarm went off anyway, they would lose the element of surprise but the IMP team would be aboard and, as Shawn assured him, it would be all over in a few minutes. All he had to do now was stay awake.

He had started the day with an intense hangover. The same bottle of tequila he drank at home seemed somehow more potent in Thailand, and while the unknown pills the pharmacist gave Robin and the warm can of Zam Zam worked their collective magic, he knew he would have felt even better if he hadn't been drinking at all. A nap would help, but he knew he couldn't risk it. He rubbed a hand across his face and took a deep breath and counted the days in his head. Shawn had said they'd be back in Phuket City by early Sunday morning, so that would make it nine days. Robin had agreed to five hundred a week plus expenses. He hadn't thought to break it down per day but

figured he'd just charge her for the week since she had to foot
the bill for Pim and her family. Besides, the bonus would make
up for the extra time.

He thought about Frankie Corynn. He could see her behind
the bar in Phuket City, hazel eyes, red hair, hot body, that you-
are-so-stupid smirk most guys thought was a flirtatious smile.
You went too far, she had said, referring to the way he handled
the bar fight; but she had said it so many times in the past, him
going one step too far then stepping back to survey the damage,
trying to find a way out of it. But this time was different. It wasn't
his show. All he had to do was open a door and step back and let
Shawn and his team handle it. It had been pretty easy after all.

"I didn't think it would be like this," Robin said, breaking
the dark silence.

He could picture her, lying on her back, staring up, just like
him, waiting. "I was just thinking the same thing," he said.

He could hear her sigh. Ten minutes passed. "What did he
tell you?"

"You'll see him tonight," Mark said.

"That's not what I asked. What did he tell you?"

"I'll let him tell you."

"Oh shit, Mark," she said, and the way she said it—another
sigh floating in among the words—he could tell she had closed
her eyes. "What has he gotten you into?"

He didn't answer and she didn't ask again.

With a gasp he awoke and jumped out of the bed, his hair
brushing against the metal frame of the upper bunk. He had
no sense of time, no idea how long he had been asleep. Ten
minutes? A couple hours? Damn it, he couldn't tell. He held
an arm out in front and crossed the cabin, feeling for the door.
In the darkness he could hear Robin's steady, even, deep-sleep
breathing. He opened the door, slipped out and closed it behind
him. The hallway was brightly lit and empty. Barefoot, he ran
to the bathroom to check the time, the alarm bypass equipment

in the cargo pocket of his shorts bouncing against his thigh. He bumped open the door and looked at the clock.

Two twenty-five.

Shit.

He turned and raced down the hallway toward the open bulkhead door. He had planned on easing his way to the fantail deck, staying in the shadows, disabling the alarm and opening the door on time, avoiding the pirate crew and safeguarding the element of surprise. That plan was gone. He sprinted past the closed doors of the passenger cabins, out into the passageway and down the steep stairway, jumping the last three steps of each short flight.

A minute late, two minutes, that could be expected, anticipated. The Gulf had taught him that. But that was it. Five minutes late and you put a mission at risk. Ten minutes late and it was seriously screwed up.

Anything more than that and you were fucked.

Mark tore down the flights, his hand reaching ahead, grabbing a support pole and spinning as he made each tight turn. He was eight flights down when he saw the crewman in the passageway. He was young, tall and athletic, his eyes bright against his dark Indian features. He held up a hand as if hailing a cab as Mark came down the stairs.

"Excuse me, no passengers allowed—" the man managed to say before Mark swung an elbow up and under the man's jaw. Blood sprayed from the man's mouth as he staggered back against the bulkhead and then, with Mark already starting down the last set of stairs, falling face-first onto the floor.

The fantail deck was darker than the others, but there was still enough light for him to see what needed to be done. He dug the plastic-cased meter out of his pocket, snapped the rubber band and unfurled the wires. The bulkhead door that led out to the landing was bigger than he had expected, twice as wide as the other doors he had seen. There was no porthole in the door, just a double-handled lever in the center that was pulled far to the right, swinging the bolts up and wedging them in place. A black rubber seal was squeezed tight around the edge. He was running a hand along the doorframe, tracing the alarm wires from the trip-box above the door, when he saw the lock. With the door secured, two flat bars slid one on top of the other, the thick rounded shackle of a padlock passing through a pair of aligned holes. He looked at it for a second, then tossed the meter onto the floor and hurried back to the coiled fire hose by the stairs.

Shawn had warned him that if he opened the door without the bypass in place he'd alert the bridge. They'd be on him in five minutes; probably less. Much less. That wouldn't make a difference now. Once he started he'd be lucky to have two minutes. He yanked the long-handled fire ax from its brackets and turned back to the door. The lock was waist high and he came in at it on a run, stepping into the swing, shifting his weight, grunting as the ax clanged against the lock and the door.

Nothing.

He stepped back and hefted the ax to his shoulder, swinging, angling each blow down on the lock. His ears rang as metal bit into metal, and through the din he could hear shouts coming from the decks above. The shackle bent away from the lock and the last blow knocked it free. He dropped the ax and threw his weight onto the lever. The bars shifted and with a dull thump the bolts pulled back. The shouts were getting louder now, more urgent. He braced a foot on the doorframe and pulled. A bell alarm sounded and red lights blinked down the passageway. Mark turned and leaned his shoulder into the door, forcing it all the way open. A block of light spilled out the door and onto the open grating of the narrow platform, five feet above the waterline. On either side of the fantail deck, couch-sized yellow drums held depth-activated life rafts and a pair of orange life preserver rings hung on the railing. Beyond the railing the churning white wake rolled out of the square of light and into the black, empty night.

Twenty-five minutes late. Seriously fucked up.

He stepped out onto the platform. His shadow stretched behind the ship, bouncing on the foamy, rabid sea. Below him, the white noise of the wake drowned out the sound of the alarm bell and the shouts from inside. There were no ropes dangling down from the upper decks, and there was no way he was going overboard on his own.

He could go back in, grab the ax and make a stand, take a couple of them out before they overpowered him or shot him. He could see it coming anyway. But then they'd head upstairs and take their revenge on Robin and Pim, the old man and the boy. It was better out here. Not for him, shit no, but maybe for them. He leaned on the railing and looked out into the black night, surprised at how calm he felt. He didn't even jump when the hand reached up and grabbed his wrist.

"You're fucking late, you worthless fucking asshole," Shawn spit out, pulling himself over the railing. "Now get the *fuck* out of the way."

Mark started to say something but Shawn shoved past, pausing at the door, pointing the barrel of his Chinese-made assault rifle into the passageway before jumping through. Mark stepped to the side as dark shapes swarmed out from under the platform, tying off their black inflatable rafts and scurrying over and under the railings like a pack of wet rats. They were Thai and Chinese, in tee shirts and nylon shorts, a few in sandals but most barefoot, and all of them shouting now. There were no uniforms, no badges, no two guns alike. He saw several with machetes, the wooden handles wrapped in duct tape. Twenty, thirty men? They were pushing past him so fast he couldn't tell. Andy Cooper, a cigarette clenched between his teeth, swung a leg over the railing. He smiled at Mark, a wolfish, dirty smile, then pushed his way through the door. From inside the ship Mark heard the rapid reports of machine gun fire and the booms of shotgun blasts and screams that came from deep in the ship. The last shape climbed from the rafts and twisted between the railing—a kid gripping a rusty tire iron.

Twenty seconds after getting the door open they were all aboard, working their way through the ship, and twenty seconds after getting the door open, Mark knew the truth.

He rushed back through the door but already knew it was too late. The smell of cordite hung in the air, and the sound of gunfire, sharp and metallic, echoed down the passageways. He had to get back to the cabins, warn Robin and Pim. He reached for the ax but it was gone, then started back up the stairs. One flight up the man Mark knocked cold with an elbow to the chin still lay face down in the passageway, but now there were three bloody holes in the small of his back, his white tee shirt scorched by the point-blank blasts.

Had he been that stupid? Had he been so desperate to be doing something meaningful that he had fallen for it so easily? Shawn had sold it all the way. If he had been gung-ho and macho, Mark was sure he would have seen through it. But Shawn had played it right, ripping the organization he was pretending to lead with the same kind of complaints Mark had heard from battalion commanders in the Corps, that same self-mocking tone that separated the pretenders from those who've been there. But Shawn had been lying from the start and he'd bought every bit of it, wanting it to be true. It's a pirate ship, Shawn had said, and Mark knew that now, thanks to him, it was.

Four flights up he found the next body, the big Australian with the squinty eyes and full beard who had caught him sneaking around earlier that evening. His eyes were wide now, wider than the bullet hole in his forehead. In his right hand he still gripped a pipe wrench, the claw end thick with blood. He ran past the body, up the last few flights and out to the passenger cabins. The gunshots had died down, so had the screams, but he could hear a lot of excited shouting and crashing sounds as the pirates claimed their prize. He leapt over the body of one of the Indian passengers that lay sprawled across the floor, ran down the hallway and flung open the door to Pim's cabin.

The room was empty. One of the bunk beds was toppled over and bed sheets and blankets were tossed on the floor. Across the hall, Robin was gone too, but their cabin seemed undisturbed. He checked the communal bathroom but it was empty, and then headed for the stairs that Mr. Singh led them up when they had first come aboard. Voices drifted up the stairs and, mixed in with the high-pitched Thai and revved up Chinese, Mark could hear Andy's fuck-laced commands.

"You go, you go," a voice shouted behind him, and Mark turned to see a pair of scrawny Thais running down the hall at him, each waving a bloody machete. He continued down the stairs, staying ahead of the blades. At the foot of the stairs he followed the voices through a bulkhead door and out onto a deck the size and shape of a tennis court, a string of floodlights illuminating the center. The confusion made it appear crowded, the pirates running out of the shadows, shoving crewmembers and passengers from one group to another, telling them to sit, then making them stand only to knock them back down again. He saw Mr. Singh, his Miami Heat tee shirt held tight against the stump where the fingers of his left hand had been, and he saw the captain, face bloodied, sitting cross-legged on the deck, a nervous gunman behind him with a vintage M16. Pim and her grandfather stood off near the shadows, Pim with her arms to her sides, eyes straight ahead; the old man, arms waving, yelling at the pirates as they went by, his tone defiant and parental. The boy was nowhere to be seen. A pistol popped twice and Mark saw a crewmember drop, the others cowering back as the shooter, arm straight out, pistol held sideways like some street-wise action hero, waited for the next person to try something stupid. Mark felt the flat of the machete blade slap his back, and he stumbled forward into the light and onto his knees.

"Well, look who decided to show up."

Mark raised his head. Shawn was dressed in the same tee shirt and shorts he had worn that first night in Koh Lanta, the wooden stock of the assault rifle balanced on his hip. Mark moved to stand, but Shawn held out his hand and shook his head. "Take a seat, Mark. You've had a busy night. Relax for a while. Just try not to fall asleep on us."

Mark continued to stand, then went down hard when a rifle butt clipped the back of his head. "Right. He said down," Andy said, aiming a kick at Mark's groin but hitting his thigh instead.

Mark didn't move. Eyes closed, he fought to clear his head, to calm his breathing. Around him the shouting continued but there was less of it. A crewman moaned and somewhere behind him one of the pirates was laughing. After a minute he leaned up to a sitting position. They were all sitting now—the real crew and the passengers—with a half dozen pirates standing guard. He could hear the other pirates in distant parts of the ship, looking for stragglers. He looked across the deck and tried to make eye contact with Pim, but she sat with her head bowed, her grandfather at her side, ramrod straight, eyes glaring at Shawn, who roamed the deck, a cell phone to his ear. Shawn said a few things Mark couldn't hear and snapped the phone closed. He walked over and squatted down far enough to keep Mark from trying anything.

"It seems I owe you a bit of an apology. You're not a worthless fucking asshole after all. In fact, if it wasn't for you, we would have never pulled this off, right Andy?"

Andy came and stood next to Shawn. "Fuckin' Man of the Match."

"They heard you coming," Mark said. "The door alarm went off and then they heard the shots. They would have radioed for help."

"Yeah, you'd think," Shawn said, shrugging. "But just so happens we had a frequency jammer with us out there, all alone, waiting in the dark. And, gee, right at two a.m. their radio went dead. By the time they figured out that it wasn't working the party had already started. No, Mark, nobody knows we're here."

Mark kept his eyes on Shawn. "Where's Robin?"

Shawn smiled. "Oh, you're gonna like this." He stood and shouted over his shoulder. "Hey *sis*, come here a second."

A trio of grinning pirates stepped aside and Robin walked out from the shadows and into the lighted area. She was wearing the khakis and polo shirt she had worn as she lay on the bunk, her hair loose around her shoulders; and as she walked closer Mark saw a coldness in her eyes she had not shown before. She didn't smile, she didn't say anything, she just walked over and put an arm around Shawn's waist. Shawn shifted the assault rifle, held it by the wooden pistol grip, put his free hand on Robin's back, pulled her in and kissed her hard on the mouth, his hand sliding down her back, ending the kiss with a sharp slap on her ass.

"I can't believe you fell for the sister story," Shawn said, draping his arm across Robin's shoulder. Mark felt the blood color his cheeks but said nothing. Robin looked away and with both hands pulled her hair behind her head.

"I don't know about you, Mark, but I'm impressed. Not with you, with her. I mean, track some missing boyfriend across town, that's one thing. But halfway around the world?" Shawn hugged Robin to his side while she continued to fuss with her hair. "I must be something special." He looked down at her and smiled; she looked back and didn't.

"I've got to pee," she said and turned and walked across the deck and through the open bulkhead door.

Two of the pirates started shouting, crossing the deck as Pim's grandfather stood up and stepped through the huddle of passengers, Pim jumping up behind him, trying to pull him back. The old man brushed her off and she stumbled backwards over one of the Indian passengers. Head high, he strode toward Shawn. The pirates shoved the old man and he stepped back but didn't fall, coming forward again.

"Oops. Busted," Shawn said, winking at Mark as he motioned to the guards to let the man pass.

Kiao pushed past the grinning guards and walked up to Shawn. With a finger in Shawn's face, the old man started yelling. It was all in Thai, high-pitched and rapid-fire and harsh, but there was no mistaking what he was saying. Pim fought her way past the guards and ran to his side, pulling on his arm and begging him to come away. She yanked on his arm but the old man did not budge, standing taller than Mark had remembered, his words sharp and his eyes filled with hate.

"You got any fucking clue what the coot's saying?" Shawn said, laughing at Mark.

Mark shifted his weight and got ready to move. "He's an old man. He's all she's got. Let it go, Shawn."

"In-laws," Shawn said and laughed, and swung the barrel of the assault rifle up and under the old man's chin, firing a quick burst that tore off the top of his head.

Mark lunged forward just as Andy brought the butt of the rifle down. The blow was as loud as a shot and Mark dropped hard onto the deck, blood soaking his hair and running into his eyes. He could hear Pim screaming, clear at first, then falling away into the blackness that swallowed him.

Chapter Twenty-eight

"Those men with the guns? They're pirates. You know what pirates are, don't you?"

Ngern nodded. "Yes," he said and the man smiled at him. He had a narrow, squished face and he talked funny and his leg bent way out even when he tried to sit, but the man had saved his life and the boy sensed he could trust him.

He had woken up late at night and gone to use the bathroom. The lights were so bright and the air conditioning so cold that he didn't feel sleepy afterward. His aunt had said they were far out on the ocean and he had wanted to see. Their room didn't have a window but he remembered seeing many windows in the first hallway they had walked down, the one where he had seen the man his great-grandfather had said was the captain. He went down the stairs and found the windows, but he couldn't see the ocean because of all the lights on the deck. He had decided to see if there were more windows farther below and he had gone down many stairs when the shooting started.

He had ducked into a corner as the crew ran by. They seemed very scared and this made Ngern scared, too. The shooting became louder and he had crawled under a row of pipes to hide. He watched as the men ran by—they looked like beggars he had seen in Phuket, dirty and wild-eyed. They raced past and didn't see him, but he knew it was not a good hiding spot and they would see him next time. He could hear more men coming down the stairs right above where he hid; and he was squeezing in tighter when the small metal door behind him opened up and a hand pulled him into the dark space, closing the door behind him. There was just enough light to see the man's face. The man held a finger up to his lips and Ngern nodded, showing he understood. He led Ngern down the passage, crawling on his hands and knees, his twisted leg bumping against the pipes. In the hallway the shooting had stopped but now he could hear people yelling. They crawled a bit further and then the space got wider and taller and there was a small light bulb hanging from a cord. Between the pipes he could see a big room all lit up, filled with more pipes and big motors. There were walkways in the room, and a table, but he didn't see any men there.

"The pirates?" the man said, "They won't find us here."

Ngern looked around the space. It was much smaller than the room he had been sleeping in, and it was hot and smelled like a big truck. There was a backpack in the corner and an open can of Coke. "Is this where you live?"

"No, I have a room," the man said, pointing up. "A cabin on one of the upper decks. But I had to share it with some other men and I didn't like them. They did not speak Thai and I think they made fun of me."

"Why?" Ngern said.

"Because of my leg. And the way I talk. But that's okay. I like to find places to hide, like this. Then I can stay hidden and watch people."

Ngern peered between the pipes. It was a good spot—you could see a lot and not be seen, unless someone came looking for you. "What will we do if the pirates find us?" he asked.

The man shook his head. "They won't. But if they do, I have these." It was a gun but not like any gun Ngern had seen before, not at the house they made him stay at, or on TV, or in any of the movies. The bottom part looked right, with the grip and the trigger, but the top part was like a box and had a bright yellow square at the end.

"Guns like these?" the man said, holding out the gun and patting several more that sat by his side. "They don't kill people.

They just knock them out. Did you see Star Wars? No? Well, they had guns like this. You pull the trigger and it shocks the person you aim at. Zap, zap, zap," he said, taking out invisible enemies. "I found a whole locker filled with them down in the engine room. You want one?" He held one out to Ngern.

The boy looked at the gun and shook his head. "No thank you. I want to go to my aunt now."

"Not now, later," the man said, then saw the look in the boy's eyes. "I promise. I will show you a way I found that will bring you close to the rooms. You can go everywhere on the ship, it's easy." He smiled.

Ngern looked at the stack of guns. "Will you fight the pirates with these?"

The man's smile vanished. "If I have to, I will, yes."

The boy paused, thinking. He wet his lips, took a deep, shaky breath and said, "I will help you."

The way the man looked at him, Ngern thought he had said something wrong. The man's eyes got watery and his head bobbed, but then he smiled bigger than ever and patted Ngern on the shoulder. "You are a brave boy," the man said, saying each word slowly so it was clear.

"Do you have a plan?"

"Oh yes," the man said, still smiling. "I think I do."

Mark ran a hand across the back of his head. His hair was dried and matted but the bleeding had stopped. The plastic baggie of ice had melted and the kitchen towel the cook had wrapped it in was dyed red with his blood. He had a pounding headache and the muscles in his neck were knotted stiff, but the nausea that often came with a concussion had faded and his vision had cleared. He was sitting on the floor of the dining hall, back against the wall just like the others. There were ten passengers—Pim and the boy not among them—and fourteen crewmen, one slowly bleeding to death from a gut shot; Mr. Singh sitting nearby, looking pale but determined to live. The tables and chairs were all pushed to the far side of the room and four gunmen, none old enough to drive, sat on a bench, their weapons loose in their hands but their eyes watching for any sudden movement.

He didn't remember, but he assumed that some of these men had carried him off the deck and up five flights of stairs to this room. And he assumed that somehow the cook had convinced the guards to get ice and towels for the wounded. A case of bottled water sat in the center of the room, and Mark found an empty bottle at his side that he didn't remember drinking. The AC was off and the room was stuffy and hot, and other than the groans of the dying man and the mumbled conversation of the guards, it was quiet, just the steady hum of the ship's engines far below. The pudgy captain and the officer in the baseball cap were missing, probably up on the bridge being forced to run the ship or, if Shawn had brought along his own pilots, dead and tossed overboard, just like Kiao.

He should have seen it coming, should have lunged at Shawn the second he saw him, or gone at Andy, got the gun, unloaded a clip into both of them. It would have never worked, of course, Andy standing behind him expecting something like that, *hoping* for something like that, but he thought about it anyway. Shawn pulled the trigger but Mark knew who had really killed the old man.

The four guards turned their heads to the open doorway and grinned as Robin came in the room. She was wearing a pair of sunglasses that were too big to be hers and a scowl that the guards read as authority. She crossed the room without glancing at them and stood in front of Mark.

"Come on," she said, angling her head back at the door. "I want to talk to you."

Mark looked up but didn't move to stand. Instead he ran his hand across his head again, looking for blood on his palm. "I don't think we have anything to say."

She sighed and put her hands on her hips and stared down at him. The oversized frames and dark lenses kept her eyes hidden.

"I need to talk to you. I could tell them to bring you and they would, they'll listen to me, but I don't want that."

"Are you taking me to see Shawn?"

"Eventually. But first I want to talk to you. Alone." She paused and when he didn't say anything, she added, "Please."

Back against the wall, Mark eased himself up. On the bench the guards stood too, looking at Robin. "It's okay," she said, the tone of her voice and her hand gestures translating the words. Mark kept a hand on the wall in case he lost his balance. He wasn't as dizzy as he had feared but the nausea returned, and as they walked across the room he stooped to pick up a fresh bottle of water. He glanced at the faces of the others in the room but they all looked away.

Robin led him down the hallway and out onto the small deck where yesterday he had helped the captain solve his crossword puzzle. The sky was overcast, but the sun was on their side of the ship. He squinted. His headache would come back now. He cracked open the plastic bottle and took a small sip, testing his stomach. The ocean stretched in front of him and he thought he saw a thin line on the horizon that might be land but it was too hazy to tell for sure. They both leaned on the railing and looked out at the water. He took a second, longer drink and waited.

"It wasn't supposed to be like this," Robin said.

"Yeah, you said that last night," he reminded her. "Before your brother arrived."

She dropped her head and looked down at her hands. She let a breath out in a long sigh. Without looking at him she said, "I met Shawn about two years ago. I had just gotten laid off from some stupid office job and I had all these bills and shit so I was looking for a job, dancing in this club." She knew she didn't have to explain what kind of job so she didn't. "Shawn was there, not working, just hanging out, and we got to talking. He had just gotten out of the county lockup. He didn't hit on me or anything, we just talked. He's real good at talking." She chuckled. "But you know that."

Mark took a swig of water and said nothing.

"So anyway, we started going out. It was great. He's so much fun, he really is. Was. And he was so good looking."

"I guess that makes up for a lot."

"It did then. He was into small-time stuff, selling weed, boosting cars, some breaking and entering. He was really good at it, too. He made it seem so easy. He wanted me to quit the bar but it was sort of fun and the tips were great. I mean it wasn't like you see in the movies, but nothing is I guess." She reached over and took the water bottle out of his hand and took a sip. "We had a place together, an apartment. It was nice. We turned one of the bedrooms into a media room with this big-screen TV and everything. We used to watch all these heist movies, pretend it was us in the movie, getting away with it. You know that line you said to me, the one Shawn told you to say?"

"Afghanistan bananastand."

"That was from a movie. It was like our special codeword. Instead of saying 'I love you' we'd say Afghanistan bananastand." She paused. "I know, it's stupid."

"We've all been there," Mark said, leaving off the part about it being back in high school.

Robin finished off the water. "Then one day he says he's going to Thailand, says that I should wait behind and he'll send for me. He emailed a couple of times the first weeks, sent a few postcards. Then…" She trailed off, took a deep breath and started again. "The dancers at the bar said he's dumping you girl, and I said no, Shawn and I, we've got something special, and they said we'll see. Then that Christmas I get an email. Just a hello, how you doing, but you know how it is. I read everything into it. For the first time in months I felt great. See? He didn't run off, he didn't dump me; I'm not just some dumb blonde he played like an idiot. Next morning I turned on the TV. I didn't even know what a tsunami was."

They stood there, looking out at the water, not another ship in sight. He slid his forearm along the rail an inch or two until it bumped up against her arm. She didn't pull away and after a minute she cleared her throat. "I'm sorry I lied to you."

"Yeah. Me too."

"I had to. If I told you the truth, if I had told you that I was a stripper looking to track down an ex-con boyfriend who had run off, would you have come?"

He wanted to tell her that her story had little to do with his decision, but that's not what she wanted to hear. "Probably not."

"The whole time I was here I kept telling myself that it would all work out, that it would be just like before, all I had to do was find him." She shook her head. "Well I found him."

For a long time neither said a word, the whole ship surprisingly quiet. Mark watched a speck on the horizon grow into a freighter twice the size of the *Morning Star*, loaded high with shipping containers stacked like Legos. It arced south miles away and disappeared. Next to him, Robin tapped the empty water bottle against her palm. "Come on. We're late."

She turned to go, but Mark stayed leaning on the rail. "What are you going to do?" he said.

"I told you, take you to see Shawn."

He looked over his shoulder at her. "You know what I mean."

She was looking at him now, but the sunglasses still hid her eyes. She drew in a deep breath, held it, dropping her hands down to her side as she let it out. "I think," she said, just loud enough to be heard, "that I've already done too much."

Chapter Twenty-nine

He had been on scores of tramp steamers and island ferries and everything from cruise liners to air cushioned landing craft, but this was the first time Mark had seen a cargo ship's bridge. He knew not to expect a tall, oaken-spoked wheel or a double-handled engine control with words like Full Ahead framed in brass but he was still surprised by how bland it all was, starting with a bank of windows that slanted in on a long counter that looked like the soundboard for a stadium-sized concert. There was one man at the controls, a shaggy-haired Thai in a black Tupac tee shirt that he remembered seeing climbing over the rail of the fantail deck.

The man sat in one of the two captains' chairs, his thumb and forefinger resting on the edge of a small steering wheel that seemed right off a video game console. There were display screens all along the counter, most of them dark, the others filled with computer-generated dials and columns of numbers. Behind the captains' chairs was a raised platform with a second counter, this one covered in unfurled maps and stacks of manila folders and a few empty beer cans. Curled up on the desk chair, one of the young pirates, open-mouthed and drooling, caught a quick nap, cuddled up to the shotgun he cradled in his arms. A second guard, this one wide-awake and jittery, watched as Robin led the way through the bridge, down a short flight of stairs and into a lobby-sized sitting room.

It was a handsome room, lined with bookshelves and ringed with built-in couches, filled out with brown leather furniture and a flat-screen TV. There were ten men in the room, maybe more. Pirates sprawled out on recliners or slept on the carpeted floor. On one of the sofas, the captain, his wavy steel-gray hair matted down on one side with dried blood, sat next to the other officer Mark had seen, the slight man in the baseball cap. The cap was missing, along with his shirt. He looked tired but unhurt. They hid their fear well but there was no mistaking the look they gave him as he walked into the room. Cigarette drooping off his lower lip, Andy Cooper sat at the edge of an easy chair, clearing a space on a coffee table to field strip his assault rifle.

"Where's Shawn?" Robin said.

Head down, Andy raised his eyes and looked at her. He took the cigarette out of his mouth, flicked the ash onto the carpet, set it back on his lip and returned to his weapon.

"I said where's Shawn," she repeated, trying to sound tough, but failing.

"Right behind you, babe," Shawn said, coming in through the bridge, a pistol in one hand, a beer in the other. He waved the gun at an empty sofa as he walked past. "Have a seat."

Shawn set his pistol on a corner of the coffee table Andy had cleared, collapsing into a leather recliner. "What a night, huh? Overall, I'd say it went rather well. But you're the military man there, Mark, what do you think?"

"Not counting the civilian casualties?" Mark said, looking straight at Shawn as he spoke but thinking about the pistol that was two steps too far away.

"Actually, we planned for worse, so in that respect, we did better than expected."

"You didn't have to kill Pim's grandfather," Robin said, and Mark was surprised by the anger in her voice.

"That one I'm laying on you," Shawn said, pointing a finger at her. "What the hell you bringing an old man with you for? I'd expect that shit from Pim, but you? Oh, boy, here we go," he said as Robin dropped her head into her hands, her shoulders bouncing with every silent sob. He smiled at Mark. "She's good, isn't she? She can turn on the tears just like that." He snapped his fingers to make his point. "I don't suppose she told you the whole story."

Mark shrugged a bored shrug. "She told me *a* story."

"Yeah, the one with the long-lost brother. Which I still can't believe you bought."

Mark gave a slow nod. "Why don't you tell me one?"

"Nah, mine won't be as good. I'd stick to the boring facts, like how Robin here was running a high-end car boosting ring when I met her, and how it was her idea to finance my little Thai adventure. Oh, and those emails where she told me that I should try to work out some sort of deal with the Phuket mob. Bet she left that out."

"You're an asshole," Robin said.

"If I know our Robin," Shawn continued, "she figured I hit a big score and just decided to cut her out, which, in fairness would have been true if the tsunami didn't wash it all away; so she decided to come here and find me and see if she could get her share, one way or the other."

She turned to look at Mark but avoided his eyes. "Don't believe him. He's a fucking liar."

"We must forgive her, Mark," Shawn said, eyes skyward in mock solemnity. "She knows she has only her looks and bedroom talents to get her through this cruel world and, well, those won't last forever, will they? And I bet she's still a bit upset about that little marriage thing. Robin darling, if it's *any* consolation, I married the bitch as a cover. And for the access to the old man's pharmacy."

"And the sex," Andy said, giggling. He peered down the barrel of his weapon, then set it on the table and pushed the takedown pins into place, lifting off the lower portion of the rifle by the plastic pistol grip.

"Is that an SA 80?" Mark said, pointing to the rifle.

Andy kept his eyes down, working a screwdriver back and forth.

"If that's an SA 80," Mark said, "you're gonna wanna put your hand over the end of that receiver."

"Piss off," Andy said, looking up at Mark as he pulled out the rear takedown pin, launching the spring-loaded recoil assembly across the cabin.

"Told you," Mark said, turning back to Shawn. "So, how much of what you told me was true?"

Shawn stifled a laugh as Andy, fucking this and fucking that, retrieved the scattered rifle parts. "The truth, huh? Well obviously there's no double secret UN police force. Well, there probably is, but I'm not in it. I do have a lot of connections with the Thai police, though. The ones I could buy off cheap, anyway."

Mark thought about the cop in the parking lot with his mirrored sunglasses and thousand-yard stare. At the time he had thought the cop was one of the good guys, the kind that earned the trust of higher-ups looking to clean house, the kind that did their jobs because it was the right thing to do. But he was wrong, the man was no better than the pirates and maybe worse. It was the first cop he had trusted in years and look where it got him.

"The terrorists wanting this ship," Shawn continued, "that's true. The cash payment, true—and let me tell you, a million bucks goes a long way out here. Oil slick, yeah, probably, but you never know when you're dealing with lunatics. What am I leaving off?"

"What's going to happen to Pim?"

Shawn smiled. "Atta boy, Mark. True to form. Here we're about to turn over a floating bomb to some crazy bastards and you want to know what's going to happen to the whore." He shook his head and laughed. "Well it just so happens that it all depends on you."

"Really? How's that?" Mark said.

Shawn finished the can of beer and tossed it onto the carpet. "There's like, what, thirty people on this boat—passengers and crew?"

"Still alive?" Mark said. "That's about right."

"Clever, Mark, clever. *Anyway*, we're gonna let them all go down to the rooms, get some sleep, hell, shower up if they want. Then tomorrow, after we hand the boat over and get our cash, we're gonna load ya all up in the rafts and take you in to Phuket. We're gonna be just outside the shipping lanes, a couple miles offshore, so it's no long ride. We'll drop you off on some deserted beach—there're a lot of those up in the north. It'll take some time but you'll get back to the main drag and by then we'll be long gone."

"How's all this depend on me?"

"Because, Mister Rohr, if you cause any disturbance, if you try anything stupid—which you seem to have a habit of doing—we'll lock the doors and leave you all right here, let the bogeymen deal with you."

"How do we know we can trust you?" Mark said.

"Hello? Haven't you been paying attention? You *can't* trust me. But it's the only option you've got. Look," Shawn said, leaning forward. "A few people got killed. All right, it happened, but it's over. Most of these guys are simple fishermen." He waved a hand around the room, taking in the snoring pirates. "They got caught up in the moment, but they're not killers. And, despite what you may think, neither am I."

Robin glared at him over the top of her sunglasses.

"Okay, so maybe I am. You'll just have to trust me on this one, Mark. I don't want to kill anybody else. It'll just get these guys all riled up and I might get hurt in the crossfire. If I *have* to, I'll kill somebody. Probably you. But it's just as easy to take you all with us. Besides, I feel like I owe you," he said standing, tucking the pistol in his belt. "After all, you made this whole thing possible."

There was a light tap on the metal door that echoed through the room. Pim eased herself off the bed, careful not to disturb Ngern. She stood and looked down at the boy, his eyes closed but puffy from crying. One way or the other, it would be over soon.

She crossed the room and opened the door just as Robin was reaching to knock again.

"How's he doing?" Robin said, looking past Pim to the bed.

Pim smiled. "He is sleeping now. He will feel better when he wakes up. Please, come in."

"I don't want to wake him."

"He is a good sleeper. Please." She stepped aside and gave a slight head bow as Robin entered.

Pim had straightened up, righting the bunk beds, folding the blankets, putting their belongings back in the small bag she carried. A pair of old sandals, too big to be Pim's or the boy's, still lay tucked under a bunk. On the deck, two men had pulled her away from the body of her grandfather and had brought her here, her shirt covered with the old man's blood. Robin had followed them into the room, yelling at the men, telling them to get out, knowing what they had in mind. They had listened to her and left but only because they feared what Shawn might do if they didn't. Sobbing, Pim had told Robin what had happened, adding that Ngern was missing, begging Robin to look for him. Eight hours later the door had opened and Ngern had walked in, alone and unharmed. Pim had told him everything and at first he tried not to cry because that was what his great-grandfather would have wanted, but it had come and now, a few hours past sunset, he slept a dreamless, cried-out sleep.

Robin sat on one of the beds at the far corner of the room. She patted a spot next to her on the bed, and Pim sat down.

"Did you get anything to eat? I can go up to the kitchen and look around," Robin asked.

Pim shook her head. "I am not hungry but thank you."

Robin looked over to where Ngern lay sleeping. "He's a tough kid."

"Yes. I wish he did not have to be, but he is."

They said nothing for several minutes, listening to Ngern's steady breathing, then Robin said, "I'm sorry about your grandfather," her voice cracking just once as she said it.

"I told him not to say anything to Shawn but he would not listen. He was very stubborn and foolish."

"No he wasn't," Robin said, reaching out and taking Pim's tiny hand in hers. "He was a brave man and he loved you very much."

Pim raised her head and looked into Robin's eyes. "You are a good woman, Miss Robin."

Robin gave a short laugh. "No, Pim. I'm a dumb blonde who fell for a load of shit because I was stupid enough to think some guy actually liked me for who I am, not how I look."

"You have also described me," Pim said. She gave a weak smile and added, "Except for my hair."

"I'm so pissed right now," Robin said, fighting to keep her voice low. "And I hate myself for what happened. If I wasn't so stupid. What the hell's wrong with me?"

"There is nothing wrong with either of us. We believed because we loved. We did not betray love, he did."

"Yeah, yeah, I've seen Oprah too."

Pim tilted her head and looked at her.

"Never mind," Robin said, and slouched back against the wall. "The kid tell you where he was all day?"

Pim gave a few quick nods that made her hair bounce. "He said a man hid him near the engines and that from there he could watch the *sà-lât*—the sea robbers—but they could not see him. He said he heard them talking. Most are men from Ranong and Chumpon, north of Phuket. Many are Chinese. He can tell by the way they speak, their accent," Pim said, her voice rising, unsure of the word.

"Did they say anything about us, the passengers? What they're going to do with us?"

"Oh yes," Pim said, smiling. "We are quite safe. My nephew said that Shawn came down and spoke to one of the men, and he told the others. Tomorrow morning, very early, the sea robbers will go back to the mainland."

"And us?"

"That is the good news, Miss," Pim said. "They are leaving us here."

Chapter Thirty

Mark was lying on one of the lower bunks, hands behind his head and feet up on a pile of flat pillows. He was expecting the knock on the door, just not so soon, and when the door swung open he expected to see Andy and a squad of grinning pirates, not Robin and Pim, with Pim dragging the sleepy-eyed Ngern behind her.

"That son of a bitch lied to us," Robin said storming in.

"You're just figuring that out now?" Mark watched as Pim shut and locked the door.

"Today. This morning. Up in that room." Robin said, her hands flying as she spoke. "They don't plan on taking any of us off. They're leaving us here for the terrorists."

"Terrorists?" Pim pulled Ngern close to her.

Mark swung his legs off the bed and sat up. "Shawn tell you this?"

"The kid heard it. Down in the engine room," Robin said, and explained what Ngern had told Pim.

"Who is this guy? A passenger? One of the crew?"

"He says he does not know, but I do not think he is with the crew because he has a crippled leg."

"What else does he know?" Mark focused on staying relaxed, hoping it would keep them all calm.

"He says the man is alone and that he is very good at hiding." Pim said, translating as Ngern spoke. "He says the man has five Star Wars guns, but I do not know what this means."

"Tasers." Mark nodded. "Some of the crew had them. Not that it helped."

Robin looked at Mark. "You think you can team up with this guy and take back the ship?"

"With five tasers?" Mark laughed. "Not happening."

"We've got to do *something*," Robin said, the frustration growing in her voice. "We can get the guns, or the tasers or whatever they are, and then get a lifeboat and get away."

"No," Mark said. "No one gets left behind."

"What are you talking about? It's just the four of us."

"It's us," he said, "and the other passengers and what's left of the crew. We all go off together."

Robin stared at him, blinking. "Are you crazy? That's like *forty people*. Getting us off the ship is going to be hard enough. The hell with that. We worry about us."

"I said no one gets left behind." He met her stare and held it for a moment before she dropped her head.

"Fine," she said, pissed and sarcastic. "No one gets left behind."

"Okay, this is what we do," Mark said, his voice changing, strong but not hard. "Pim, ask Ngern if he can find the man who hid him down in the engine room."

"He says yes, he can take you there," Pim said, translating.

"The boats the pirates used are probably still tied up under the fan deck. I'll go down and make sure the alarm is off the door, get the boats lined up so we can just load up and go. I'll send Ngern back up with a taser. When he gets here, Pim, you go to that first cabin on the end, that's where they put some of the crew. You tell them to start sending people down to the fantail deck."

"What is a fantail deck?" Pim asked.

"Just tell them the back door, they'll know. Tell them they have to be quiet and fast or we'll never pull it off."

"What do we do?" Robin said.

"After Pim tells the crew, you three hightail it down the back stairs. The odds are you won't bump into anybody but if you do, you get past them, I don't care how. We'll get you in the first boat and I'll get Ngern's mystery man to take you to shore."

"Whoa, what about you?" Robin said. "You're not going to stay on the boat and pull some hero bullshit on us, are you?"

"Me? Hell, I'm going to be right behind you."

A pair of engines, each the size of a singlewide, ran the length of the brightly lit room. Only one was running, idling, but loud enough to drown out the small sounds. From a darkened catwalk, Mark could see a middle-aged man sitting in front of a bank of dials and buttons. The man's right leg bounced uncontrollably as he tried to stay focused, chewing his thumbnail to the quick. Behind him a pirate guard half his age, a sawed-off shotgun in his lap, balanced his chair on its back legs. Even if he knew where to look the pirate would never spot them up here, too many pipes and shadows in the way.

Last night it had been the *Morning Star* and the crew had been professionals with assigned watches, but even then Mark had only encountered one man. Now, with an untrained pirate crew, Mark had assumed the passageways would be empty and he was right. Ngern led him down several flights before taking Mark's hand and pulling him through a narrow door and onto the catwalk that branched off high above the engine room. Mark kept an eye on the men below as they crossed, stepping off into a second dark bay, following Ngern up a ladder and onto a grated landing. The boy stopped and looked back at Mark and smiled, then turned back and spoke to the shadows.

At first Mark saw nothing, then movement, shades of gray on black. The engine still roared, but he could hear the sound of leather sandals dragging on the grating as the man stepped into the dim light. He was wire thin and his clothes hung limp, several sizes too big, his deep cargo pockets weighed down on either side, his baggy tee shirt almost to his knees. His body dipped to the side as he maneuvered his twisted leg around a stand of pipes and hissing valves. There was a yellow tint to his eyes but he was grinning, his head bobbing as he stepped closer.

Mark tapped Ngern on the shoulder. "Go on," Mark said, knowing that the boy didn't understand but hoping he'd remember what his aunt had told him to say.

Ngern nodded and began speaking, the Thai words coming out impossibly fast. As he spoke he pointed up at Mark, then down to the lower levels, then back up above them in the direction of the cabins. He made gun shapes with his fingers and then seemed to start all over again. The man watched the boy, his eyes following where Ngern pointed as if he could see the spots from here. The man nodded and asked a few questions, both of them nodding as they went over it all a third time, then stopping and looking up at Mark.

"I guess that means we're ready," Mark said and motioned for them to lead the way.

They squeezed between columns of pipes and ducked under dangling cables, stepping out into the passageway two flights above the fantail deck. Mark's hands felt grimy and smelled of oil. He took the lead now and moved down the stairs. It was dark, the lights either turned off or busted out by errant gunshots, but like last night there was still enough light to see. At the bottom of the steps he paused a moment to let his eyes adjust, then moved toward the door. It was shut and the double-handled lever was pushed back in place, but this time there was no lock. The meter still lay on the floor where he had dropped it the night before. He picked it up and untangled the wires. Behind him, Ngern and the man watched, the man talking to the boy in low tones, the boy's eyes wide as he listened.

Mark ran his hand along the rubber seal of the door, his fingers finding the bundle of alarm wires, tracing them along the edge of the door. He knelt down and set the meter on the floor, stretching up the black set of the wires. He separated one of the door alarm wires from the bundle and attached the alligator clip. He squeezed the tip of the clip until it bit through the wire's plastic coating. He attached the rest of the black wires, then did the same with the green and red sets. The hair-thin needle on the meter jumped, then settled low on the scale, just like Andy said it would. He stood and grabbed the handle.

"Well, here goes nothing," he said and yanked on the bar. There was a grating sound and a sharp click as the bolts slid back, but there were no alarm bells and no flashing red lights. He pulled open the door and the humid salty air rushed in. High clouds obscured the stars and none of the ship's lights were aimed down on the open grating of the fantail deck.

Ngern stared out the door and for the first time since they left Phuket the boy seemed nervous. The scrawny man hobbled closer, put his arm around his shoulder and spoke softly in his ear. Mark smiled at Ngern, hoping that whatever the man was saying would keep the boy calm. "Wait here," Mark said, pantomiming the message. "I'm going to untie the boats. Just wait here." He patted the air in front of him several more times, as if repetition would make them understand.

The ship was stopped. Although he couldn't see them in the darkness, Mark knew that the anchors had been dropped, that earlier that night they had arrived at the rendezvous coordinates. To the east the lights of Patong Beach lit up the horizon, two miles away. The island's hills and stretches of empty beach melted into the darkness. To the south and the west he could see the lights of cargo ships and tankers far out in the shipping lane. The sea was calm and the ship so large that the platform was as steady as a cement dock. They were lucky. If the sea had been rough, with waves crashing over the railings, they wouldn't have a chance.

Through the open grating Mark could see the small flotilla of rubber rafts and long-tails that the pirates had used to intercept the ship. A few had taken on water and one of the long-tails looked ready to capsize, but there were enough to get them all to Phuket.

No one gets left behind—the Marine Corps mantra coming back to haunt him.

One arm on the railing, Mark lay on his stomach and hung below the platform. He'd start with the boats near the edge, string them out so they were easy to climb aboard. There would be enough crewmembers to operate the boats, just outboards on the inflatables and small cylinder chain drives on the long-tails. Phuket was in sight and with even a five minute head start there was no way Shawn's men could catch up to them. He untied the first raft, an inflatable that was in better shape than most, and tugged it into position, with the nose of the raft just under the platform so all they'd have to do was step down into it. He didn't want to make it hard for Ngern's new friend to get in the boat. He needed the man to move fast—no one gets left behind but somebody gets out first; and those somebodies were going to be Robin, Pim and Ngern. Mark knew he'd get out too, but he'd go on one of the last boats, towing the empties far enough out to cut off pursuit.

Mark ran the rope through the grating and tied it off, then climbed down onto the raft, looking under the platform for anything that might catch on the raft when they pulled away. It was clear and he turned to pull himself up. The scrawny man was standing above him at the railing, his arm extended straight out at Mark, the yellow cap of the taser just visible in the light.

Mark heard a toy gun pop, then a roar in his head as his body went rigid, the pain indescribable and everywhere at once, his arms stiff and flailing and legs twitching, rocking the raft. He clawed at his chest, tearing at the twin metal prongs, his wrist brushing the wires that completed the circuit. He forced his fingers to close and pulled, the metal dart ripping free just as his knees buckled and he fell to the bottom of the raft. The pain was gone but his muscles refused to respond; and gasping, he fought to sit up, get out of the boat. He was leaning forward, a shaky hand reaching for the railing when he saw the man draw a second taser. He arched backwards as the hot darts bit into his neck, the pain rushing up again, blinding, nauseating, every muscle convulsing, his hands curling backwards, blacking out then snapping back as the man pumped the trigger.

And then it was over.

Chapter Thirty-one

Sometimes things just come together.

Two hours ago he had been starting to panic. He had no idea where the ship was going or what the pirates would do to him if they found him. Sure, he had told the boy that he had a plan but what was he supposed to say? That he didn't know what he was doing, that it was all a big stupid mistake right from the start, that he should have never even followed the American in the first place, that it was Jarin's problem, not his? Or should he have told the boy what everyone in Phuket used to say about him, how he was a nothing there and just a big stupid nothing here, too?

But then the boy and the big American were standing right there in front of his hiding place and *that* was scary because he didn't even hear them coming. And then the boy tells him what the American wants to do, about getting everyone off the ship and leaving it for the pirates; and right there, just like that, it all came together. He really *did* have a plan.

While the American was turning off the alarm he had been whispering with the boy, telling him that when they got the door open they were going to have to make sure it was safe for the others, and how he sure hoped the boy wasn't afraid of sharks because there were going to be a lot of them, big, hungry sharks that could tell if you were scared, just like dogs; and oh yeah, would he mind running back up to the cabin and checking on the women while they stayed here and took care of the sharks? The boy nodded so fast he thought his head would pop off, and no sooner had the American stepped out onto the platform than the boy raced up the stairs.

The American made it so easy. Of course he had to do everything himself, jumping down to untie the boat, acting like he was the only one who knew what to do. Typical *ferang*. He didn't want to use two of the stun guns, but when the American pulled out the dart he was glad that he had the other gun ready. This time he held the trigger till the American just lay there twitching and kept his finger on the trigger, ready to zap him again if he moved. But he didn't and it only took a minute to use that wide, gray tape to tie his hands behind his back and tape his ankles together around that chain. If the American tried anything he'd toss the cinderblock anchor overboard and that would be it. But the American still wasn't moving much. His breathing sounded normal again—as normal as it could sound with his mouth taped shut—and he was blinking a lot like he was trying to clear his vision, but he didn't seem strong enough to stand. Still, he steered the outboard with one hand and kept a third stun gun aimed at the man's back. You never knew with *ferangs*.

He kept the bow pointed at the big house on Surin Beach, five minutes away. It could have been better, he could have gotten the Thai whore and the other American man too, but this was good. He'd really make a name for himself tonight.

Jarin had a hundred men working for him but he'd be the one to deliver the American, right to his door.

With her palms pressed tight together and her head bowed so that her forehead touched the tips of her fingers, the housekeeper crossed the living room to kneel at Jarin's feet. He was sitting on the couch, a drink in one hand, the remote in the other, watching a game show where obese people humiliated themselves for prizes. She waited silently for him to acknowledge her presence, listening as the TV audience's laughter faded down and the Kara shampoo jingle began.

"Yes?" Jarin said, not bothering to lower the volume for the commercials.

"Sir, there is a security guard at the back door."

"Why do you tell me this?" he said.

She said nothing and with her head down she could only guess at his reaction. She heard him give an angry sigh and she knew that she should tell him the rest, but her mother had taught her that those who give bad news are often punished, so she said nothing. Swearing in English and Thai, he stood and stormed past the kneeling housekeeper. He cut through the kitchen, startling the cook, who was napping in a chair, and continued down the hall, past the servants' quarters and the entrance to the garage area, down a flight of stairs and across the footbridge that spanned the indoor koi pond to the screened in-porch. He pushed open the door and the guard snapped to attention.

"Sir, we caught two men on the beach, sir," the guard stammered out.

"You call me for *this*?"

"No sir," the man said, shaking now. "The men, they arrived by boat. One is a *ferang*. He is tied up. The other man is Thai."

Jarin's eyes narrowed as he listened, none of it making sense. "Where is this boat?"

"It was a raft, sir. We pulled it far up the beach, up behind the shed."

"And the men? Where are they now? Who is with them?"

"We took them to the game room at the boathouse, sir," the guard said, falling in alongside of Jarin as he strode across the deck and down to the beach. "There are four security guards and four of your…associates, sir. Your driver, Mr. Laang and also three others."

"These men in the boat, were they armed?" he said, knowing that his men would be.

"Yes, sir. The one man, the Thai, he had several stun guns with him."

"Stun guns?"

"Yes, sir. They are electric devices—"

Jarin swung a sharp backhand into the man's face. "I know damn well what they are. Why do they have them is what I want to know."

The guard said nothing, focusing now on staying a step behind, then rushing forward to open the boathouse door. Jarin stepped inside and the uniformed security guards straightened up when they saw him, each taking a step back to give him more space in the huge room. Laang was standing next to a pool table, the non-driving driver holding a pistol to the ear of a thin-faced, bony youth, no more than twenty, who sat in a folding chair. The man's eyes were wide and he shook with fear but when he saw Jarin enter the room he smiled, something Jarin had not expected. Jarin walked over and stood in front of the little man. He took a fresh pack of cigarettes from his shirtfront pocket and tapped it several times against his open palm. "What are you doing at my home?" he said.

The man brought his hands up under his chin and bowed his head. "*Sawatdee krup*. Sir, my humble name is—"

"That is not what I asked," Jarin said, tearing the cellophane off the pack. He nodded and Laang struck the man with the butt of the pistol, not hard but enough to get his attention. "I will ask you again. What are you doing at my home?"

The man winced but didn't move. "Sir, I have brought you the American you were looking for."

Jarin did not let his excitement show, taking his time to select a cigarette and getting it lit. He took a long, satisfying drag, blowing the smoke straight at the man's face. "What American?"

The scrawny man smiled again. "The one who stole your whore."

Laang didn't wait to be asked, smacking the man again for his rudeness. This time the man brought a hand up to rub the side of his head, a trickle of blood smearing across his fingers. "Where is the other one?" Jarin said to the driver, the driver pointing to the door that led to the enclosed boat slip.

Jarin walked over and opened the door. They had only turned on the one light, leaving the rest of the boathouse dark, but he could make out the smooth silhouettes of his matching speedboats and the line of jet skis his children used. Under the lone light, two of his men stepped aside so that he could see the American sitting, knees up, on the concrete dock. His hands were secured behind his back and there were bits of tape still stuck to his ankles. A wide piece of tape covered his mouth but Jarin still recognized him from the descriptions that Won and the longhaired hotel owner had given him. He stepped back out of the room and walked to the pool table. He motioned, and his driver pushed the man's chin up with the barrel of his pistol. Jarin looked into the man's frightened, yellowed eyes and said, "Why?"

The man opened his mouth but said nothing, his head moving from side to side, his confusion clear in his expression.

"Why do you bring this American to me?"

The man wet his lips and swallowed. "I knew you were looking for him, sir, and I found him."

"Why do you bring him to me? What do you want?"

"*Want?*" the man said, shaking his head again. "Sir, I do not want anything. It is *Náam-jai*, my respect for you, sir. That is all, sir."

"*Náam-jai?*" Jarin said and took one last drag on his cigarette, the embers glowing fire red, and stepped forward, leaning into the man with the cigarette, the man tensing as it neared his face, but not moving away; Jarin leaning past, stubbing the cigarette out in an ash tray on the edge of the pool table. This man, this forgettable little man with his funny lisp and his bony little frame and rat face and a leg that hooked out at that weird angle—he would have never brought on a man like this, but he had done what his best men had failed to do, he had found the American.

Rule Number Two: It's not the size of the dog in the fight, it's the size of the fight in the dog.

There was always a need for someone like that, some runt of the litter who had to fight his way up. Wasn't that what he had done, fought his way up off the streets of Bangkok, fighting still? This runt had that kind of fight in him and Jarin knew that despite his size and his gimpy leg, he'd be a good man to have around, the tough little bastard.

Still, the man had brought this business to his home, and he'd have to pay for that. Rules were rules.

Jarin held out his hand and Laang gave him the pistol. Jarin racked the slide, ejecting an unfired round and chambering a new one. There was no reason to do this, the gun was already loaded, but it looked good and he could see from the man's eyes it had the desired effect.

"What is your name?" Jarin said, holding the pistol down by his side.

The man looked at Jarin then down at the gun. They waited as he sat there, not moving. Then, slowly, he raised his head back up, meeting Jarin's eyes full on, sitting up straight, his chest out, his chin forward. "My name?" he said, his voice strong, even loud, "My name is—"

"Stop," Jarin said, swinging up the gun.

The room fell silent and the man looked at Jarin, still holding his stare.

Jarin smiled. He wanted to say something to the man, something about pit bulls and never giving up, but instead he said, "I think now that it's better I don't know. In case I change my mind. Now get off my island."

Jarin walked back to where they held the American, closing the door behind him, and for a full minute after he had gone no one moved. Then the man stood, and when he walked out of the room, Laang and the others watching him go, not one of them noticed his limp.

Chapter Thirty-two

When Jarin walked back in the room the first thing Mark noticed was the gun.

No one told him it was Jarin, no one had to. He could tell by the way the others stepped back when he walked toward him, the way he looked past people as if they were invisible, which, to a man like Jarin, they were. And he could tell by the way the two men had brought him in the room. The security guards had been rough, jerking him out of the boat and dragging him down the beach. But these two didn't have to play tough. They lifted him up by the shoulders—one of them flicking open a knife to cut the tape from his ankles—and walked him into the boathouse and out onto an enclosed dock. They were professionals and they wanted him to know it as well.

The ride in on the boat had been the worst of it. So far. The shocks had left him nauseous and with the tape over his lips he was afraid he'd be sick. He thought he had seen the man somewhere before but wasn't sure, not that it made a difference. And he had had a good idea where the man was taking him—not this spot, this house on the beach, but to Phuket and, eventually, to Jarin. Nothing else made sense. But Mark knew he was lucky. It could have been days before he'd be taken to see Jarin and by then it would have been too late for anything. But now, with Jarin right in front of him, there was still time.

He knew he'd have one chance and that's it.

It had worked before but this time was different.

He'd have to be faster, better—no, not better, perfect.

It would all come down to him, and he had to play it through, right to the end.

He had planned it in an instant, the parts falling in place. Now, as Jarin walked toward him, the automatic at his side, Mark felt himself relax.

It was time to cast.

"Stand him up," Jarin said to the guards in Thai, stepping off to the side to light another cigarette, stepping back as one of the men ripped the tape off Mark's mouth. "Mr. Mark Rohr, you have made me very angry. You have shown me great dis–"

"I don't have time for this shit," Mark said. "You're already in enough trouble as it is, Jarin, so don't piss me off and make it worse." He doubted that the others spoke English but there was no mistaking his tone and from the way that he looked at him—mouth dropping open and eyes blinking—he was sure Jarin understood as well.

Jerk the line, bob the lure.

"Your brilliant decision to bring me here may have just screwed up an operation *months* in the planning and if it falls apart, *you* are taking the blame, you got that?" Mark grit his teeth and gave his best disgusted headshake, waiting for Jarin to start speaking, then cutting him off, keeping his words hot and angry but under control. "We left you alone—*gave* you this island—and you pick *tonight* to fuck with us? *Tonight?* What is your problem?"

It was just an eyebrow twitch, a half-second, but Mark knew that the hook was in. Head up, nostrils flaring, he waited for Jarin to run with it.

"I do not know what you are talking about. You are just—"

"Don't *fuck* with me, Jarin. You know damn well who I am and who I work for, so cut the bullshit."

"You work for Mr. Shawn."

"*Work* for him? Is that what you think?"

Jarin blinked once.

"I should have known you were going to be trouble," Mark said, chuckling as if he was recalling some inside joke. "That cop over in Krabi, Captain Jimmy, he said you were behind my *visit* to the police station. Well he's paying for that little screw up. Bangkok came down hard on him. Didn't you realize *something* was up when he let me go?"

"I…I do not know what you are—"

"The IMP, Jarin, or are you gonna pretend you don't know?"

"I do not know the IMP," Jarin said. There was a strange lost quality to his words, as if someone else was speaking through him. Mark noticed the guards' grip shifting, their feet shuffling, unsure what was being said but certain something was wrong.

"Jarin, you run this island, you can *not* be that stupid." He sighed. "The International Maritime Police, a UN task force. You *do* know the UN, right?" When Jarin nodded he knew the hook was deep. The Noble Lie, American-style. "Well in case you haven't heard, I'm the Section Chief for this part of the world and you, Jarin, have put a major multi-national anti-terrorist operation at risk. If I'm not at the rendezvous point on time, it all falls apart and I *will* take it out on you."

"You are forgetting that you killed one of my men."

Mark shrugged. "Cost of doing business. I had to infiltrate Shawn's organization and that was my way in."

Jarin brought the gun up and held it level, pointing at Mark's chest and Mark felt the two guards leaning away from him. "No one knows you are here. If you disappear it can not be connected to me."

Mark made a show of rolling his eyes and said, "GPS."

Jarin said nothing. He licked his lips and swallowed.

"Global Positioning Satellite?" Mark said. "There's a transmitter on the boat. Microscopic," he added, hoping it wasn't too much. "They know exactly where I am. And when I don't show and this mission fails, they will come looking for me."

For a long moment Jarin held the gun level but when it dipped, just an inch, Mark knew it was time to reel him in.

"You've got three options, Jarin. One. You shoot me and get rid of the body." Mark shrugged. "I think it's a stupid idea but I put it out there just so you can see that I know what you're thinking. They know I came here, our people in your organization will confirm it and that's it, game over. Two. You let me go and one of your goons drops me off in Patong. This is the one you're considering but it's also stupid. You do that, I miss my rendezvous and the mission fails. Tomorrow, me and one hundred of my closest friends raid everything you own and take you down. Here's what you do instead. You listening?"

Gun still out but arm lower now, Jarin nodded.

"Good. Now, how many men you got?"

Chapter Thirty-three

The cruiser cut through the water as dark as the starless night. The wind had picked up and so had the waves but at over sixty feet long the Fairline *Targa* cabin cruiser barely rocked. With the running lights off even the hazy glow of the instrument panel was too much and someone covered it over with a beach towel. A mile ahead, the *Morning Star* sat anchored just outside the shipping lane. The deck lights were on and there was light behind most every window, but there were no fire hoses spraying down the sides of the ship and the pivot-mounted searchlights were all off. It was well past midnight, hours since he had left, and he didn't know if the lack of activity on board meant an opening or a trap.

There were twenty men on the cruiser but no one made a sound. It had taken Jarin less than an hour to assemble his men, one SUV arriving with boxes of black tee shirts, loose-fit black warm-up pants and all-black sneakers, another with a rack of SWAT-style MP5 9mm submachine guns and an assortment of handguns, most fitted with suppressors. The shirt was a tight fit and the sneakers a bit snug, but the shoulder holster felt right.

Jarin was somewhere on the boat, down in one of the salons. Mark was surprised when he had climbed aboard back at the dock, not bothering to change out of his red and white Aloha shirt. There had been a moment when Mark was sure he was a dead man, Jarin staring down the barrel of his handgun and the bullshit deep and getting deeper. And while Jarin had given a nod and the tape binding Mark's hands had been cut and Mark's demands for men and arms had been met, he still felt as if it was all just a short reprieve, Jarin simply amused or curious.

"How will you get on board?" Jarin had asked as they waited for the men to gear up.

"The fantail deck. The door is open and unlocked," Mark had said, hoping it was true. "Send a few of your men to the lower decks—there's only one of Shawn's men in the engine room, a kid with a shotgun. The rest of the men should take the bridge and work down from there. Warn them that there're passengers aboard, so just don't go spraying everyone."

Jarin drew on his ever-present cigarette. "These are my best men. They are professionals but they are not mind readers. If they encounter someone in the hallways they will shoot them."

"That's not the way it's done."

Jarin had raised his head and looked at him, his eyes narrowing before he turned away.

The boat was angling past the *Morning Star* toward the dark waters far off its stern. They would come at it from the seaward side, an approach that would be less expected and one that didn't pass them in front of the distant lights of Patong Beach. Mark was watching the water rush by, focusing on his breathing when someone tapped his arm.

"*Long bpai,*" one of the men said, pointing down the short steps into the ship's dark interior. Mark started for the steps but the man placed a hand on his chest and withdrew the pistol from Mark's holster, another man taking the MP5 from his hands. "Okay," the man said, spreading the word into three syllables, then letting him pass. Mark eased around the man and made his way down the stairs. Black shapes filled the room. He felt a hand on his shoulder guide him forward, that hand dropping off and another taking its place as they moved him through the salon to a door, another unseen hand knocking. The door opened and a sliver of light shot across the salon. Mark brought a hand up to cover his eyes and stepped into the room, the door shutting behind him.

Jarin sat behind a built-in desk of golden-hued wood, two armed men to each side, the muzzles of their assault rifles aimed at his chest. The room was thick with cigarette smoke, and already, there were three butts in the ashtray. "My pilot says we will be in position soon," Jarin said, and Mark nodded.

"I want the truth, Mr. Rohr." It was the way he said it, not raising his voice, as if he already knew the answer, that told Mark that his bluff was being called. Mark waited, not offering anything.

"Is Shawn on that boat?"

"Yes," Mark said, still in the game.

Jarin drew on his cigarette. "What you said about terrorists and the oil spill, is that true?"

Mark nodded. "That's what Shawn told me."

"Who are the terrorists? What organization?"

"I told you everything I know," Mark said, the truth sounding like bullshit now, and Jarin watched him as he smoked. Mark leaned to his right as the boat started a wide arc around the stern of its target, Jarin and the guards leaning too.

"I have fought the terrorists for years," Jarin said.

"I know. It was in the reports I read about you," Mark said.

Jarin chuckled, blowing smoke out of his nose. He ground the cigarette out, pulling a replacement from the pack on the table. "You *read* it in your *reports*," he said, and chuckled again as he flicked his lighter to life. "You are American, yes? Tell me, do you love your country?"

He hadn't expected the question and he paused, but then said, "Yes."

Jarin drew on the cigarette. "And would you kill to protect your country?"

Mark paused again, this time for other reasons. "I have."

"And if someone told you that your country was in danger and that you could protect it, would you act?"

"Yes."

"So tell me, Mr. Mark Rohr," Jarin said, leaning forward as he spoke, "why would this not be true for a Thai?"

Hands cupped around his cigarette, his eyes just visible through the curl of smoke, Jarin waited, and Mark knew then that his truth no longer mattered.

"We will talk later, Mr. Rohr," Jarin said, sitting back, dimming the light down. "But now you have a ship to catch."

Mark climbed the short stairs to the back deck of the cabin cruiser just as the pilot cut the main engines. He could hear switches being thrown at the helm and then the low hum of a small electric docking motor and the rolling waves that slapped the sides of the boat. The sheer stern of the *Morning Star* towered above them, the outline of the superstructure backlit by deck lights that angled every direction but down. The cruiser rode higher than the fantail and through the open grating Mark could see the outline of rubber rafts and wooden long-tails bobbing below.

The fantail hatchway was closed with no light visible around its edge. Mark couldn't tell if it was simply pushed shut from the outside or secured down from within.

One of Jarin's men leapt onto the fantail and guided in the cruiser's bow while five others, barrels up, scanned the ship for movement. The vinyl boat-bumpers squeaked as the pilot drew the cruiser alongside, the men scrambling out onto the fantail and shouldering up against the hull of the *Morning Star;* Mark jumping out with them. The man tossed the rope back onto the cruiser and it pulled away, disappearing into the darkness.

A row of men squatted at the outer edge of the fantail and kept their weapons trained on the superstructure while the others lined up on both sides of the door. A few of the men looked at him, waiting for him to lead them in.

Mark shifted his MP5 to his left side and reached for the door's handle.

Maybe the alarm bypass had fallen off or failed to work correctly and the hatch had been relocked hours ago.

Or maybe his taser-wielding kidnapper had attracted too much attention in his rush to deliver him to Jarin, bringing someone down to investigate.

Maybe one of the pirates just happened past and pulled it shut, throwing the lock.

The kid could have got it wrong and told Pim and Robin that everything was ready and they told the others, and when they rushed down and it wasn't ready, somebody panicked. There could be piles of bodies inside with dozens of edgy pirates waiting in ambush.

But if it was locked, it was over.

Mark wrapped his fingers around the handle, nodding once to the man beside him, the man nodding back, slipping inside as Mark pulled the hatch open. Mark felt his breath catch in relief, then stepped through, the others silently pouring in behind them.

Nothing had changed. The passageway was still empty, the bypass was still in place, but Ngern was gone. He was a smart kid and he knew his way around. Mark just hoped he'd stay low till this was all over.

The first man through turned and signaled to the others, a squad of men splitting off toward the engine room, any noise they made lost in the steady hum of the ship's machinery. The man tapped Mark on the shoulder and pointed to the stairs, his eyes asking the question. Mark nodded and took the lead.

He moved up the stairs one step at a time. So far no one knew they were aboard, and the longer they could keep it that way the better. The open frame of the MP5 stock at his shoulder, Mark came around each bend of the staircase ready to fire. On the fourth flight up, he did, dropping a pair of Shawn's pirates as they walked down the corridor toward him, the suppressor reducing the shots to airy thumps, the metallic clack of the bolt and the clatter of the six brass casings on the metal deck the loudest noise. Two flights later Mark heard the same rhythmic clatter coming from below. A hand-signaled message worked its way up the line letting him know that there were three fewer pirates onboard.

When they reached the main passenger level, Mark stopped and stepped to the side, gesturing to the man behind him that he was staying here and that they should continue to the bridge. The man looked hard at Mark, his jaw set, his eyes burning, then waved the others on, throwing Mark one last hot glance before heading up. Mark waited for the last man to go by, then cut across the passageway to a shadowy alcove near the open bulkhead door that led to the passenger cabins. He went low and popped his head around the corner. The corridor was empty, all the doors shut. He was two steps away from Pim's cabin when he heard a toilet flush in the communal bathroom at the end of the hall.

Mark moved fast, reaching the end of the hallway and sliding up against the wall just as the bathroom door swung open, the door swinging out, hiding him from view, swinging back shut as Andy, head down, zipping up his fly, walked past. Mark crosschecked Andy into the doorframe of the first cabin, slamming his knee up into Andy's crotch and shoving the side of the rifle hard against his throat. Bug-eyed and wheezing, Andy fought to catch his breath, bringing both hands up along the side of his face.

"Unarmed," he managed to gasp, wiggling his fingers as if to prove the point.

"Where is he?" Mark whispered.

Andy tried to shake his head but Mark held the weapon tight, pushing in until Andy said, "Cabin."

"Here? One of these?"

Andy opened his mouth to speak but only gasped. Mark shoved him against the door again and stepped back, shoving the barrel of his submachine gun into Andy's gut. "You shout, you die," Mark said. "Which cabin?"

Andy sucked in a shaky breath. "Fuckin' bastard," he said, his voice just audible.

"Which cabin?"

"Not here. Up on the other deck, four flights up. First cabin on the right," Andy said, and Mark remembered the ship's diagram taped up on the back of his cabin door. Then Andy smiled and added, "Shagging that whore."

It was a quick move and Andy never saw it coming, Mark jerking the barrel up, the heavy suppressor catching him on the chin, Andy's mouth snapping shut on his tongue, a string of blood streaking up into his face, Mark jabbing the barrel back into his gut before he could move.

"Bastard," Andy spat out, his hands coming up to cover his bloody mouth. Mark let him, wondering now what to do with his prisoner. It was one thing to shoot an armed man and he had done it minutes ago without hesitation, another thing to gut shoot a guy with his hands in the air. It had only been seconds since he had first slammed him against the cabin door, but Mark knew that he didn't have time to waste on Andy Cooper, didn't have time for honor. He thought of Pim and Robin and the boy and was drawing in a halting breath, his finger moving for the trigger, when the door behind Andy swung open and Andy fell backward into the cabin, landing at the feet of Mr. Singh. The remnants of the original crew climbed off bunk beds and moved to the door to stand behind their officer, the low murmur in Thai stopping when Singh raised his bandaged hand.

"You need to keep your men inside until this is over," Mark said, looking into the man's dark brown eyes, Singh giving the slightest nod to show that he understood. Then both men looked down to Andy.

"We will take care of this one," Singh said as his men dragged Andy, screaming, into the cabin, Singh keeping his eyes fixed on Mark as he slowly shut the door.

Mark listened as the lock turned in place, then stepped away from the door and started back to the stairs.

There were shots now, choppy machine gun bursts and booming shotgun blasts coming from above and isolated pops from handguns below. The suppressors on Jarin's men's weapons kept the sounds of the battle one-sided. Mark took the steps three at a time, leaping over the crumpled body of a pirate on one landing and the black-clad body of one of Jarin's men on another. He was rounding the last set of stairs when the shots came, a line of sparks and deadly ricochets passing inches over his head.

He pushed on, springing out low, hitting the deck on his side, his MP5 firing off a dozen silent shots, catching the two pirates as they brought their Chinese assault rifles around, the men seeming to dance in place as the rounds ripped through them. Instinctively, Mark rolled the other way, dropping a third man before he could raise his shotgun. He stood up and put his back to the bulkhead and scanned the hall, looking for movement or odd-shaped shadows, a lifetime of skills taking over.

Mark slid along the bulkhead, stopping at the edge of the second hall of passenger cabins. He risked a quick look around the open doorway. There were four doors on both sides of the short hall with no communal bath at the far end, just a spiral staircase that led up somewhere in the direction of the bridge. According to Andy, Shawn and Pim were in the first cabin on the right. But was it the first cabin from this end of the hall—the door he stood in front of now—or was it the first cabin from the spiral staircase end, making it the last door on the left? He could blow off the lock and kick in this door, a fifty-fifty chance he'd have the right room, catching Shawn off guard and ending it quick. The same odds that he'd be warning Shawn and dooming Pim.

Keeping his eyes trained down the hall, he leaned in and pressed an ear against the door. He could hear muffled noises but those could be ambient sounds resonating through the ship.

Fifty-fifty.

The same odds that the door would be unlocked.

Mark slung his MP5 across his back and drew the Beretta from his shoulder holster. He pushed down on the door handle and he felt it turn, pulling the door toward him to keep it from creaking open before he was ready, inching the door open until the latch was clear. He took a deep, silent breath and in one move, swung the door open and swept the barrel across the empty room just as a scream echoed down the hall behind him.

Shawn was stepping backwards out of the far cabin, his left hand coming up to the four deep scratches that raked his face, his right arm aiming a pistol back into the cabin. "You fucking *bitch,*" he shouted, firing once before Mark emptied the automatic, the first two shots slamming into the side of Shawn's head, Shawn's lifeless body crumpling sideways as Mark sprinted down the hall. Mark dropped the Beretta and swung the MP5 down into his hands as he ran, the gun hip-level as he came in the room. Pim was on the floor, leaning up on one hand, staring down at the blood that flowed from the hole in Robin's shoulder.

He threw the gun on a bed and lifted Robin off Pim's lap. She was unconscious but her breathing was steady, her shirt already soaked in blood. He propped her up on her side and ran a hand along her back. "Good. The round went straight through."

Pim stripped off a pair of pillowcases and knelt down beside Robin. "Hold this tight please," she said, wadding up the white cotton cover and placing it over the exit wound, high on Robin shoulder; placing the other over the hole in the front of Robin's shirt. "If it did not cut an artery," she said, hitting every syllable, "she will be all right. When I worked in my father's pharmacy on Phi Phi, we saw many stab wounds, much worse than this. Now hold here as well."

"I got it," Mark said, shifting his position so he could press the bandages between his hands. He looked at Pim and saw her glance out the door to where Shawn's body lay, the pistol still in his hand, his head blown open. "What happened?"

"Shawn made Miss Robin and me come to this cabin. He heard the shots. Then he…he was going to…" she stopped—her breath coming in short gulps—then looked into Mark's eyes, and through clenched teeth she said, "I scratched his face."

"Why did he shoot her?"

Pim shook her head. "No. He was going to shoot me. Miss Robin, she jumped in the way and knocked me over. Then Shawn fell and you were here."

She stood and pulled a sheet from a bed, tearing it in half then rolling it lengthwise into a long bandage. Together they wrapped the sheet tight around Robin's chest, a mix of Marine Corp first aid and makeshift clinic practicality.

"Where's Ngern?" Mark said, looking around the room.

Pim's eyes widened. "He is not with you?"

"No. But I think I know where he is," Mark lied. Robin stirred and gave a low moan. "We need to get moving. She going to be able to get out of here soon?"

"Yes. She needs to be taken to a real doctor, before she is infected."

"Don't worry," Robin said, blinking her eyes open. "I've had my shots."

"Miss Robin," Pim said, the tears coming now, bending down and hugging her neck. "You are so brave. You should not have saved me."

"Tell me about it." Robin winced as they helped her sit up. She looked at Mark. "Did you kill Shawn?"

Mark nodded and Robin looked past him, out the door and into the hall. She breathed a long sigh. "Oh shit no."

"Robin, he killed Pim's grandfather, he tried to kill Pim, and he almost killed you. If I didn't shoot him he would have killed me, too. I'm not sorry I shot him."

"I'm not sorry either," she said, tilting her head to the door, "but they look kind of pissed."

Five men in black tee shirts and matching black pants stood at the open door, their weapons all pointed at Mark.

Chapter Thirty-four

Jarin grunted and flipped his phone shut. "Bring us in," he said, and the pilot spun the wheel, maneuvering the cabin cruiser back to the empty fantail deck.

It had only taken ten minutes for his men to secure the ship. Pirates, he knew from experience, were not disciplined fighters and they lacked even the basic organizational skills. According to Laang, the operation had gone as planned, just one man killed and two wounded. They had done well and he was proud of them, but he certainly wouldn't tell them that—that's what he paid them for. He also paid them to get information and they were doing that, too. The few pirates still alive were eager to talk, assuming foolishly that it would matter. And apparently they had something interesting to tell.

The boat crept alongside the fantail and two men jumped out, this time tying the ropes off, locking the cruiser's gangplank in place before signaling to Jarin that it was ready. Jarin took the pilot's nine millimeter from the man's holster. In the old days he would have tucked the gun into the front of his pants but his overhanging gut made that impossible now. Instead he used it as a pointer, directing the three remaining gunmen off the cruiser and through the fantail door. A moment later, one of the men gave the all clear and Jarin stepped down the gangplank, across the open grating and into the *Morning Star*.

It had been years since he had been in this part of a ship, but it still seemed familiar. The steady hum of the auxiliary engine, the smell of oil, that strange lighting and how the rows of pipes seemed to run on forever. Ships were different now, all that computer crap making it impossible for a ship to disappear. He had had some good years in the eighties, before every ship worth stealing installed a GPS system. The best was that freighter out of Oman. That had set it all up for him, allowed him to move into Phuket, take over, even allowing him to get out of the piracy game altogether. Just in time, too.

His men were moving ahead, two checking the stairwell, the third on his phone, getting directions to the bridge, when Jarin saw the boy. He was squeezed in between a pair of standpipes, pulled back into the shadows, and Jarin would have missed him if the yellow cap of a stun gun hadn't given him away. Jarin stopped and the guards moved back toward him, but he waved them off. Still, they kept their weapons trained on the gap. Jarin bent down and looked at the boy. "*Sawatdee krup,*" he said, bringing his palms together around the butt of his pistol, giving his head a slight nod. He felt himself smiling, and it surprised him.

"*Sawatdee krup,*" Ngern said. He bowed his head but kept his eyes and the stun gun on Jarin.

"You're what, ten years old?" Jarin said. "I have a daughter your age. Her name is Jaa."

"I am Ngern and I am eight and a half years old."

"Really? You look older. Tell me, Ngern, why do you have that gun?"

The boy wet his lips but didn't say anything.

"If you are going to carry a gun like that you should learn how to use it. You have the safety on so it won't shoot. There, just above your thumb," Jarin tapped the spot on his own pistol to show him. "You need to flick that little lever up."

Ngern tilted the gun to look. "This?"

"Yes, just push it up. There, it is armed," Jarin said, not knowing if it was or it wasn't, just knowing that the boy now trusted him. "If we see any pirates, you will need to zap them, all right? Come on, get out of there before you get stuck."

Ngern turned his shoulders and stepped out, lowering his arms. Jarin patted his shoulder. He let him keep the gun. "Are you a member of the crew?" Jarin said, and off to the side he could see that that made one of his men smile.

"No, uncle. I am on a trip with my aunt and her friends. They are from America."

Jarin's eyes narrowed. "From America? What are their names?"

"My aunt's name is Prisana but we call her Pim. There is also Mr. Mark and Miss Robin. They are the Americans."

"You are Pim's nephew," Jarin said, and grunted once. "I did not know you were so young."

"My great-grandfather was with us too, but my aunt's husband, Mr. Shawn, he killed him." Ngern looked down at the gun in his hand, then back up at Jarin. "I don't like Mr. Shawn."

"Me either," Jarin said.

"Can we go see my aunt now? Please?"

He looked at the boy—at his big puppy dog eyes—and sighed. "Yes," he said, standing, "it's time we get this over."

"Stop looking at me like that," Robin said.

Smiling, Pim reached over and brushed a stray hair out of Robin's face, Robin slapping her hand away.

"What do you expect? You saved her life," Mark said.

"Yeah, keep reminding me."

They were on the floor of the dining hall, Robin lying down, her feet up on a chair to keep from going into shock, Pim sitting on one side, Mark on the other. Two men leaned against the wall on either side of the door, their weapons lowered but their fingers still on the triggers, a third pacing the room, a cell phone held to his ear. The man had a deep voice for a Thai, and by the way he waved his free hand—angling up flights of stairs and hooking left and right at each turn—it was obvious he was giving directions. In a dark corner of the dining hall, under an overturned table riddled with bullet holes, one of the pirates stared out at Mark, a look of surprise frozen on his lifeless face.

"How you feeling?" Mark asked Robin.

"Like I want to puke. And a little cold."

Pim slid her hand under Robin's shoulder, holding her fingers behind Robin's head to show Mark the blood.

"I will get you a blanket," Pim said and stood, the two guards snapping their weapons up to their shoulders, shouting at her in Thai as Jarin entered the room. He raised his hand and they fell silent, lowering their weapons.

"*Excuse me, sir,*" Ngern said in Thai, squeezing around Jarin's legs, pushing the stun gun into the man's fat hand before running into Pim's outstretched arms. For a moment no one said a word.

Jarin cleared his throat. "Congratulations, Mr. Mark Rohr. Your UN mission is a success."

"*UN mission?*" Robin said, leaning up on her good arm.

"I'll explain later," Mark said to her as he slowly rose, the guards' guns rising with him.

"Oh, I suppose that any minute your men will be swarming over the ship, helicopters in the air. Perhaps even a submarine?"

"Everything I told you about Shawn's plan was true. Ask your men about the pirates or get one of the crew members up here, they'll confirm what I said."

"All of this," Jarin waved his pistol as he spoke, "it all started when Mr. Shawn lied to me. His lies cost me one hundred and eighty thousand US dollars. Now you lie to me. What new problems will this bring for me?"

"None," Mark said. "It's over. Shawn is dead."

Jarin stepped closer, the guards stepping in with him. "And I am still owed the money. Who will pay for that? You?"

"The terrorists will pay you. They're coming at daybreak, just a small group of them. And they're bringing the money. More than enough to cover the debt."

Jarin's smile disappeared. "You are a proven liar, Mr. Mark Rohr," he said, wagging the barrel of the pistol like an accusing finger. "But you picked a good time to tell the truth. My men learned about the payment from some of the pirates they...

questioned. We do not have much time to prepare, but I am certain we can give them a warm reception when they arrive."

Mark nodded. "We can put a few men—"

"*We* will do nothing. *You* are leaving."

"I'm not going anywhere without my friends."

Jarin glanced down at Robin, Pim, and Ngern. "They are your problem now," he said, walking away, the guards backing out with him. He stopped at the door, turned back and pointed the pistol at Mark's chest, the guards stepping aside. "I will ask you a question. You will tell me the truth."

Here it comes, thought Mark.

"Do you follow any rules?"

Mark stepped forward, moving away from the others, Jarin's pistol following him, a clear shot now if that's what he wanted. "What kind of rules?"

"Rules to live by. Do you have any?"

He was ten feet away from the end of the barrel, impossible to miss. He took a deep breath and closed his eyes, clearing his mind. Ready now, he looked at Jarin. "I have a couple left."

"Then allow me to give you one more. It is called Rule Number Ten," he said, lowering the gun. "Every dog has its day. This is your day, Mr. Mark Rohr. Make the most of it."

Chapter Thirty-five

"How's your squid omelet?" JJ pulled the fat curls of his dreadlocks behind his ears.

"Different," Mark said between rubbery chews.

"See? That's why this place could be a gold mine. It's got everything." JJ held up his hand and counted off. "One. Great location. It's the closest restaurant to the beach and it's surrounded by all these nice, inexpensive hotels that tourists love."

"And if they're looking for something different," Frankie Corynn said, "there's always the Phuket Inn by the Sea."

"*Exactly.* Okay, two. Unique menu."

Mark looked down at the stubby tentacles that poked out of a mound of scrambled eggs. In the five mornings he had eaten here it was the most recognizable meal so far. "No argument there."

"Three. You can *not* beat the view," JJ said, gesturing toward a trio of Australian tourists in matching bikinis who sashayed down the beach, past the spot where Pim and Ngern played in the surf, Ngern's laughter louder than the waves.

"Beautiful," Mark said.

"Yeah..." JJ said, his eyes glazing over as he stared, snapping back when a scooter roared past. "And Patong is safe, too."

Frankie shook her head, which made her frizzy red hair bounce. "That's not what I heard, JJ."

"What are you talking about? It's a hell of a lot safer than Phuket City."

"Maybe," Frankie said. "But according to the scuttlebutt, the police found the bodies of some suspected terrorists on this drifting long-tail a couple days ago."

Mark sipped his pineapple juice.

"Oh that," JJ said, waving it off. "That's different. I'm telling you, this is the closest I'll get to paradise."

"That's true for all of us," Frankie said.

"Pim says we can get a good price on the lease on this café, that way we can offer package deals, like stay the night at the inn and get breakfast or something. She's smart," JJ said tapping a finger to the side of his head. "Got all sorts of ideas."

"Watch it, you'll be working for her before you know it."

"If I'm lucky. Hey," he said, raising his voice. "Don't look now, here comes trouble." He pushed out a metal chair with his foot and Robin sat down, setting her stuffed backpack by her feet. Her eyes were red, her hair was still wet from the shower and there were green and yellow tints to the fierce bruises around her bandaged shoulder, yet somehow she was still more attractive than the models trolling the beach. "How you doing this morning, sweetheart?"

"Hung over," she moaned. "What was in those drinks?"

JJ held up his hands. "I warned you that Frankie mixes a mean Mai Tai, but no, you didn't listen. Look at Mark here, you didn't see him slamming down the drinks, getting all crazy."

"I didn't get crazy," Robin said.

"Relatively speaking."

Mark took a bite of his eggs. "You find an internet place?"

She nodded. "I checked in online. Up to Bangkok, anyway. Oh, and I found this, too." She pulled a folded paper from the back pocket of her shorts and tossed it on the table. "It's a list of arrivals at the port in Chennai. The *Morning Star* docked yesterday, delayed due to engine problems off Phuket."

"So what time's your flight?" Mark said.

"One o'clock. Which reminds me." She bent over and unzipped a side pocket of her backpack. "Here's your return ticket. It's an open booking, you just let them know a few days in advance when you want to leave. And then there's this." She held out a plain white envelope. "It's only eleven hundred. I'll send the rest to you when I get back to Ohio. It'll take a couple months, but I'll get it to you."

Mark took the envelope and opened it, pulling out five twenties before handing it back. "That's plenty. You'll need it more than me. I'm all set here."

JJ laughed. "You're not staying at the inn if that's what you're thinking."

"And I hope you're not thinking you can get that bouncer job back," Frankie said.

"No," Mark said, finishing off the last tentacle, "I'm heading south. Koh Lanta. I've got to tell a Canadian woman that she and I are the new owners of F and A Divers."

Robin looked at JJ and Frankie and they all looked back at Mark. "You? A business owner? In *Thailand?*"

Mark smiled and raised his empty juice glass. "Would I lie to you?"